CRUDE POLICY

CRUDE POLICY

JOEL ALBERT

iUniverse, Inc.
Bloomington

CRUDE POLICY

iUniverse books may be ordered through booksellers or by contacting:

iUniverse
1663 Liberty Drive
Bloomington, IN 47403
www.iuniverse.com
1-800-Authors (1-800-288-4677)

Because of the dynamic nature of the Internet, any web addresses or links contained in this book may have changed since publication and may no longer be valid. The views expressed in this work are solely those of the author and do not necessarily reflect the views of the publisher, and the publisher hereby disclaims any responsibility for them.

Any people depicted in stock imagery provided by Thinkstock are models, and such images are being used for illustrative purposes only.
Certain stock imagery © Thinkstock.

ISBN: 978-1-4620-6777-0 (sc)
ISBN: 978-1-4620-6776-3 (hc)
ISBN: 978-1-4620-6775-6 (ebk)

Library of Congress Control Number: 2011960959

Printed in the United States of America

iUniverse rev. date: 11/29/2011

"There is danger from all men. The only maxim of a free government ought to be to trust no man living with power to endanger the public liberty."

John Adams

To my mom, who taught me the joys of reading . . .

To my dad, who taught me to see a project through . . .

To Jim, who told me to rewrite the manuscript six times, and then start over . . .

To John, who told me I had a diamond in the rough, when there was no sparkle . . .

To Cade, who put up with hours of me buried in my computer . . .

To Val, who challenged me to do my best, or don't do it at all . . .

And to everyone who has influenced me over the years, you are all in the book . . .

Prologue

The room was still warm at 2:00 A.M., musky and humid from the warm summer day, dimly lit and filled with cigarette smoke. They were in a remote and abandoned house nestled on the outskirts of Tripoli near Kfarhata, Lebanon. Like all of their communications, information about their location had reached Jamal a week earlier through a highly encrypted Internet message board. Very secure.

The room held an oppressive silence even as it slowly filled with Arabic men without a trusting bone in their bodies. Jamal felt his blood pulsing through his temples as beads of sweat pearled down his forehead onto his cheeks. Breathing was difficult, as if someone pushed a pillow into his face. He had been dreaming of his mission for years, and now that it was upon him, anxiety was taking over, not the determined focus expected of him.

Jamal studied each new arrival with suspicion just as they stared at him with obvious misgivings, only causing his anxiety to rise. Every steely glare was steeped in an aura of hate that was also meant to convey an air of confidence. He had never met a single one of them before this moment, and he assumed the same was true for each of them.

In Jamal's world, the first rule was the most important: trust no one. Jamal understood each man had his unique role, painstakingly recruited based upon his individual skill sets and blind dedication to their interpretation of the Islam faith. The situation was tense;

however, all the men had two things in common: their distrust of everyone and their Jihadist intentions.

Jamal might not know the men populating the room, but he had received information on their capabilities. Each had a background in the petrochemical business, including three with Ph.D.s in chemical engineering. Impressive. Telling.

After the sixth man arrived, Jamal slowly moved to his knees and whispered a silent prayer. Each man followed, and the room filled with their low toned voices in different Arabic dialects saying their individual prayers. After a few minutes, each man returned to his seat.

Jamal rose to his feet, knowing that once he spoke, there would be no turning back. He took a deep breath, doing his best to gain composure. He was going down a road of personal sacrifice that would ultimately end in his own martyrdom. But he was certain his death would be glorious.

Jamal stood tall in front of the other six men and pointed to a detailed distribution map of the United States natural gas pipeline network.

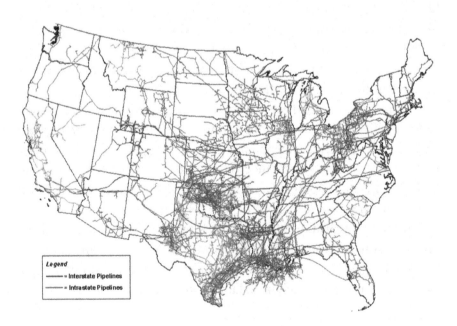

"Seven major natural gas transfer and compression stations are here, which include forty-eight in-feeds, and seven major out-feeds," said Jamal.

His voice was soft and accented, but his English grammar was otherwise perfect and easy to understand. Jamal had explicit instructions to speak in English, as his journey over the next year required him to integrate seamlessly with the American public, as if he just walked off the campus of an Ivy League graduate school.

"Our targeted pipelines are located in the state of Oklahoma, near the state capital of Oklahoma City. Many natural gas pipeline companies deliver gas through these stations. These evil companies are the primary exporters of this region's natural gas to other parts of the country."

Jamal paused for a moment, and turned to look at the men. They all remained silent and expressionless. He stared into their eyes to discern if their stoicism was lack of commitment or mere distrust. He was disappointed in their apparent lack of enthusiasm, and had an exposed feeling as if he were on an island alone. This was the first time any of them had heard the objective of their mission, and Jamal had no idea what to expect.

Jamal continued, "This is the primary gathering point for twenty-four percent of the natural gas distribution for the southwest United States, and represents four hundred and nineteen million cubic feet of natural gas per day."

Then Jamal turned and said, "And my brothers, we will make the ultimate sacrifice to destroy these compressor stations, transfer manifolds and pipelines. With Allah as our guide, we shall deliver devastation to the energy market in the United States."

The anxiety in the room was beyond the stress point, but after hearing this, the men smiled, then cheered and laughed out loud. The roomful of strangers became instant brothers. Jamal felt the tears stream down as the tension left his body. Years of planning had brought him to this point. He was finally with his family.

Jamal shouted over the group, "My brothers, come and review the map closely, and we will begin discussing each man's assignment for . . ."

Suddenly out of the corner of his eye, Jamal saw the entire wall across the room disintegrate. The force of the explosion blew him backwards and he hit the ground with more velocity than imaginable. The blast was so loud his head felt it was about to explode. He could hear the screams of one of his brothers across the room, his mid-torso bloody and exposed. Jamal heard the shouts from other men, no doubt American, as they yelled orders. In the haze, Jamal saw men in assault uniforms enter the room, fully clad as commandos with camouflage gear, night vision scopes and automatic weapons.

Jamal was grabbed by the back of his head, and then a soldier put him in a choke hold which he could not escape. Then Jamal witnessed a scene of evil, one for which he was not prepared. The commandos dragged each of his brothers to the center of the smoldering room as they reeled in pain and confusion. They were ordered to stay on their knees while his brother with his torso blown away was dragged directly in front of everyone. Jamal was once again standing upright directly in front of his companions, this time in dramatically different circumstances.

At that moment an older soldier entered the room, wearing an American uniform that Jamal recognized from his days in the military. The soldier walked directly to Jamal and clamped his hand on his face.

The soldier said, "Let me be clear, the days of Islamic terrorists operating on our soil are over. We know everything you do, how you do it and how you plan it. Now, watch closely what happens to your kind."

Then one of the commandos walked to each one of his brothers, and fired a bullet through the back of their skulls. All six of the men lay lifeless as blood oozed on the old wooden floor. Jamal screamed as his knees collapsed, forcing the soldier to hold him upright. He was shaking violently from the total panic and shock of the last few moments. Sweat poured from his body and tears streamed down his face.

The older American scanned the room, and then turned to Jamal with a steely glare, "We're watching you, everything you do. You and your kind have no chance of fulfilling your missions. We have a reminder for you to think of this lesson every day."

Suddenly, another commando approached Jamal with a large knife. Jamal started screaming, trying to fight out of the neck hold. The man quickly grabbed Jamal's chin with his left hand, and then slashed his face from the bottom of his left cheek to his right eye. He felt the razor-sharp blade dig through his skin and cut into his bone, leaving him with a permanent scar across his face. Jamal cried out, and then fell to his knees as the commando released his body.

Jamal heard the sounds of the helicopter as the soldiers exited the room in an instant. He was alone, bleeding and left to his shock and desperation of the moment. Years of planning were destroyed in moments. He rolled from his knees to his back, weeping, confused and betrayed. He felt the warm blood flowing down his face to the back of his neck. He put his hands on his face to try and stop the bleeding, and then looked at his hands in horror, totally soaked in blood. He lay alone in the silence of the room, trying to comprehend the gruesome scene next to him.

Then it hit Jamal. He came to the realization that his mission from Allah would not be completed, and his life was a failure. He let out a blood-curdling scream as his very soul left his body.

Manish and Hakeem sat in the corner of the coffee shop. The smell alone made Manish and Hakeem sick to their stomachs at the thought of American capitalism, as they drank the $4.00 espresso with a 300 percent cost markup. Both men were in a foreign land in the middle of a silent war, helpless to support their cause. They sat in melancholy as their commitment to Allah seemed a distant dream slipping further and further away.

"They're getting smarter, more clever," said Manish in a low and subtle voice as he rubbed his hands across his face. "I don't know, but I think they're following me."

Manish was at the table with Hakeem, but not really speaking to anyone. He was engrossed in deep thought as he stared out the window into the ninety-five degree heat and seventy percent humidity, typical of a summer evening in southeast Texas.

"We opened the Internet portal through the cable company in North Dakota. It must have been monitored. Hassam posted logistics for the meeting in Kfarhata using all our encryption tools."

Manish looked out the window with his arms folded across his chest. "From what little I know, the meeting was raided. Six of our brothers were killed; only Jamal escaped. No doubt he was allowed to go free to spread the word of their counterintelligence. We think it was American mercenaries hired by the CIA. I don't think it was American soldiers, or we would have heard about it by now, and nobody would be alive to tell about it."

A moist-eyed Manish continued, "My efforts to find the perfect communication channel were a failure. I'm the reason for their plight. It feels as if they wish us to plan, they wish us to dream. This is unbearable."

"Allah will guide us, brother," said Hakeem in a depressed tone. "We shall find a way to our mission."

"Brother," said Manish with regained composure, "I shall speak candid with you. So I ask for your forgiveness."

"Please, speak your will."

"We can no longer plan acts for political purposes on our own. We can no longer post videos to weak-minded journalists for media sensationalism. These are futile efforts," said Manish in a deep and determined voice while his eyes pierced Hakeem.

After a long pause, Manish said, "We must leverage our strongest ally to avenge our brothers."

"Who's that?" asked Hakeem.

"Greed."

Chapter 1—Hope of a Great Day

Brian Larson's Apartment—Downtown Houston, Texas

"This is the day," Brian said as he disarmed the alarm clock ten minutes before it would have started screeching.

Today was the day Brian Larson would become president of the largest oil company in the world, and the youngest president in the history of the big fives. Brian would control three million barrels-a-day of oil and ten billion cubic feet-per-day of natural gas, and have influence over seventeen percent of the world's natural energy resources.

Brian had been dreaming of this day for years. The day that made his sacrifices worthwhile. All the sixteen hour days, overseas assignments, achievements of the most critical projects, and unbelievably stressful situations. His personal sacrifice in the name of GeoGlobal Energy and the worldwide distribution of oil had finally paid off. No family, no real relationships and no hobbies. His lost personal hours seemed insignificant now.

Brian literally jumped out of bed, almost like Christmas morning when he was a boy growing up in Longview, Texas. He was brushing his teeth when his cell phone rang. Brian smiled as it was no doubt Doug from the public relations department. Brian just let it go to voice mail, as Doug was way too energetic early in the mornings, fueled by far too much caffeine.

After his cell phone gave the familiar chirp noting a new voice mail, Brian pressed the button to listen. "Hey Brian. It's Doug. We've been monitoring the news lines this morning and fielding calls from

1

the media companies. This American Morning called . . . actually Kathy called herself. She wants you on the show this afternoon, in time to beat the five o'clock cycle. I told her you'd call after nine. I think one of the other cable channels might be better. We need your face in front of a younger audience as the new face of energy . . . ."

Doug launched into his chess gambit of publicity maneuvers that he recommended for the day. Although Doug was a valuable asset, he quickly became annoying. Brian chose to ignore Doug until he was officially The Man.

Brian had the appearance expected of up and coming executives in the oil and gas industry. His dark brown hair with a touch of gray conveyed experience, but a cool and modern style to show he was up on the latest trends. He had a small scar on his left front temple from a drilling rig pipe chain, proving to the world he was tough and had been in the field as a roughneck. Brian wore designer suits, fashioned appropriately to show confidence, but just cool enough to not be considered a pompous financial type. His 6' 2", 195 lb. frame, deep brown eyes and thick brown hair with modern haircut made him an image straight out of GQ.

Brian not only had the looks, but the attitude required to be a leader in the business. Every meeting was completely thought out and planned, even days before the event. Project goals were aligned to his benefit. All financials goals were managed and overseen. Sophisticated petrochemical processes were understood and potential revenue and customer markets were targeted. Every division from Geo Sciences through Refining liked and respected Brian. Just as important, Wall Street had faith in him. Brian had become the heir apparent president of GeoGlobal.

Outside the company, politicians, society elite, media and business leaders desired his support. Every man was somewhat jealous of him, but felt comfortable in his presence. These qualities made him one of the most recognized names in the industry, and the most sought after personality at high profile events in Houston.

Without a shadow of doubt, Brian was the most sought after man in a town full of multi-millionaire bachelors. Brian's love life was about the only unstable area of his life. Different social circles in Houston, and around the globe for that matter, often found Brian at the center of the conversation. While many women would blast Brian as being a vain and pompous ass with no concerns for others, any of them would do almost anything just for a date with him. Brian's recent appearance in People Magazine's most eligible bachelors issue only added fuel to this fire.

These charismatic features might seem natural to most, but they're not. In actuality, these attributes were constantly tuned and refined. Brian's work was his hobby. It was his life. His entire personality had become a finely tuned act, all centered on achieving the goal of becoming the most powerful businessman in the world. GeoGlobal had become his family, his mistress and his hobby.

But for Brian personally, he truly loved his company and his associates. Brian never really considered himself a boss, more like the uncle who rose up to be the family patriarch. Although he understood what was required of him on a daily basis, and the daily act of changing personalities based upon the situation, he considered these things a requirement of the business. His family might be dysfunctional occasionally, but nonetheless, it was his family. As the successor to the President of GeoGlobal Energy, he would make sure it stayed in good hands for many years to come.

This morning, the 30-minute workout couldn't end fast enough. The slow timer on the treadmill started to piss him off, and tried his best to forget the stopwatch. He ran faster, hoping his endurance and pride would overcome the slow workout. He stared over the Houston skyline. His $4,000 a month loft over the city gave him the most incredible view. To most, Houston lacked the elegance and romance of New York or Paris, but to Brian this was the most beautiful city in the world. Houston was power, energy and real money. Every other city (and person for that matter) was submissive to the powerful people of this town, one way or another.

Brian smiled at the thought of being the ultimate business influence in the world. Every senator would beg for his capital dollars. Every governor would lobby for one of his plants. Every company associate would long for his attention. Every shareholder would pay dearly for the smallest bit of insider scoop. Every competitor would shake at the thought of his takeovers by a simple signature. He would be—The Man. Complete control over $350 billion. By the time he was done, he would be the first man to lead a $500 billion company. He would make GeoGlobal not only the largest company in the world, but also the most admired and respected. And to some, the most feared.

Or so he dreamed . . .

Chapter 2—Politics of Rising Energy Prices

4th Floor Conference Room
Department of Energy / Fossil Fuel Division—Washington D.C.

"I can feel the sharks circling," said Glen Abbott. "We're looking at $220 per barrel pricing and pump prices at $5.50 per gallon within the next few months. Congress is screaming about lowering energy costs. The President's been advocating this for years. We either loosen the regulations for a new refinery, or we'll find ourselves in the private sector. Then we'll have to work for a living."

The room let out a light chuckle, but the atmosphere was anything but lighthearted. For the past four months, the small group of men and women had a glaring spotlight on them, and the pressure was to the boiling point. Even Glen's name had become a focus of every American's wrath. His initials GA were commonly referred to as "Government Asshole." Ever since the gas crisis of 1976, the ultimate goal of Glen and his team was to take every step possible to limit America's dependency on fossil fuels, not increase the production of them.

To an outsider, this team might seem like a group of Ivy League educated bureaucrats with no real power, but in actuality, it was an extremely talented team with very high influence. Years and years of industry knowledge were in the room, with a deep understanding of energy trends, political forces, environmental issues and the worldwide energy market. Glen had dedicated his entire career to building the perfect team with a well-understood mission statement, and an initiative plan for success that would rival any Fortune 500 CEO's so called "Performance Driven Culture."

Now it seemed to be falling apart. Glen had been leading the Fossil Fuels division at the DOE for around 20 years, and he was very content and competent in his job. Glen had never even tried for a promotion to the head of the DOE, as it was too political in nature. Glen found his job to be very important and rewarding. Radio hosts and television personalities loved to speak of a lack of energy policy, but Glen and his team knew every possible thread of energy policy, and the long-term impacts it posed to the economy. And just as importantly, the government looked to Glen for advice on energy matters, which gave him and his team the personal satisfaction of guiding such an important topic.

Glen very seldom if ever found himself mandated to make swift changes. His job was one of methodical and well-focused objectives, which Glen always achieved. Glen felt his team's contribution made major improvements in oil and gas safety, produced a drastic reduction in CO2 emissions and, until recently, stabilized pricing at a good level. Many times in government work, your efforts will not pay off for years down the road, and they were truly beginning to see the fruits of their labor. Until the past four months.

As every leader of a large organization would tell you, no matter how good things look, something bad will happen tomorrow. Taking the bullet for the team was one thing, but knowing where the bullets were coming from was another. For Glen this was especially true. Glen simply hadn't predicted that oil prices, reserves and stability could get so out of control. As typical in Washington, every politician did a masterful job of avoiding any blame and hammered someone else for the big disasters. This time, the blame fell to Glen and his team.

The nightmare began about four months ago, as a small tropical depression evolved to a massive hurricane, wreaking heavy damage to the oil industry of Louisiana. At the height of the President's popularity, he gave an impromptu press conference while traveling through the devastated Gulf Coast after Hurricane Consuelo. The first question out of the press was not about humanitarian aid, shelter, support or help, it was about gasoline prices. At the moment, oil had just surpassed $110 per barrel on the news that the off shore platform named "Beachhead" had been critically damaged, and a gas transfer station near Port Islas, Louisiana was shut down as well. Gasoline at the pump sold for nearly $4.85 per gallon, with no limit in sight.

President Rhea stood on the front porch of the ruined home of a low income family near Sulphur, Louisiana.

"Well, the problem isn't having enough supply of raw petroleum; the problem is the Washington bureaucrats in the Department of Energy," said President Rhea.

The President quickly glanced at the reporters, attuned to reading their immediate reactions, which helped make him an exceptional orator and media manipulator. The President chose to continue speaking in his educational tone, trying his best to get his point across without looking like he was giving a lecture.

"Our great gas companies have the oil, but they can't refine it, and I don't believe Americans completely understand this situation," said the President while giving an incredulous look to the reporters.

"The Department of Energy and the EPA have steadfastly refused to authorize a new refinery in the U.S. for over 30 years. Now our production is limited to a fixed amount because of our lack of refineries. We have no ability or reason to transfer existing reserves to another refinery, because they're already running at 96 percent of their production capability. This is crazy!" said the President with a dismayed look on his face.

"I mean, this should be obvious. If we're limited on potato chips, we build a potato chip factory. If we're limited on cars, we build a car factory. But in the energy market, we need more fuel, but we build no refineries. This makes no sense at all!

"So, in today's situation, the refinery in Lake Charles depends on oil from the Gulf which is not available because of the storm, so we've effectively knocked out our ability to produce almost 15 percent of our gasoline. The only choice is to import more refined oil from other countries, and that's expensive. Let me ask the obvious question: Who do you think pays for that?"

The President glanced at the reporters for a moment, letting them ponder the rhetorical question. "Yeah, the price at your pump, high commodity pricing, you name it. The American consumer pays for this situation. If not for the bureaucrats in Washington, we would have more refineries and we wouldn't have this problem today. More refineries give us more bandwidth, and room for unexpected situations. Oil and gas executives have been saying this since 1982. It's now time to pay for our government's arrogant blindness towards the realities of today's economy and energy market."

The President sensed the media's immediate reaction. Seldom did the press learn a lesson from a politician, but they were genuinely interested in his message. If they were interested, then Americans could be influenced.

The President gave a deep sigh, giving the impression of trepidation. "Look, there will be lots of debate about my opinion here from a wide array of so-called consultants and experts, especially from the Democrats who unfortunately control the House of Representatives at this moment, unlike my close partners in the Senate."

The President held his hands out. "Americans need to hear me loud and clear, and completely absorb this message. This problem isn't unlike the California electrical energy crisis from a few years back. In California, the problem was limited capacity to produce electricity, identical to our lack of capacity to refine gasoline. To compensate for this, electrical power must be purchased from bordering states at extremely high rates. At the end of the day, the only thing that happens is the average Californian pays four times the average rate for electricity. Then they sit and watch the utility companies make millions of dollars from extra cash flow with no additional infrastructure cost! It's a ridiculous situation."

The President glanced out again, pausing at just the right time to let every point sink into the reporters' heads. Just to make his message even more poignant, he pulled out his ace card.

The President lowered his tone a bit, implying a feeling of disgust: "And just as concerning, the commodity and private equity firms are the biggest winners in all this mess."

"They set the prices. The utility companies aren't the only ones to blame. They can't build plants because of the EPA and DOE, and don't set prices because of trading regulations. California learned its lesson about the EPA, DOE and Wall Street. Those people don't have to worry about paying bills or feeding their families. They're bureaucrats, Ivy League finance types and lawyers. California's now finally in the process of building six new power plants. Interestingly enough, none of the plants are online yet, but electrical power now costs one half of what it was one year ago. Pretty interesting . . . don't you think?"

The President was rolling, and seized this moment to lock his grip on the upcoming elections. He sensed he had made the coveted "simple" connection. He made the gas problem an easy one to understand, got his most loyal campaign contributors the support they needed, and placed the blame on a power area he desperately wanted to control.

The President paused for emphasis, "Americans, I beg of you, look closely at the voting records of your local Congressmen. If they've refused to support a comprehensive energy policy, then send a message and get them out of Congress. Under my leadership and support of Congress, we'll fast-track new refineries in the United States. Give me the help of Congress and our oil pricing situation will go away."

That evening, as the whole country watched coverage of the hurricane devastation on the different news networks, they listened to a confident President give a clear and simple message to a problem affecting millions of people. Every Democrat went on the defensive, talking about how he would give his unbridled support to a refinery bill. The President's approval rating went up an additional eight percentage points the next day, and the Democrats were all but destroyed for the upcoming elections.

To make matters worse for Glen and his team, the oil and gas commodity traders paid the media handsomely to make gas reserves the top story, just adding to the panic of the movement. Glen seriously underestimated how low, far and fast the financial investors and traders on Wall Street would go to raise gas prices. His team had to accept the growing fact that large media outlets lacked a moral compass when it came time to decide whether to present the truth or cover the stories in a manner that directly benefited the companies buying advertising.

But, Glen ultimately understood what greedy investors and first-level thinkers did not: with prolonged irrational oil prices, nothing was too big to fail. No government or governments could stop the economic collapse once the tipping point was crossed. All citizens would be negatively impacted no matter their socioeconomic level. After the real estate collapse, many of the major financial players gambled their remaining fortunes on oil and gas futures and they would go to any length to guarantee their risks paid off. Enron might seem like a disaster to main street America, but to Wall Street, Enron was a beautiful thing as long as you got out in time.

For the average American, the source of pain was a clear one. The new generations of Americans had grown accustomed to instant solutions, and were absolutely unwilling to wait things out. The people of America allowed the EPA and DOE to destroy the American economy and America's dominance of the global market. To Americans, Glen and his team were the reason for all these problems, and there was little he could do to defend himself. Right or wrong, they were to blame. Understanding the price and demand balance for oil was very complicated, and there were no simple answers to complicated topics. However, the President's speech made sure there was no real debate. America wanted refineries, and wanted them now.

Glen had clear orders from the President, the Secretary of Energy and the Energy Committee in Congress, to accelerate the approval process for a new refinery. The President made it very clear in a personal conversation with Glen: he either drafted the legislation for a new refinery within 30 days, or the entire Fossil Fuel Leadership team would be eliminated. As powerful as the President had become, Glen had little doubt he would uphold his word; no matter that he really didn't have the authority. To make matters worse, the last four months had damaged the credibility of his team in the energy industry. Getting a plush job now would be as difficult as a Nixon advisor in the 1970s. His team needed to perform.

Glen said to his team in a direct and blunt tone, "Call your families. Let them know you won't have time for anything else but work. Call your staff, and let them know to be on call 24-hours a day for any purpose. We'll have legislation completed on a new refinery in 30 days. This process typically would take three years. Everyone be back in here in one hour."

Chapter 3—Succession Planning

GeoGlobal Headquarters—Downtown Houston, Texas

"Cocky son of a bitch!" screamed Chuck Gordon as he paced around his overindulgent office overlooking the Houston skyline. "He only wishes he knew the business like I do. How in the hell am I supposed to leave this company to an arrogant bastard like that. My granddaddy would have my ass!"

Chuck Gordon talked to his CFO and grabbed another drink from his liquor cabinet, at 9:00 A.M. His CFO just sat there silently, hoping to get through this situation with as few words as possible. Charles "Chuck" Gordon, president of GeoGlobal Energy, was a legend in the business; at least his family was legendary. He certainly thought himself the legend. The aged and definitely out of touch executive wore $1000 suits with the cheesy cowboy boots, and of course, his initials were on them. He was overweight, with a balding head, white hair, vintage 1980 glasses and a deep Texas accent. He always seemed to wear Windsor knotted tie on a shirt too small for his double chin. The good timing and good living executive only commanded respect because of an intimidating title and a quick temper.

Chuck had the big oil executive office of deep wood with thick shag carpet, open bar with the Jack Daniels, minus the desktop computer because only those who worked for him used those "things." The office was adorned with pictures of himself with industry and political leaders, and pictures of himself with large dead animals from safaris in Africa. To convey the not so subtle point a little further, he had three different exotic deer trophy mounts hanging on the wall, as if to convey a killer attitude to those who entered. The company headquarters' lobby had pictures of himself and the young owners of champion Herefords from the Houston Livestock Show and Rodeo. The pictures of himself with eleven year old girls were the running joke of the company.

Chuck acted like he was important, but in reality he hadn't made an important decision in years. The Board of Directors and other leaders in the company made all the decisions, and only communicated them to Chuck if it was good news. Everyone was just fine with letting him "think" he had anything to do with GeoGlobal being so large. The third-born grandson of the original founder was there by name association only, and was the image Americans and the world hated about big money oil executives.

But Chuck did have one great skill, one that was valuable in today's media. Chuck paid very handsomely to know the backgrounds and secrets of those in powerful places. He had spies of all sorts on his personal payroll, and was very secretive about it.

Chuck caught the eye of his grandfather when he was just a boy. One day while running around the office of his grandfather's oil business in Pasadena, Chuck overheard a heated conversation between his grandfather and a foreman on a pipeline. When the foreman left his grandfather's office, he stormed to another office and slammed the door behind him. Chuck, being a nosy kid, moved closer to the foreman's office door and overheard him talking on the telephone to somebody; he mentioned taking down a well to teach the old man a lesson. Chuck immediately went to his grandfather and let him know of the conversation.

Chuck's grandfather gave him a big smile. "Boy, you've learned the first rule of business. Information is everything."

Chuck's grandfather immediately called a telephone number and offered somebody a $500 bonus to tell him of the conversation he just had with the pipeline foreman.

Chuck's grandfather hung up the phone and said, "Stay here boy, it's time you learned how the world works."

A few moments later three other men, including the foreman, walked into the office. Chuck noticed how all three men were breathing heavily and seemed nervous, but Chuck's grandfather was cool and relaxed.

Chuck's grandfather leaned back in his reclining chair and put his boots on the desk. "Mike, I understand you called Jacob down at 23 after our conversation, and asked him to blow the head off the compressors."

The pipeline foreman's eyes were wide as saucers and he was white as a ghost. No words were spoken.

Chuck's grandfather never took his eyes off the man. "That's what I thought. I always knew you were a sad excuse for a man, with no backbone to back it up. I just wanted to make sure you knew I had the balls to say it in front of others, instead of sabotaging you behind your back. You're fired."

As the ruined man was escorted out of the building, Chuck was pulled aside by his grandfather. "Lesson one, all men are replaceable. Just remember the Gordons rule this place, and never let anyone get in a position to make you vulnerable. Always let others do the hiring, and let the Gordons do the firing. Always have an ace in the hole on all your employees. Lesson two; fire a few people a year, just to keep everyone else on their toes."

Taking his grandfather's advice to heart, Chuck over the years had evolved to nothing more than a real prick with information. As usual with business folks lacking real skills or brains, Chuck mostly resorted to confrontational conversations with business associates to establish the alpha male. His unique ability to create total business disasters, with no operational team, actually evolved into a unique business culture at GeoGlobal. Processes involving capital, acquisitions and strategic decisions didn't require his signature or his input; they only required the CFO's and Group VP's. Because Chuck failed to create an atmosphere of teamwork, other lone wolves in the company took advantage of the every-man-for-himself system and found ways to make decisions without his input or signature.

Typically this would be a problem at other companies, but Chuck was too ignorant to know the difference.

"Arrogant prick," continued Chuck to his CFO, as he crashed down into his desk recliner. "Brian thinks he's a slam dunk for this position. God, the cocky fucker is almost daring me to not select him!"

Chuck waved his hand while pointing towards the door as if someone was standing there, face bright red with anger. "He's talking to Mergers and Acquisitions about acquiring Continental Pipeline. He's talking to the fucking press about our future. Jesus, he's even talking to the goddamned Russian government about a new refinery! He ain't got that authority. He hasn't even spoken to the Group VP of downstream about a refinery!"

"Why are you so upset, Chuck?" said an exasperated Mark Dye, sitting CFO of GeoGlobal and long time business associate of Charles Gordon. "Upstream's delivered over seventy percent of the profits for us for three years running under his control. Not to mention, production made a complete turnaround in nine months under Brian. He's dedicated his life to this company. I think we're lucky to have him."

Chuck stared out the window with a pouting attitude as Mark said, "Come on Chuck, you should be thankful to the man. He's added millions to our bank accounts. Without him, we'd be another generic energy company with $18 stocks. We need visionary leaders like him in the company. Brian is someone who strategically thinks five years ahead, but can perform on a tactical level if needed."

Mark Dye had been dreading this day for over six months, ever since the day Chuck announced his retirement. Mark removed his eyeglasses and rubbed the bridge of his nose with his eyes shut. He tried his best to remain calm as Chuck went on his rant. Over the past 10 years the board made certain Chuck made no major decisions, because they were always a fiasco. In 10 years, Chuck had made only one real decision. And that was his replacement. The board made sure there was only one choice, and as predicted, Chuck made it painful.

After a long and successful career, Mark simply wanted to make it through this conversation and spend the rest of his life relaxing. His 68th birthday was two weeks away, and he had no intention of working a day thereafter. He had sold his majority shares in the bank he founded, and only needed to begin his transition out of GeoGlobal, and he would call it done.

Mark's long and treacherous career as a banker had grown old, and he was ready to get out of the game. Doing double duty as CFO for GeoGlobal and president of the bank he founded had left him completely mentally exhausted. GeoGlobal was the only major oil company to exclusively bank with his company, but the bank was intensely involved with other oil and gas support companies. Many smaller firms such as engineering companies and original equipment manufacturers used UnionTrust. UnionTrust had a way of making sure its clients received the most lucrative contracts from the major oil and gas players. This "negotiating" capability might seem unethical to those on the outside, but to the oil and gas world in Houston it was simply a way of taking care of your own. There was plenty of money to go around, just make sure everyone stayed stable. Mark had the influence now to make sure the 1980s oil and gas depression wouldn't happen again.

"His leadership! You saying we ain't successful under my leadership?" yelled Chuck in a pissed off tone.

Mark said, "Chuck. I understand your pride. The young buck is replacing the old man. But come on. Please, for me and the board, make this transition an easy one. Just announce Brian as your replacement. Let's share the last years of our lives traveling the world with our old ladies and playing golf and poker. Brian's an exceptional leader. The company's in good hands."

Chuck fired back, "Kiss my ass, Mark! Don't talk to me in that demeaning tone. I've been President here for so long because I've made a living keeping people like Brian Larson under control, and milking them for all they're worth. Nobody knows the business like I do. Cocky punks like him are a dime a dozen, and easily replaceable. I'll choose who I damn well please."

Mark felt his pulse rise. Too many years of attitude from Charles Gordon pretending to be the badass of GeoGlobal was now overwhelming and his delusions of grandeur had long run their course. Instinctively, Mark resorted to the skills that made him one of the most powerful bankers in the world.

Mark said, "Charles. The board, Wall Street, management and I believe Brian is the most qualified candidate. I hate to be so candid with you, but frankly, you're the one who doesn't understand the business. You had a hand in the old wildcatter days of building gas wells, but now the company is completely different. GeoGlobal is about refining, pipeline management, commodity trading and consumer products on a global scale. You're not anywhere near qualified to decide who should run GeoGlobal. This company has long since bypassed your understanding of the business."

Chuck gave Mark a look of rage that would burn a hole through solid iron. In his entire career, nobody had spoken to him in that tone, except for his grandfather. "Boy, are you saying I'm a pawn in your game, and the decision isn't mine?"

"That's exactly what I'm saying. You're only here as a figurehead. Jesus Christ, the board even has quarterly offsite meetings with the VPs just to keep you out of the loop. Grow up for once in your life. When Brian gets here this morning, you'll do as you're told and announce him as replacement. Good God, Chuck, Brian's constantly and steadfastly been a supporter of yours and GeoGlobal. You would've long since been terminated if not for men and women like Brian. The board has allowed you to stay so we wouldn't disturb our stocks and out of respect for your family name. As a board member, I'm asking you to calm down and make the right decision. This conversation's making me uneasy, as your undeserved pride will affect my net value and thousands of others. GeoGlobal staffs over 80,000 good people, and its economic impact is phenomenal. I simply won't sit here and let you make a mistake of this magnitude."

The room fell into an unbelievable silence. Both men pondered the turn of events of the last few minutes. Mark felt the personal satisfaction of putting Chuck in his place. *It's about time someone told him how the world works,* thought Mark. *Just stand your ground, and we'll get over this situation.*

Both men were breathing heavily as they stared each other down. Memories of their long-term relationship flooded their minds. Both men knew the stakes. The importance of this moment was extremely high to GeoGlobal and millions of shareholders and 401K owners around the world.

A wry smile came across Chuck's face. "Mark, you and the board can kiss my ass. This is my company with the majority shares, and I'll choose who I damn well please. And it ain't Brian."

Mark screamed, "You arrogant idiot! You'll regret this! The board and I will meet within the hour to unanimously vote to terminate you! I'll make it my mission to seize your stocks, and leave them in legal shambles for years! By the end of the day, you'll be a joke in Houston and be in financial ruins!"

"You won't do that, Mark," said Chuck. "You think I don't know about your arrangement with Mitchell-Nelson Consulting? Man, it was really interesting how every member of the Integrity Capitol 'Texas Tea Fund' got indicted except yourself."

Mark's body was frozen in a moment to which he was not accustomed. Chuck's comments made him go numb. Mark was always the one in control. Now this brainless cowboy had completely caught him off guard.

Chuck couldn't help but giggle, "Oh, and how's—Michael is it? Man, he's a fine looking young boy. I wonder how the media would handle it: the most powerful banker in the world, I mean the founder of UnionTrust himself, is discovered to be both a money launderer and a homosexual. Wow, that's some story!" exclaimed Chuck as he paced near the wall-length window.

"I can just see it at the top of the Chronicle—*Mark Dye, President of UnionTrust, is a thief, adulterer and homosexual.* Wow, that's a great story!" said Chuck as he broke out into deep and lengthy laughter.

Mark literally felt his knees start to bend. "How, how . . . . could you possibly . . . . Michael and I never . . . . how do you know about Michael . . . . ."

Chuck's laughter instantly stopped and spoke in his tone direct, "Mark, I never want to see you again. Oh, by the way, let the board know I have even better dirt on them. You'll . . . how did you say it with such bravado? Oh, I remember, 'Do as you're told' and release a statement today that the board has complete and total confidence in your current president, and fully endorse whoever I damn well choose!"

Just to lay the mortal blow, Chuck said the words that no father ever wanted to hear: "How's your daughter? Boy, I remember the time she and I . . . Well, some things are better left unsaid. It's just . . . man, I can't get that smell of her out of my mind. I mean, the way she . . . ."

Chuck talked off into the distance, "I understand she has a little family and a young and aspiring lawyer husband. I'd hate to call Judge Lettermer and let him know some things. Hell, I bet he couldn't get a job anywhere in this state, maybe not even in the country. Well that's not true, the world could always use a legal clerk to help research some things . . . Well, I'd just hate to see her lose her husband and daddy in one horrible week. Don't you agree, Mark?"

Mark was now bent over; both hands on his face, his mind reeled with the pain of the words.

"Say it Mark," said Chuck as he walked towards him. "Say it boy! Look at me and say it!"

With every ounce of strength he could muster, Mark stood upright and looked straight into Chuck's eyes. "I'll support any decision you make for president of GeoGlobal."

A big smile crossed Chuck's face. He picked up his phone. "Get security to escort out Mr. Dye, and execute the replacement plan. Remove Dye and the leaders of upstream and refining. I better not see an operational leader in my sight."

Mark was stunned, and looked at Chuck with a perplexed and scared expression. The crazy old bastard had actually done it. Chuck had already planned the removal of the operations leadership at GeoGlobal. Anything related to petroleum gathering and production was now in his hands completely. He had put the fortunes and careers of thousands in jeopardy, just to prove he could. Mark's mind raced, absolutely shocked, trying to comprehend these actions.

In short order, the security guards opened the door to the office. As they escorted out a ruined man, Chuck shouted orders to the head of security, "Get rolling on it. Remove all three division VPs from the building. Verify their cell phones have been deactivated. Don't let a single one of those fuckers on any GeoGlobal property with only one exception. Have Brian Larson come to my office the moment he walks in the door."

Chapter 4—An American Crisis

4th Floor Conference Room
Department of Energy / Fossil Fuel Division—Washington D.C.

Glen rubbed his temples while waiting for the rest of his team to return to the conference room. He had just read the confidential update on the latest oil and gas news, which only added more stress to an unrelenting situation.

Glen turned to Dr. Jennifer Liepert, who stayed in the conference room while the others left to call their families, as she had no family to tend to. "This is bad, Jenny. We're in a full economic war. This kind of financial collapse causes historical revolutions. How in the hell did all this fall to us?"

Glen acting this way was incredulous to Jenny, and she gave an almost frightened look back at him.

"How bad is it?" asked Jenny.

Glen let out a deep sigh, and spoke while he rubbed his temples, "It's bad. It's real bad. China's forecasting a twenty-five percent increase in their petroleum usage over the next ten years. This is utter bullshit. This kind of increase isn't feasible."

Jenny's eyes flew wide open, and she quickly grabbed the document. "Glen, they don't have the reserves for that kind of oil . . . . Oh my God. They cut a deal with Venezuela. They have first rights to sweet crude in Latin America."

Glen looked up at Jenny, actually relieved that someone as astute as he picked up on the information so quickly.

Jenny, stunned at the words she read, quickly looked up at Glen. "We're not the primary customer to Latin America anymore. We have a supply crisis now as well. This will push oil pricing to incredible levels."

"Yep," said Glen. "When this information hits the press, oil and gas trading will move sky high. China has just delivered a business shot across the bow. Petroleum prices at this level will effectively stop our economy and put us in a permanent recession."

A frazzled Jenny asked, "How did the meeting with Congress go this morning? I'm guessing it was dreadful."

"It's a disaster, Jenny. The only thing that kept me from getting blasted even worse is they're scared to death. Beating me to a pulp seems insignificant now. Even the most bearish economist didn't see this coming," said Glen in a tone of dread.

Jenny listened to his every word as Glen said, "We had a couple of high end economists talk with us, and they both essentially said the same thing. With most energy crises, the economic curve is about a six month event. The high gas prices limit spending on expendable income, you know, travel, vacations, higher end items like boats, electronics and things like that. Then manufacturing starts to trend downward as existing inventory plans are met at a faster pace. Then manufacturing companies idle their plants, layoffs occur, bargain shopping commences, then spending almost comes to a halt."

Glen continued, "So, the lack of cash flow is a devastating event, causing existing bank loans to go into default, and new loans are shut off so banks can hoard their cash reserves. Things like this create a cascade effect that takes months for the full impact. Usually the good news is the economy rebounds at about the same pace."

Glen then moved towards Jenny to make sure she fully comprehended his next comments. She was his most trusted associate, and he needed her to perform.

"Jenny, this one's different. Gas prices go down in a depression, not up, and definitely not exponentially up. Energy prices aren't coming down, they're going up. Nobody even considered this kind of effect. You understand what I am saying?"

Jenny was on edge, not really sure how to respond. "I understand, but I might not be grasping your full intention, Glen."

A frustrated Glen almost angrily said, "Gas prices are going up. It's actually costing more to make the most basic of commodities. They're not coming down. This cycle can't last. We're in a major recession, and prices are actually going up."

"What're you saying, Glen?" asked Jenny, almost scared to hear the words.

Glen looked towards the door to make sure nobody heard their conversation. "Congress is scared to death, Jenny. Our meetings are all classified because this information isn't supposed to be out, but I need you to understand the full story."

"What do I need to know, Glen?" asked Jenny.

Glen almost whispered, "This cycle can't last, it can't last. We don't know how to get out of it. Imagine it, Jenny. Imagine not having a job, and clinging to your money. Basic items such as milk go from $4.00 a gallon to $8.00 a gallon. Inflation isn't based upon demand, it's based on real cost. Everything comes to a halt. We're talking a total economic collapse. Total."

Glen shook his head back and forth, and took a deep breath. "They're secretly beginning to ramp up the National Guard for fear of riots. Read your history tonight, Jenny. This kind of meltdown ended the Czar rule in Russia, brought the Nazis to power; I mean this is truly historical. Petroleum is the basis of our entire economy, it's now truly unaffordable. We either get energy back where it needs to be, or you can only imagine what our country will become."

Jenny leaned back, almost like the words were pushing her.

Glen said, "And they're looking to us to fix it. That's exactly what you need to know."

Chapter 5—Hopes Shattered

GeoGlobal Headquarters—Downtown Houston, Texas

While driving his company-owned SUV to the office, Brian winced at the news of oil going to $190 per barrel. *I'll have to make the TV news circuit,* thought Brian. *People need to calm down and come up with real solutions.*

Although rising prices to this level made most oil and gas executives celebrate, Brian understood what this really meant. Pricing at this level drastically reduced the usage of petroleum, further expedited the expansion of alternative fuels such as ethanol, and ramped up the development of hybrid automobiles and hydrogen-based fuel cell research. Plus, to limit the embarrassing stock dividends at the end of the quarter, GeoGlobal would be forced to announce drastic capital investments for the future. Over the past two years, GeoGlobal Engineering had been systematically devastated with the workload already. Another billion dollar capital project announcement would push engineering and design over the edge.

Brian was already thinking as president of GeoGlobal. He really had over the past three months. At one of the offsite meetings with the other VPs and the board, he felt an overwhelming sense of satisfaction and respect when the team unanimously selected him as Chuck's replacement. The support, friendships and genuine commitment from the other VPs only deepened Brian's sense of pride for GeoGlobal, and firmly established the board's support for his efforts.

A daydream took over Brian as he drove, and he thought of the many steps required as leader of the company. Seeing the entrance to the company headquarters snapped him out of it. Brian was surprised he had a few moments to himself, assuming his cell phone would be ringing off the hook as usual. He just assumed most people were giving him some space on the big day. As Brian pulled to the security gates, he found it difficult to keep his smile in check.

"Morning, Mr. Larson," said the security guard. "I have an urgent message for you. It says you're to see Mr. Gordon the minute you walk in the door. Skip going to your office and see him immediately."

The security guard had been at this post for many years. Though a stickler for process and details, his usual warm demeanor gave everyone a sense of personal security. The guard seemed a little stern today, which was a little odd.

The security guard said, "Just skip the parking garage and go directly to the main lobby entrance. We have a spot reserved for you there already."

Most times, this request to see Mr. Gordon would only concern Brian. Chuck only spoke to Brian on rare occasions, to act important. But this morning, Brian understood the urgency. He was sure Chuck wanted to get the formality of the process out of the way, and begin scheduling meetings, press releases, interviews and things like that.

"No problem," said Brian. "I'm heading there right now."

The security guard nodded, and the gate and concrete barrier gave way to a clear driveway. Odd, thought Brian. The security guard was usually much more conversational. No matter. Today was a great day in the life of Brian Larson.

Brian entered the massive lobby of GeoGlobal Headquarters. The entire lobby was made of high-rise glass casings that give an ambiance of a bright future. The floor was adorned with miniature models of refineries and offshore platforms. The walls proudly displayed years and years of awards, patents and accomplishments of the massive company. Three large corridors lead from the large glass encased entrance. Down one corridor was the "hall of fame" for GeoGlobal, which held numerous hand-sculpted copper busts of founders and important members of GeoGlobal. Brian had no doubt he would one day be in that group.

Brian walked toward the elevators and gave the good mornings and hellos to other associates of GeoGlobal. Brian had a remarkable memory. He pretty much knew every person he saw, and his or her function in the company. Brian's ability to recall almost everyone he met further cemented his reputation as a good guy.

"Mr. Larson!" shouted someone behind him.

Brian turned and saw a lobby security guard jogging towards him.

"Mr. Larson, I'm here to escort you to Mr. Gordon's office. We have strict orders to make sure you go there first."

"This is a little overboard isn't it?" quizzed Brian. "I'm heading there right now and doubt I need an escort."

The guard said, "Sorry, Mr. Larson. Orders are from Mr. Gordon himself."

The security guard resumed walking immediately to the right and behind Brian. He attempted no further conversation and had a very serious look on his face.

"Wow," said Brian.

The ride up the elevator was awkward. Mr. Gordon's office was on the 14th floor, and the security guard didn't allow anyone else to join the ride. In the lobby, the security guard shouted orders to other associates to wait for the next elevator as Mr. Larson needed a speedy ride to the executive offices. Brian, feeling pompous, did his best to avoid eye contact. Everyone knew who he was, and he was sure the associates felt one of the big shots was playing the part. Neither the guard nor Brian attempted conversation the whole way up.

As the elevator door opened the guard said, "To your left and down the hall."

Brian stopped and looked at the guard. "I'm well aware of the way to the office. I think you need to remember your place here."

The guard made no comments or gestures. He simply continued to stand next to Brian on the lavish floor of the executive offices with his finger pointing down the hallway. A flustered Brian chose to ignore him and walked at a high pace towards Mr. Gordon's office.

As Brian paced down the hallway, he sensed something wasn't right. The offices of the Executive VPs were closed and the floor was eerily quiet. At this time of the morning on most days, you heard nearly everyone on the telephone with their teams all over the world, conducting important business situations. The support staff sat quietly in their cubicles, and made no attempt at eye contact. Brian's senses were now at full alert. Instinctively, he reached for his phone to call his counterparts.

"I am stepping in here for a moment. I'll be right back," said Brian.

With that, he ducked into the men's room, not offering the guard a chance to protest. Brian walked straight past the urinals and into a stall. He stooped down to see if any others were in the bathroom. It seemed he was by himself. He started to find his contact list on his cell phone, and to his amazement, it said "no service."

"What the hell is this?" Brian couldn't even begin to comprehend what had happened. Instead of panicking, years of crisis solving kicked in and he pieced things together. He made the conclusion that Chuck Gordon had pulled one on him.

Brian had considered approaching Chuck first about becoming President, but the board insisted they communicate with Chuck. It was well known you didn't give Chuck the chance to say no, because he would. During his rise through the executive ranks, Brian sometimes worried that he should have a better relationship with Chuck, and he thought it rather sad the old man had so little involvement with the great company. In all these years of phenomenal growth, Brian had never built any type of relationship with him. Although his direct boss on paper, Brian had never discussed any major business decisions with him. No problem for Brian on a professional level, the more power he had the better, but on a personal level the situation was rather bothersome.

Brian knew he couldn't stay in the bathroom forever, and had to face the situation. He left the bathroom with a different attitude, as his jovial outlook 10 minutes earlier had now turned to business survival. This meeting wasn't going to be a good one, and Brian had no idea what his life and career would be on the other side of this conversation.

Chapter 6—Anxiety

Dr. Jenny Liepert's Office
Department of Energy / Fossil Fuel Division—Washington D.C.

Jenny excused herself from Glen for a few moments to collect her thoughts prior to the meeting. She shut the door to her office, grabbed a diet soda, and sat in her chair to reflect on the moment. Jenny's years in the oil and gas business had prepared her for energy policy, not crisis management.

Dr. Jennifer "Jenny" Liepert led the O&G Supply Division at the Department of Energy, and her long track record of success and achievements seldom left anyone to doubt her capability. But now, even Jenny wondered if she could be depended upon to navigate energy policy in a dramatically changing world. She was accustomed to giving advice on the U.S. petroleum roadmap for years to come, not dictating exactly what the U.S. should do to stop an economic crisis. Jenny took a deep sigh, and stared blankly out her office window.

Jenny was an outgoing and friendly woman in her late thirties who was extremely confident in her job, but was somehow always introverted in her personal life. Being known affectionately as the local roughneck was a fun joke, but few doubted her ability to run the department or her intimate knowledge of the oil and gas business. Jenny somehow was able to carry on a conversation with any person, but also had natural leadership ability with deep insight, wit and wisdom. Jenny's personality was mostly attributed to her Texas upbringing, a down to earth attitude towards people and their families. Although Jenny was single, she often attended family outings with her associates at the DOE, no matter what job title they had. Work was her life and constant obsession, except for her commitment to her horses on Sundays. If you wanted to meet with Jenny on Sundays that was fine, but it would be at the stables on the outskirts of Chantilly, Virginia, where you'd be riding horses with her. Her long blonde hair, deep brown eyes and wonderful smile gave her the natural southern girl look, and she often found many single and married men needing to have a conversation on a Sunday.

Jenny was raised in the small East Texas town of Kilgore, the original oil capital of Texas. She and her mother lived alone in a small, two-bedroom house in an average to lower income neighborhood. Although the neighborhood might not have been the best, Jenny and her mother were constantly working on their house, where Jenny learned about building something together and the importance of people you can trust. Jenny knew little about her father, but she had felt the void her whole life. Her mother had never gone on a date with another man, and Jenny understood her mother only had one true love. Jenny's father had chosen the oil business as his true love, and he never looked back.

Her mother had worked at the local Texas Oil Museum for as long as Jenny remembered, and still does to this day. Through her mother, Jenny learned the true roots of the oil business. Jenny and her mother would read books together on oil production, chemicals and major companies. They would take trips all through East Texas to view the different oil production facilities, tank farms and pipeline booster stations. It might seem like a strange family hobby to most, but Jenny understood it was her mother's way of coping with the loss of her true love. Somehow, keeping the oil business close made her mother feel more comfortable, and allowed her to come to terms with her loss.

No matter to Jenny, she loved every minute of it. Oil and gas insiders knew her as a natural and it was in her blood. No words were truer. While most girls dreamed of being cheerleaders or prom queens, Jenny dreamed of being a roughneck. Not in the literal sense of actually connecting drill pipes to 3000 horsepower equipment, but she desperately wanted to be in the game.

She remembered her first job at an oil and gas company. She walked into the Republic Gas production offices in Kilgore when she was 13 years old. It was the start of summer vacation, and she rode her bicycle three miles to the office from her home.

She walked in the office; her stomach was filled with butterflies as she asked the receptionist, "My name is Jenny Liepert and I would like to have a job. Can I please have one?"

"My word!" said the receptionist. "Honey, you should be out playing with your friends. School just got out last week. Does your mother know you're here? Who's your mother?"

"She's at work ma'am, but I'll do anything you need. Please let me have a job," begged Jenny in the most sincere voice a 13-year-old girl could manage.

To her left next to the coffee machine stood a tall man with faded Jeans, Republic Gas blue long sleeve shirt, worn out steel toed boots and Ranger Boat hat. In a booming voice he asked, "Young lady. Why in the world would you want to work here?"

Jenny said, "Well sir, I think Republic Gas is the most wonderful company in the world. I've read how Republic Gas has the best geologists, and how you almost never miss when you drill! Oh, and how you understand the piping of the gas after separation, it's just amazing. I know where all your gathering stations and compressors are, but how do you know to drill in the places to get the pipelines? Why do you use electrical motors for compressors sometimes, and not just use natural gas engines? I mean, you have all the gas in the world right there!"

The tall man and the receptionist stared at the young girl in amazement, not knowing what to say next. Jenny heard a shuffle in the office behind the receptionist. A heavy set man with a deeply dark skin from years of outside labor stepped through the office door, and gave Jenny a deep stare.

"Mrs. Johnson," said the man from the office, "I think we've found our office assistant you need for the summer. How does $4.50 an hour sound, young lady?"

The receptionist turned to Jenny with a huge smile, and the tall man slowly walked towards Jenny with his hand out. "Welcome aboard!"

With that, Jenny got her start in oil and gas. Jenny continued to work for Republic Gas year round, full-time in the summer and part-time during school. Republic Gas gave Jenny a scholarship to Texas A&M, where she earned a double degree in Chemistry and Petroleum Engineering. From there, Jenny went to work for Gulf Star Refining in Saudi Arabia straight out of college. Jenny longed for international travel, plus the starting salary of $70,000 a year was more money than she ever dreamed of. Jenny had a rough breakup with her college boyfriend, and the thought of starting fresh in another country was perfect for her.

Although Jenny deeply loved the fast-paced work of the refinery and the industry, she eventually found the lack of good friends, and almost no other women, to become straining on her life. Being a blonde-haired woman in the position of authority in Saudi Arabia became quite stressful. She was very lonely, and longed to have some outlet in her life.

Jenny soon discovered a small group of young college graduates from the United States, while visiting the American embassy in Riyadh. Over time the embassy became her home away from home, and she quickly grew interested in the politics and finance of the oil and gas industry. During her time at the embassy, she became close friends with many Ivy League trained students with a completely different perspective on life. Their careers were in culture, politics, money and society issues. To her pleasant surprise, most of these embassy employees did not have the pompous attitude she expected. Instead, they were deeply motivated to understand the culture of the Saudi people and to do their best to have American business and ideals integrate with Saudi residents. Jenny actually helped one of her friends teach a class on basic engineering principles to a group of young students. Since Jenny was a woman, the students of the class were stunned when she walked in and began teaching. Moments such as these were the small but impactful steps her friends implemented to integrate American culture.

With much persuasion and support from her new friends, Jenny became convinced she needed to better understand finance if she were to be a leader in this industry. Jenny applied to the Harvard School of Business where she was immediately accepted, and went on to earn a Masters Degree in Business and a Ph.D. in Economics. After completing her degrees, Jenny joined the Department of Energy Fossil Fuel Division, where she'd been ever since.

Jenny, now at 37 years old, was actually a 24-year veteran of the business with deep knowledge of the technical and business side of energy. Most people in her field didn't underestimate her; at least they never had until four months ago, when America's oil-driven economy threatened to grind to a halt. Now for the first time in her professional career, Dr. Jenny Liepert was being looked upon as unable to perform her job, and seemed to have critics all over the place. Her years of forecasting predictability in petroleum supplies had been her hallmark of success. Suddenly it seemed she didn't have a handle on U.S. petroleum supplies at all.

The world now seemed to only focus on one area of the Department of Energy: O&G Supply and Delivery. Ironic actually, O&G Supply was typically the most mundane of all the divisions. Infrastructure issues were extremely political in nature, and involved much more input from the Department of Transportation for interstate commerce and tax issues, and the Department of Interior for quality of life, visual appearance, environmental concerns and land rights. Infrastructure additions were so difficult to get passed that the oil companies had become quite competent at upgrading their existing equipment, and didn't even bother requesting new pipeline routes, let alone ten to twenty new pipelines required for a refinery.

However, O&G Supply was the biggest factor in pricing of the commodity, and data was the name of the game. Wall Street analysts, politicians, prospectors, and lobbyists were constantly trying every trick in the book to get the inside scoop on their futures report. O&G Supply influenced billions of dollars in price fluctuation with any indicator of supply, weather concerns, energy usage or infrastructure capacity. The tricks and games major financial players used were phenomenal, and the associates in O&G Supply were well accustomed to their ways. Economics was the big focus for the O&G Division, and everyone thanked God every day for spreadsheets and the glorious invention of relational databases.

Jenny returned to the conference room and took her seat at the end of the table next to Glen Abbott. She was completely devoted to the effort he requested over the next 30 days. Through all the pressure, Jenny continued to look like a million bucks. She wore a long pleated beige skirt, long brown boots up to her knees, and a very attractive white blouse that was cut just low enough to show hints of her chest. Her long blonde hair was in a well-groomed ponytail that pulled over her left shoulder. Jenny was taught long ago by her college boyfriend to always look the part, and give an appearance of control and outside composure, even if you're dying on the inside. Jenny was as prepared for this journey as she ever could be.

Chapter 7—Corporate Reality

GeoGlobal Headquarters—Downtown Houston, Texas

Brian was almost overcome with emotion while walking toward Gordon's office. He had chosen his career over a family and long-term relationships, dedicating his entire life to this company. He now had the sinking feeling that he made the wrong choices.

Brian was completely confused, but sensed that Chuck had done something. He'd let Chuck take him down a road, trying to set the bait. But Brian would be ready, and had no intentions of taking a sword to a gunfight. Although he had no idea of what "ready" meant, he wouldn't let Mr. Gordon have the satisfaction of the last word.

Or should he? Maybe the best idea was to be submissive to Mr. Gordon, let him win the battle, but Brian would win the war. He decided to not be angry and just be cool. His mind was probably imagining things, but he doubted it. At the end of the day, the board was the major decision maker, and they supported him. He took a deep breath, and then confidently knocked on the door while entering Mr. Gordon's office.

"Mr. Gordon, you asked to speak to me this morning?" said Brian in the most middle-of-the-road voice he could manage.

"Sit down Brian," said Chuck Gordon. He was reading some GeoGlobal documents, but never bothered to look up or shake Brian's hand.

Brian sat in the chair for what seemed an eternity while Chuck read the documents, not saying a word. His bad feeling about the meeting was getting worse.

Chuck finally started in a slow and inquisitive voice while never looking at Brian, "Why don't you tell me about these quarterly offsite meetings with the board."

Now it clicked. Chuck discovered the leadership team circumvented his approvals. Chuck was acting like a jealous high school kid who didn't get to start on varsity and wanted to get even.

"Sure," said Brian. "Would you like to know about the overview of the meetings, or are there some specific details you'd like to discuss?"

Chuck looked up with his all-knowing smug expression, throwing his papers on his desk. He leaned back in his chair with his hands behind his head and said, "I want to know everything, boy. I've got all day."

Now this was the hard part. Brian could easily manipulate Chuck's thoughts, but he wasn't sure how much he had already discovered. This might turn out okay, but Brian couldn't be caught in a lie. As of right now, Brian still felt he would be president with or without Chuck's approval, but the less Chuck contested his new role, the better.

Chuck played his mind game as well. Unfortunately for Chuck, he couldn't find any good dirt on Brian. Brian had a ton of different girlfriends, but nothing out of the ordinary for a millionaire bachelor. Brian always seemed dedicated to the company and led a pretty quiet life, which highly annoyed Chuck. He even planted a few traps for him, including drugs and prostitutes, but he never took the bait. As far as Chuck could tell, he managed his money well and did a masterful job of avoiding career-limiting moves.

Instinctively Brian resorted to his sales tone, with the full intention of making the meetings sound unimportant with mundane topics. That way, Chuck wouldn't think he'd missed something important, but would only be pissed he wasn't invited to the party.

Brian said, "Well, with the crazy growth over the past few years, the board constantly find themselves talking to one another about situations they really don't understand."

Chuck stared at Brian with no emotion in his face, so Brian continued, "Uh, for example, you remember the fiasco we created on the LNG terminal in Asia? Well, the board kept getting many questions about things like that, and having to scramble to call operations, VPs, each other. All this really only got half of the story. So to make life easier, they started having meetings to discuss operational issues, sales trends and things like that. Personally I think the meetings could be much more productive and strategic in nature, but they're mostly 'is everything going okay?' meetings."

Brian chuckled, "I think the BP thing got the board so freaked out, they want to look at operation guys in the eye and threaten their firstborn if things aren't exactly how we say they are."

Brian continued to smile after the speech, but Chuck looked at him with a deep stare without any hint of a grin on his face. Brian knew what Chuck was doing; he was trying to read the signs of a liar via leg movement, eye contact or a stressed face. Chuck would find no clues here; hell, Brian could give seminars on beating a lie detector test with the stress and training of his career in this godforsaken business.

Brian did the same, but Chuck didn't have a clue he'd already read the signs. From the moment Brian walked in the room, he was looking for the human clues just like a Fortune 100 senior sales representative. Chuck was nervous, and having difficulty keeping focus. Chuck's labored breathing was obvious, and he read the same document three times while sitting in silence when Brian first entered. He knew Chuck was pondering the only avenue he understood, and that was one of confrontation.

But something was holding him back. *Is Chuck afraid of something or someone? What the hell is bothering him so much?* Brian knew he had the advantage here, so he would throw a curve ball to see how Chuck reacted.

Brian asked, "Mr. Gordon, it seems awfully quiet around here this morning. Not a single VP is in their office, and no one has called me. It's really strange. Is something going on?"

Chuck fired back while pointing his finger towards Brian, "Maybe they're having an offsite, and you weren't invited!"

Okay. Now we're getting somewhere, thought Brian. He'd first go for stroking his ego.

Brian held up his hands in a defensive motion and said, "Hey, hey, Mr. Gordon. If I've offended you by attending these meetings, I apologize."

Chuck leaned back in his chair again, with a deep stare of hate beaming towards Brian.

Brian said, "I asked once about you being there, but the board said there's no need to bother you with trivial details. As a matter of fact, Mr. Dye once said, 'GeoGlobal pays me a lot of money to worry about these problems, and it's my job to solve them, not Mr. Gordon's.'"

This was the important moment. If Chuck came out of his chair, then Brian would be the winner. Mr. Gordon would put the punk in his place, feel satisfied, and then go on with the details of the president transfer. If Chuck responded otherwise, then Brian was terminated from GeoGlobal.

Chuck looked Brian straight in the eye, and delivered the message he had been dreaming about for six months. Chuck lashed out with an evil veracity he didn't expect. "Brian, I know you take me for a fool. Guys like you are a dime a dozen, who wouldn't be shit without my company making you everything you are. Look at you, all dolled up like some pussy hitting the news channels today. Because of me, you are what you are. When you eat dinner, it's my company that put the food on the plate. When you get laid by some bimbo, it's my money they're chasing. You're nothing without me, boy. Fuck you, and fuck the board for pressuring me to choose your sorry ass."

Brian gave a steely glare to the old bastard, contemplating jumping the desk and beating this sack of shit to a pulp. All the years of dedication and personal sacrifice he gave to this company, and this is how the son of a bitch thanked him! Brian's fists clenched in his chair, and the adrenaline ran through him. But again, this was probably a trap. The old man was pulling a stunt to get Brian busted for assault or something, just to sabotage his new role. Brian played it cool for the moment.

Chuck said, "I won't stand by and let you and the board force me out, or force a decision I don't want to make. It gives me great pleasure in saying you won't be president of GeoGlobal Energy. Your blatant abuse of your authority by bypassing me to the board is insubordination of the highest order. You're fired."

Brian said, "We both know your total lack of ability to run a company like this. I have the full support of the Divisional VPs, the support of Wall Street and the board. If you terminate me, then you'll be the one explaining why this company is being run by someone with no capability, no brains and definitely no knowledge of the business. By noon today, you'll be begging me to come back. And you can bet it'll be a cold day in hell before I give you any more satisfaction of my services."

Chuck laughed out loud, "Boy, you have a lot to learn, and sound an awful lot like a meeting I had this morning. First of all, the Operations VPs have already been terminated. Secondly, you might want to read this."

Chuck handed the document over to Brian with the most pompous, arrogant smile imaginable. Brian sat stunned as he read the words.

From: GeoGlobal Board of Directors
To: Public, Press, Shareholders, Stakeholders and Associates of GeoGlobal Oil

For immediate release:
Six months ago, Chuck Gordon, our longtime president, announced his retirement. To date, Mr. Gordon has not felt confident in the candidates interviewed to replace his position. Mr. Gordon has decided to remain with GeoGlobal for an extended period until a qualified candidate is selected for this important role, and a proper transition plan is in place.

In addition, we announce operational changes at GeoGlobal. In today's environment of rising oil and gas prices, we feel leaders more adaptive to the changing global energy needs are required. Over the next month, GeoGlobal will announce replacements for all three Divisional Vice Presidents with the company.

The Board of Directors fully supports Mr. Gordon in his decisions. GeoGlobal will be announcing our new leaders as they assume their roles.

Regards,
Mark Dye
Chief Financial Officer and Operations Liaison

Brian couldn't believe the words he read. His temper was severely overshadowed by his profound confusion. How could the board betray him this way? He couldn't take his eyes off the document. The next thing he knew was the sound of security coming in the office.

Chuck shouted, "Have him escorted him off the premises! And all the way off. Don't let him drive out of here in his pussy SUV. That's company property!"

Two security guards moved briskly towards Brian, and literally picked him up out of the chair. As Brian was whisked out of the office, he couldn't even begin to speak. There were simply no words, just utter confusion and dismay at the circumstances of the past 30 minutes.

As the elevator door opened in the lobby, another security guard joined the group, and they began the long walk across the main foyer. Everyone stopped and stared at the commotion. Brian held his head low at the total embarrassment of this moment. He walked past many associates he knew, and they stared in confusion at Brian with the three security guards, including one with his hand firmly on Brian's arm.

In the middle of the lobby, one of the security guards stopped the group right in front of a bunch of people and said, "I need your office keys, company credit cards, company computer and any other items. I need them immediately."

Brian actually felt his skin get a sensation of a thousand small needles pricking away at him, a common first sign of an anxiety attack. His face was bright red, and the sweat rose through his shirt. He briefly looked up and saw two of his close associates watching this scene with shocked and sad expressions. He briefly felt an urge to break down, but just told himself to hold it together. He slowly handed his keys, company credit card and cell phone to one of the guards. His PC was in his (now old) office.

The walk across the parking lot was even worse. It was already a sweltering 89 degrees with high humidity at 10:00 A.M., and the Texas sun ripped right through him. The heat of the day and his expensive dark pinstriped suit melted Brian. As he walked, other associates of GeoGlobal stopped their cars and stared at the unusual scene unfolding before them. As they got to the security entrance, Brian looked up to see the sad face of the gate security guard. With this, it was too much. Brian felt his chest swell up, and his eyes got moist. The tears started flowing and couldn't be stopped.

As the guards walked Brian to the street, they stepped away from him. Brian was suddenly standing on a busy street sidewalk, no ride, no job, and no phone. Brian was embarrassed, confused, and alone. For the first time in many years, Brian didn't know what to do next. He jogged across the road to a wooded park area. Once he was sure no one from GeoGlobal saw him, he sat on the ground leaning against a tree and buried his face in his hands.

As he sat in the park, he fell deep into thought about life choices. He remembered back to when his parents were killed in a horrible accident, and how he chose to run from any real relationships ever since. Only one person truly knew Brian, and he let her go for the sake of his career. Oh how he longed just to talk to her at this time in his life. He had made a huge mistake.

Chapter 8—Presidential Focus

White House—Washington, D.C.

"The logistical issues confronting the DOE team at this moment are astounding. I don't want any unnecessary noise. If I see anyone's face on CNN, Fox News, MSNBC or whatever, I promise you complete and total lockout in regards to this refinery," proclaimed President Rhea.

The majority leaders of the House and Senate were listening anxiously to the President. All were thrilled to be a part of this meeting, even though there was little actual power entitled to them specific to the refinery. His scolding just proved the point even further. Ever since gas passed $6.50 per gallon, the media frenzy surrounding the politics of a new refinery had become an absolute circus. Most news headlines began with inflation, lost jobs and the discussions about the new world order revolving around China. The Congressional leaders were all dying to get their faces on the news, but the President would have none of it.

"I'm fully aware of the possible economic impact this will have on your collective states, the environmental concerns and the political pressure you all feel from your constituents. But please, just let the team at the DOE put together a plan. This plan is critical, as it gives structure to our conversations and debate. Until that point, all discussions are a waste of time. After the plan's done, we'll call a closed-door, joint emergency session to debate the plan. I'll give Congress five days to review, and that's it. This refinery's too important, and it'll raise above all political concerns."

"How can you have confidence in Glen Abbott after all of this?" asked Senator Kelly from Tennessee, longtime Senator and even longer alcoholic. "As far as I'm concerned, this whole DOE plan will be laced with holes."

The President stared with amazement at the ignorance of so many so-called leaders on Capitol Hill. Some of the congressional leaders were so far out of touch with reality that having direct dialogue was becoming impossible. They commented on things as facts which in reality were nowhere near accurate. The President's current power and popularity gave him the confidence to say what was on his mind.

"Senator, do you even know Glen Abbott?" asked the President.

The Senator sat expressionless as he considered the political ramifications of any direct question. This type of conversation drove the President crazy as he felt any real progress just wasn't possible in Washington anymore. The President didn't give him time to respond, and just waved him off.

"Look," said President Rhea, "Mr. Abbott has a tremendous team that's been blindsided. Yes, I agree they should've seen some things coming; however, now isn't the time to reflect on what should've been. Right now, we need the best energy consultants we know to be working on this energy legislation, and Glen has the best team for this. Glen and I had a very frank conversation. I gave Glen the ultimatum of either getting this legislation drafted, or find the door. We can reflect later about DOE emergency preparedness, but as of this moment, there's not a better team on the planet."

An obviously agitated President Rhea continued, "Tell me senator, can you get a better team in here in less than five days?"

The room remained silent as the President studied the leaders in the room. "Are there any more questions about the refinery?"

"Fine," said the President. "Please have all congressional management and lawyers prepared to focus on this legislation. Any and all decisions required for this legislature that the DOE requests from Capitol Hill will have to be answered within the hour. With everyone's cooperation, we'll have this legislation ready for the floor in 30 days. I request your full support of this bill. We'll have a few days to debate, but that's all I'll allow. With that, everyone is dismissed except the senators from Texas."

Senator Les Matthews and Senator Meredith Johnson stayed behind as requested. As the door shut to the Oval Office and it was just the three of them, everyone relaxed a little bit. The two Republican senators were from Texas and President Rhea from Georgia. All knew and respected each other from many years in government leadership positions. Senator Matthews headed the Energy Subcommittee, and Senator Johnson lead the Transportation Subcommittee. The power in this room was enormous, but luckily for Americans, none of them behaved that way. This team was legendary for their decisions and proactive leadership roles and, much to the Democrats' pain, very seldom made mistakes. But more importantly at this moment, they all understood the energy business.

"What's the deal with GeoGlobal?" asked the President. "I read a memo a few hours ago that the operational leaders of the company have been let go. At a time like this, the last thing anybody needs is a major management shakeup there, especially considering the only one running operations is that idiot Gordon."

"We're not sure yet. Really strange," said Senator Matthews. "Our team's been trying to contact them all day, but with no luck. I've even tried personally to call Mark Dye, but he's been unavailable. Their stock dropped six percent today alone on this news, and their company has no comment other than the weird press release about Chuck Gordon."

Senator Matthews shook his head in frustration. "To make matters worse, the SEC is raising all kinds of flags. Every board member and most vice presidents have issued formal documents stating their intention to sell all their stock. This accounts for eight percent of the entire damn company. After-hours trading is showing an additional five percent loss. With the profit and growth they have going on, it doesn't make any sense. It's almost like something disastrous happened and everyone wants out. It's bizarre, and I'm growing tired of not getting any answers."

"Oh Jesus. This thing's going to tank the market even further," said the President in an exasperated voice. "Have your office get some folks on this. At least get someone from GeoGlobal in here informally so we can get some answers."

Senator Johnson started in her esoteric tone, "With this management shakeup, I've no confidence in GeoGlobal's ability to build the new refinery, not even the pipelines. We need strong corporate leadership in making sure this project gets the attention it needs."

"Who are the top candidates?" asked the President.

"All the typical O&G big players. We have some good international candidates, but I'd think they're not an option," said Senator Johnson.

"All are capable of running a refinery, and certainly have the cash to fund a project of this scope. But as we all know, they'll drag their feet. It's certainly not in their best interest to ease supply issues. I'm just not sure if we can trust any of them."

She continued as she pondered the very limited options, "Although they're the first to blame lack of refineries, very few people are aware of their efforts to support the EPA in limiting refineries. Over the years, both groups have actually found a happy medium with one another."

The President reflected on this comment for a moment, remembering back to his press conference when he stated oil and gas companies wanted refineries, which actually often wasn't the case.

"Then what do we do?" asked President Rhea. "This whole effort of getting everything through government bureaucracy in record time is worthless without the same level of expediency from the owners of the refinery."

"Well," said Senator Johnson, "we'll have an evaluation starting tomorrow. Within three days, I'll come back with a recommendation. But I won't lie to you; I don't have a good feeling about anyone building a refinery within a year. The only one I would completely trust is Brian Larson with GeoGlobal. But as of today, it seems he no longer has GeoGlobal behind him. The timing of all this GeoGlobal mess isn't good at all."

"Hmmm," said Senator Matthews with an inquisitive look on his face and a renewed excitement. He stood from his chair and paced back and forth while rubbing his chin.

"I have a thought. What's the best way to do this financially? What if the government built the refinery on our own, and then sold the refinery to the highest bidder? That would completely reverse the game. Once the gas companies understand that regulating supply isn't possible, they'll resort to the next best thing, and that's market share. With this option, we wouldn't have to wait on the gas companies, we control our own destiny. And I'd bet we could get triple our money back on the investment, and ease gas prices almost immediately."

"Sounds good," said the President. "But we have no intellectual property or talent for something like this. Not to mention this adds a whole other layer of politics to it. Getting permitted is one thing, having taxpayers foot the bill is another."

Senator Matthews and Senator Johnson looked at each other. Senator Matthews spoke up with a tone of brilliance, "Brian Larson knows how to do this, and he seems unemployed at the moment. He's a good guy who worked for a bastard. Brian has everything we need."

Senator Johnson said, "Plus, I think your political power at this moment is enough to get the money you need. Especially if we put in a bylaw that states the refinery would be sold. We will have converted this project from nationalism to capitalism, which is full Republican."

President Rhea learned a long time ago to rely on his experts, and to always take their advice. He picked up his phone and called the director of the FBI. "Find Brian Larson. He's a former employee of GeoGlobal Energy. Find him and get him to the White House as soon as possible. Make this a top priority."

Chapter 9—Bottom Dwelling

Downtown Houston, Texas

It was about ten in the morning, and Chase Stockton was looking over one of his client's files when his cell phone rang. It was his wife, so he immediately answered the phone.

"What's up girl?"

"Hey Chase, Brian just called here, and was frantically looking for you. He said he needed to talk as soon as possible."

"Okay. Why doesn't he just call my cell phone?"

"He said he didn't have a cell phone, and had lost all his programmed numbers. He used directory assistance to get our number. But the really weird part is he made a collect call from a payphone. He's in some park in downtown Houston."

"What the hell?"

"He gave me the number to the phone, and wants you to call him. He gave it to me three times to make sure I got it correct, then made me promise to take his collect calls if he calls back. I'm really worried. Brian's never acted like this."

Chase quickly wrote down the number and called. The phone had just started ringing when Brian answered, "Chase! Is this you?"

"Yeah Brian, it's me. What the hell's going on? You need some help?"

"Oh thank God. I need you to come get me. I'm at the small park opposite the entrance to GeoGlobal. No questions right now, I'll let you know everything when you get here."

"I'll be there in 15 minutes."

Chase was Brian's college roommate from Texas A&M and longtime friend. Actually, Brian considered Chase more of a brother than a friend, as Chase was the only person he could totally confide in and know it was completely between them. Chase had gone to Law School at St. Mary's and had become a great O&G Lawyer, but he steadfastly refused to be Brian's lawyer on any matters, including GeoGlobal. Chase always said if anyone actually knew their real college stories, he would be disbarred and indicted as a criminal immediately.

Chase had two residences, a cheap apartment near downtown Houston, and a house in the countryside near College Station, Texas on ten rolling acres. Chase usually spent about three to four nights a week in Houston, and the rest of his time with his family and home office in "God's country" at a beautiful house straight out of Southern Living, decorated by what seemed like a Martha Stewart apprentice. To Chase, any place within 15 minutes of the Dixie Chicken and Kyle Field qualified as God's country.

Funny, thought Chase. Brian had always been the responsible one, and Chase had been the fuck-up. Chase never thought the day would come when he had to save Brian from the winos and homeless in a park in downtown Houston. As Chase pulled up to the park, he saw Brian sitting on the curb in his suit, sunglasses on his head, staring down at the pavement. As Chase pulled up next to Brian, he stood up and slowly opened the door to get in.

Chase had been thinking of what to say to Brian, and saved his best, "Damn man, I knew one day you would get caught fucking a senator's wife."

With that Brian and Chase were laughing out loud. Chase immediately headed the truck towards Highway 290. The Dixie Chicken, lots of beer, old George Strait music and dominos are what's needed. For two hours few words were said, but Chase was there. Brian's life was already getting better.

They got to the Dixie Chicken about 2:00 in the afternoon, took the best table and started drinking ice-cold beer. They both started with a Bud Light, as they had been successful enough in their careers to move up from the 95 cent Lone Star Beer. The Chicken, as it is known in College Station, served the most beer per square foot of any bar in the whole country. The bar had been a mainstay of the Northgate section of College Station for more than 30 years, a small, dirty hangout to play dominos, shoot pool, listen to legendary Texas music, and of course to drink ice-cold beer. The greasy food, dozens of mounted deer racks, live rattlesnakes and old wood floors made this bar one of the best in Texas. The hot college girls didn't hurt matters either.

Chase started laughing, "Lay it on me, Brian. It can't be that bad."

"Man, it's that bad." Brian went through his life over the past five years and then detailed what transpired earlier that morning. The more Brian talked, the more he drank. Chase just sat there and let Brian do all the talking.

Once Brian finished his story, Chase said, "Holy shit! That's one crazy ass story. I bet this would make the cover of the Houston Chronicle tomorrow with this juice! Why didn't you go back to your apartment instead of sitting in that shitty park?"

"It just seemed too plastic and lonely. I need to get away for a few days. I really can't face any of the insiders, fake friends, bankers, who the hell ever. I just don't know what happened. I guess I'll go away for a week or so and kind of show back up somewhere and see where it takes me. I can never repay you for helping my crazy ass out right now."

"Aw, whatever. No need to thank me. You alright with money? Do you need anything?"

"Last I checked I had about twenty million in assets and five million cash, so I'm okay."

Chase's mouth opened wide. "Son of a bitch! So, you can buy the mobile phone company; you just can't get one of their accounts. Damn! You know how many times my wife and friends have asked me about your money? I've always lied to cover for your sorry ass with some lame story about giving it all to charity or something. This bar bill's on you!"

Chase said, "Do you remember the time we got busted with beer in the dorm parking lot, and the cop was your old high school football buddy from Longview? On his first day on the job as a policeman! He didn't know if he should arrest us or join us! To this day, I can't imagine a more fucked up situation in that poor guy's mind . . . ."

Brian and Chase reminisced about college life the whole afternoon, evening and night. They flirted with college girls and talked about anything but work. Brian didn't remember much of the evening, but somehow they got to a cab that took them to Chase's house near College Station around 2:00 A.M. Twelve hours at the Chicken definitely wasn't a record, but probably in the top five for their mutual benders.

The next day, Chase dropped off Brian at his apartment in Houston. The apartment ran about $1000 a month, and was a completely disastrous bachelor pad. It simply served as a place to sleep and crash for Chase during the week, and had no décor of any sort. He did splurge $40 a week on a maid who kind of cleaned the place, and another $40 a week to keep the fridge at least stocked with the basics such as beer, bread and bologna.

Brian lounged on the couch and watched lame TV stations all day. Whenever he ran across a news story about GeoGlobal or energy, he changed the channel. He didn't want to hear or know anything. The more Brian relaxed, the more he became comfortable with the thought of being a consultant, farmer, wave watcher, whatever . . .

This was actually the most relaxed he had been in 19 years. Nobody in the world knew where he was except Chase, and it felt damn good. Brian thought of his college girlfriend, and how he could contact her again. Was she married, kids, would she even talk to him . . . ? People kept talking about this Facebook thing on the Internet . . . maybe he could find her that way. The last he heard, she had left Gulf Star to go back to school, but that was 15 years ago or longer.

Brian lounged on the couch and was deep into daydreaming when Chase came in the door.

"Come on man, enough is enough, go crash somewhere else," said Chase as he entered the apartment.

Then Chase pulled up a chair and took a serious tone. "Man, we need to talk. Some serious people are looking for your ass."

Chapter 10—Corporate Downfall

GeoGlobal Headquarters—Downtown Houston, Texas

The media frenzy that engulfed GeoGlobal was amazing. Security that seemed so in control yesterday now thought they weren't as powerful as they perceived themselves. Tight control was impossible with folks who cared less if they were arrested for getting a story or a picture. With the resignation of the board imminent, and the termination of the VPs, GeoGlobal's stock was off by more than 14 percent and dropping fast. The market capitalization loss was staggering, and the SEC was considering an emergency stop on all trading of GeoGlobal. On this news, every single mutual fund manager panicked and pulled his shares at a frantic pace.

"Keep those motherfuckers off my damn phone!" screamed Chuck Gordon to his assistant. "If I hear another reporter on my phone, your ass is fired!"

"Sir, it's not a reporter who called. That's Doug from our communications department looking for some answers. Our employees are nervous and investors are fleeing. I've taken more than a hundred calls today. Please let us know what's going on. You owe this to your employees at a minimum."

"I don't owe the employees a goddamned thing! They get their fucking paychecks, don't they! Tell them to keep doing their jobs like they're paid to do. I don't have to explain anything to anyone. Everything's under control."

"Sir, e-mails are circulating around from Internet reports. They say this is another Enron, and investors will be lucky to get 10 percent of their money back. Rumors are the SEC is going to shut down trading, and you're the one they'll investigate. How in the world did all this happen in two days?"

A red-faced Chuck said, "I already told you, I don't have to explain anything. Only idiot computer people use the Internet anyway! Now get out of here!"

"I can't do that anymore. I need some answers! People are screaming at me, constantly saying they will find a way to get at me if they don't get answers. I can't handle this. I don't know what to do! Both of my kids' college funds and our retirement are based on our stocks. My husband is screaming at me, and powerful people keep calling! Please tell me what to do!"

"I'm going to count to five. If your ass isn't out of my sight, then you can kiss your job and your retirement goodbye."

The assistant stared at Chuck, and then quickly headed toward the door. While walking out, she turned her head and said, "The FBI called and they'll be here in 10 minutes with the Securities and Exchange Commission. You can deal with them."

She rushed out and slammed the door behind her. Chuck stared at the door, frozen on the FBI comment. Usually in situations like this, Chuck enjoyed the attention, but not this time. Typically, he would have a well-fabricated lie prepared, but he realized he knew so little about the business that he couldn't begin to come up with anything in a few minutes. And now, there was no one to turn to for help on an executive level. Mark Dye always handled media-based problems, but he definitely wasn't available. Chuck did the math in his head, and realized he had personally lost about $6 million in value just in the past day. Chuck was panicking. His short-sightedness and ego were now a major problem for him personally. His instinct told him to run, but he knew better.

He called his law firm.

Chapter 11—Financial Value

Offices of Integrity Capitol—New York City

"We're losing our ass on GeoGlobal. In today's energy market, how's that even possible!" screamed the president of Integrity Capitol, the largest mutual fund company in the nation. "How can the single most profitable company in the world lose 21 percent market cap in three days! We've already lost 16 percent on our positions and the SEC won't stop trading! Leaving Gordon in charge is some kind of sick joke. I swear we're suing somebody's ass over this. Somebody, somewhere, has full liability on this nightmare."

The fund managers were completely at a loss on this situation. Days earlier, when the rest of the market was in a panic, Integrity Capitol sat in high cotton, having long selected the secure market of O&G as their core assets. While the rest of the market crashed on inflation and decreasing revenue, Integrity Capitol was the most solid investment as O&G was the only rising value on the entire stock market. That was until GeoGlobal leadership seemed to dissolve overnight, sending the entire O&G market into a tailspin.

"Sir", said one of the fund managers, "we're completely confused at this situation. All we know is this. Two days ago there was a meeting with the division leaders of GeoGlobal and the Board of Directors without Chuck Gordon or Brian Larson present. About two hours after that meeting, they began selling their shares like crazy. Mark Dye then had a meeting with the SEC this morning, and the outcome of that meeting isn't known. As crazy as this seems, it's like the leaders have quit, pulled their stocks, and are running away from GeoGlobal. We can't contact Mr. Dye, can't find Mr. Larson, and Mr. Gordon will only speak through his attorney. The Board will only speak through Mr. Dye, and he's only speaking to the feds. It's just crazy."

The president of Integrity Capitol stared at his team. He knew this was a great team, and they had no answers and saw no future.

What's our five year return on GeoGlobal as of right now?"

"Twenty-four percent as of this moment, and dropping fast," said one of the traders.

"Dump it and let's move on."

On the news of Integrity Capitol dropping GeoGlobal, the stock price dropped an additional 15 percent by the end of the day, and financial portfolios from around the world felt even more pain. The once most valued company in the world, worth $550 billion in market capitalization, was now valued at $300 billion. The venture capital sharks and breakup lawyers started smelling blood. The breakup value of GeoGlobal was now a serious discussion.

Chapter 12—Possibilities in a Crisis

White House—Washington, D.C.

Sandy Everett sat on the couch in the Oval Office, feeling like every word he said landed a cross punch to the powerful group in front of him. He was leader of the Securities and Exchange Commission, and usually let his employees deliver bad news, but the President insisted he do it himself in order to limit any possible press leaks. Sandy was nearly sweating as he listened to the senator yell after every comment.

"Oh you have got to be kidding me," said an exasperated Senator Matthews. "In today's media world, everyone's scared to death about dirt. Hell, we have more dirt on Chuck Gordon than the entire board combined!"

President Rhea said, "Just so I'm clear, Chuck fired the refining and pipeline production leadership without any authority from the board. The board would fight back, but they're afraid of what Chuck would tell the media about their personal lives? So Mark convinced them to resign as well?"

"Yes, sir. That seems to be the situation narrowed down to a few words," said Sandy. "It seems they got together, realized they're all multi-millionaires, took their money, and are leaving the fallout to Gordon."

Senator Matthews almost yelled at Sandy, as if he were the one that caused the problems at GeoGlobal, when he only delivered the message.

"This situation is dire, Mr. Everett, and we need GeoGlobal stable. What else did Mark Dye say?" said Senator Matthews.

Sandy slowly shook his head, not wanting to say the words. "Mr. Dye confided in me about a relationship he has with a young man, but swears it's just a mentoring relationship."

Senator Matthews rolled his head and threw up his hands.

Sandy continued, pausing a moment between each emotional outburst, "Mark said that Gordon threatened to twist the story into one of a sexual nature. Gordon also said he would ruin the lives of his daughter and son-in-law. So, he told me flatly he won't allow his family to go through this kind of disgusting behavior."

Sandy paused a moment, "And, uh to make matters worse, the SEC recruited Mark to help us catch some hedge brokers manipulating energy commodities. Mark worked with us to create a small fund called 'Texas Tea.' He helped us put those guys behind bars. All of this was very confidential. Somehow it seems Chuck Gordon found out about it, and is threatening to blame Mark for somehow being involved with the bastards."

Sandy said, "I apologize, Mr. President, I thought GeoGlobal was a shining beacon of management. I would've never guessed it was so close to a house of cards. I know this timing is bad. I didn't see this coming."

"What about Gordon?" quickly asked Senator Matthews, not willing to take any emotional commentary from a finance guy.

"Well," said Sandy in a more enthusiastic tone, "we finally got the judge to issue an order for a meeting with him. He'd only speak with his multiple attorneys present. When asked about corporate guidance, board approval, blackmail and coercion, he said none of it happened, and denied any knowledge of meeting with Brian Larson or Mr. Dye. When I asked about his feelings in regards to GeoGlobal going on a disastrous spiral downward, he said it was the board's problem and not his. That's why he pays them so much money. So, Gordon isn't giving us any information."

Sandy continued, "I told Gordon his unwillingness to cooperate was grounds for me to freeze his public stocks until this mess was worked out. We've also issued a restraining order on him, ordering him to stay within 25 miles of his residence. His attorneys started screaming, but there is little they can do until an initial hearing. I decided to go off the record for a moment, and put a little more fear in Chuck. I mentioned Texas Tea, and let him know that was a government sting. If he even remotely mentions it to anyone, we will have him arrested for obstruction of justice. We have Chuck trapped, so I feel he'll eventually be quite supportive if we need him."

The President and Senators sat there for a moment contemplating this situation, pondering the ways they could make use of this apparent disaster.

"Do you have any idea where Brian Larson is?" asked the President.

"No sir, I don't. I really didn't ask though," said Sandy.

"How much market cap has GeoGlobal lost?" asked Senator Matthews.

"As of a few hours ago, it's lost $250 billion in market cap, and still declining. I think we'll put an emergency stop on all trading this evening. So, I would guess, somewhere around $280 billion to $300 billion is where it will wind up. Mr. President, are you okay with us stopping trading on GeoGlobal?"

The President pondered this for a moment, as this recommendation went against his capitalistic instincts.

"Yes, stop it tonight. Okay, thanks, Sandy. This is the information we needed. It helps us put the pieces together much better. I'll be in touch."

An extremely relieved Sandy Everett quickly walked out the door. The President and Senator Matthews look at each other knowingly.

"The oil industry needs the government to save it. This is actually playing into our hands," said Senator Matthews.

"Scary how much we think alike," said the President.

Chapter 13—Visit From the Feds

Chase Stockton's Apartment—Houston, Texas

"I don't know what's going on, but I think there's some serious shit happening," said an alarmed and uptight Chase. "First of all, the only thing the news is talking about is GeoGlobal. There's major speculation about how it's an Enron and all this crap. Nobody at GeoGlobal is talking, so it's just getting worse. Even my boss is asking me to call you and find out what's going on."

"Well, tough shit for Gordon. It's his mess, he can deal with it," said Brian.

"You might think it's his mess, but I think it's your mess."

"What do you mean?"

"Well asshole, let me tell you what I mean. Two FBI agents and a federal marshal came by the office to talk to me. You don't even want to know the shit-pot this stirred at my office, but that's another story. Damn man, you're a pain in the ass! What the hell did you get me into?" said Chase, always trying to gig Brian a bit.

Brian continued to lie on the couch, now fully alerted to Chase.

"Look Brian, they want to talk to you as soon as possible. They don't want to alarm you, and insisted you're not in trouble, but some very important people want to see your ass as soon as possible. I said I didn't know where you were, so they promptly asked why I called a pay phone across the street from GeoGlobal yesterday, why I missed work, why I had a $200 Dixie Chicken bill, and why my house received a collect call from the same pay phone."

Chase paused for a second, and then pointed his finger at Brian, "By the way, how in the hell did I wind up paying for your fried food and beer binge, you cheap bastard?"

Brian grinned at Chase, not knowing whether to laugh or to be concerned with this conversation.

Chase waved his arms at the situation and kept talking, "Anyway, they swore me or you weren't in trouble, but they needed your assistance in a matter of high national importance, and recommended I quit fucking around with them. I'm certain they followed me here. Sorry dude, but you need to speak to these guys."

"Damn it!" exclaimed Brian.

He was now fully upright on the couch, still in his boxers and two day worn, old button down shirt. Brian walked to the window to see if anyone was outside. There didn't seem to be anyone, so he moved to open the door and take a peek. As he opened the door, there stood three men.

"Mr. Larson. I'm Agent Walker with the FBI, and this is Agent Watters and Agent Sene."

All three men automatically pulled out their wallets and showed them to Brian. Brian stood there, not knowing what to say.

The federal agent said, "Do not be alarmed as you're not in any trouble. However, your presence is requested in Washington, D.C. as soon as possible."

Brian turned to Chase with a stunned expression. Chase had a huge smile, and then shrugged his shoulders and held out his hands in a *see, I told you so* type response.

Chase, without hesitation said, "Good luck, dude. Happy I'm not your fucking lawyer."

Chapter 14—Choices

Glen Abbott said, "As requested, I hope everyone checked their egos, political and financial motivations at the door. These next few days are critical. As a first order and decision, where should we build the refinery?"

The tension in the room was palpable, and the group of bureaucrats literally felt the public and political pressure on them. The Fossil Fuel Division of the Department of Energy was separated into six areas of responsibilities including Natural Gas Delivery and Regulations, Clean Coal, Carbon Sequestration, Hydrogen and Clean Energy, Strategic Reserves, and Oil & Gas Supply and Delivery. Each division manager was present for the meeting. Additionally, the team was joined by Jim Jackson with the Blanchard and Blanchard Law Firm. He was considered an expert attorney for legal matters with new oil and gas mineral rights, particularly eminent domain and property concerns.

Jenny never hesitated. "We build on a military base, ideally abandoned or on the list to close. We own the property, and they usually have military spec infrastructures such as reinforced concrete, high volume water pump stations, firm soil and high voltage electrical substations. It'll require about three thousand acres, so we need all the help we can get to bypass the eminent domain issues. The President and Congress can deal with the environmental and political concerns."

The roomful of DOE leadership sat quiet for a few moments. Glen said, "Any objections?"

Jim Jackson said, "That's a good idea. The DOD's been considering for some time what would be good use of the land from abandoned or scheduled-to-close military bases. Even with abandoned bases, the DOD carries a huge price tag for just maintaining these old facilities."

Glen gave a knowing look to Jim, thinking to himself that he was way ahead of this damn consultant. About two years ago, when the price of diesel and gasoline prices began to rise, Glen Abbott had started working on a draft proposal jointly with the DOE and DOD to consider the building of new refineries. A core piece of this legislation was a refinery located on a closed military base. Since it would be on federal property, acquiring the necessary federal and state permits would be considerably easier. Glen was on the right track, but too late to make a difference.

"Okay, now geographically, where do we build it?" asked Glen.

Jenny said, "Well, the biggest problem with a refinery is the physical logistics associated with it. Typically a refinery has at least eight major pipeline inputs from multiple upstream sources and as many as sixteen pipelines as an output."

The management team listened to Jenny, always impressed with her knowledge on oil and gas infrastructure topics. They all knew the trap she was in, one of understanding the business, but with real issues understanding the influences of the business.

Jenny said, "These output pipelines feed a huge tank farm, but usually with different petroleum types. Before we decide the location, it's my opinion we decide what customer type we target, and how we could immediately increase supply in critical areas. This will go a long way toward understanding the facility type."

Jim said, "Well, the U.S. military is one of the largest consumers of petroleum in the world. For instance, the U.S. Air Force consumed over three billion gallons of aviation fuel last year, which is more than half of all fossil fuel used by the government. In fact, the total Air Force bill for jet fuel last year was a whopping $4.7 billion.

That's more money spent on just fuel than the average Fortune 500 does in total revenue. I would guess the total government bill to be around $7 billion per year in just aviation fuel."

The room remained silent. Most of the leaders in the DOE weren't so much political, but more introverted in their personalities. They took the term "two ears and one mouth" literally, and computed in this recommendation in their minds.

Jim didn't sense any immediate objections, so he continued, "So an easy answer is aviation fuel. Plus, U.S. commercial aviation accounts for nearly thirty billion gallons of fuel per year, or better stated over five hundred million barrels of crude. If we focused solely on aviation fuel, that would ease supply issues dramatically, and would force refiners to go into deeper competition on other products."

Jenny said, "We could ask the Department of Defense to make a commitment to purchase fuel from this refinery. That would force existing suppliers for the DOD to retool their refineries for different product types. This would really put some money in the economy, and drive competition in the oil and gas market."

Jim asked, "On that note, who's going to own this refinery? Shouldn't the companies bidding on this thing be here?"

Glen stared at the room for a moment while all eyes were on him. Glen was always careful around a consultant. Everyone here understood what was at stake, fully aware that major refiners would want this factory. Once the green light was given to build new refineries, then market share was the game. The scramble to get the rights to this refinery would be an epic battle among the big five gas companies.

Glen gave an even-keeled look to Jim. "Senator Matthews and Senator Johnson are evaluating that topic at the moment. I should have an answer by sometime tomorrow."

"Okay", said Jim. "But as a thought, if this refinery produces jet fuel to meet the needs of aviation in general, then more commercially refined products would be available. Just like Dr. Liepert said, the automotive, rail, and motor carriers will benefit from more supply.

These days a couple of pennies per gallon sure mean a lot. Plus, the government would be in a better position to supply the nation with petroleum in an emergency. You wanted my apolitical opinion, and boy that's about as direct as it gets."

Glen said, "Good ideas, Jim. Well, does anyone object to the line of thinking here? To recap, we build on a military base, focus on aviation fuel, and recommend it's a government owned refinery with the DOD as our primary customer."

Son of a bitch! Glen thought to himself. Glen had made his first mistake, and knew it immediately.

"Who recommends it be a government owned refinery?" asked Jim without hesitation. "If that's the case, then your problem isn't just infrastructure and policy, the problem's getting enough intellectual property. You know, people who actually know how to make these things work. How in the world are you going to pull that off?"

Jim aggressively pointed to Glen, "I would think the government would need to hire at least five thousand people in short order, and not to mention, hire the best oil and gas guys in the world. In today's market, those people are very hard to find."

Glen gave a stoic look at Jim. "I made a mistake by saying that. I'm implying the government is taking the lead on the justification, not the construction or operations of the refinery. We're considering many options."

Although Glen gave his best poker face, he might as well have had a mirror showing the table his hand.

Shit, thought Glen, *I can't believe I said that in front of a fucking consultant.*

The room remained silent, but actually the data wizards that worked for Jenny were deep in their notebook computers. They were calculating the total consumption required to lock up the aviation fuel market in the United States. It didn't take long to reach a pretty profound realization.

After a few minutes of silence except for the key strokes of the computers, Jenny said, "If these are the goals, this refinery would need to refine nearly two million barrels per day. This would be two times the size of the world's largest refinery. That's simply too much crude to get to one location."

Jenny paused for a moment and thought deeply about her next comments. She had to draw upon all her years of experience in the oil and gas business to come to this moment.

Finally, Jenny said, "We could target 800,000 barrels per day. That'd represent 15 percent of U.S. annual output, and be one of the largest refineries in the world. It'd cost more than $18 billion to build, and probably cost on the scale of $2 billion a year to operate and maintain."

Everyone at the table leaned back in their chairs. Building a refinery this big was an unbelievable undertaking. The U.S. hadn't built a new refinery in over 20 years; the team was scrambling in their minds to comprehend this type of infrastructure.

Glen said, "Where are we building it, Dr. Liepert?"

Jenny said, "We build on the abandoned Kelly Air Force base in San Antonio, Texas. We can get oil from the Gulf of Mexico and East Texas. The freeway infrastructure is reasonably capable for logistics, and in close proximity to Mexico and the Corpus Christi ship channel for international crude deliveries. That's your spot."

Jim spoke up, "Texas has minimal politics when it comes to oil. No unnecessary issues there to deal with in that state. I can get this legislature drafted fast."

After a few moments of thought, Glen said, "Let's do it. Get to work. I'll meet with the President to discuss the highlights. Dr. Liepert, you're going with me to the White House and giving the presentation."

"Do you need any help or support for the meeting?" asked Jim, hoping to be in this high level meeting.

"No. Just me and Dr. Liepert," said Glen.

The disappointment on Jim's face was obvious. Pulling attendance in that meeting surely meant partner for his firm, plus a much larger salary for being in the know.

Jenny froze in her place. She realized her role was important, but never really considered her position to be at this level.

"The President of the United States?" asked a stunned Jenny in front of everyone.

"Well, you do work for the United States government. So if you know of a different President, I'd sure like to know who that is," said a grinning Glen with everyone else staring at her. "We'll be meeting the two Senators, the President, and our first advisor for the new refinery."

"Who's the advisor?" asked Jim way too quickly.

"Not sure," said Glen. Although everyone in the room knew he was really saying "I know, but I am not telling a damn consultant."

Chapter 15—A New Reality

White House—Washington, D.C.

Most people would be thrilled at riding in a $22 million Gulfstream G500 at 44,000 feet. But Brian's mind raced a thousand thoughts a minute on anything but his first class ride. Plus, this ride was anything but a friendly one. The FBI agents were deep into their notebook computers and didn't say a word.

How in the hell did I wind up here? was all Brian thought. *Man I must be in big trouble. The board or Gordon somehow blamed the GeoGlobal disaster on me. What did I do to piss off the feds? Should I get a lawyer, the agents swore I wasn't in trouble, but the government needed my help??*

Brian told himself he was a vice president of one of the biggest companies in the world, and he could handle almost any situation. But this one was different. He was always in control of the state of events, and directing them. But this time, well . . . well this was just crazy.

At least the agents let him go by his condo to take a quick shower and put on a suit. Brian was quite accustomed to packing quickly and catching a private jet out of Houston, but taking a shower in plain sight of multiple men in his condo was a little disturbing. The agents only agreed after cutting a deal that Brian could never leave their sight. Plus, the tracking monitor on his ankle pretty much sealed his fate. Being able to hide was no longer an option.

Brian was deep in thought when the plane's Rolls-Royce engines started decelerating. The co-pilot walked through the cabin to announce they would be at the hangar in ten minutes and everyone needed to buckle up, with the same level of enthusiasm as the FBI agents.

The plane dropped altitude so fast that it felt like a ride at Six Flags. The plane seemed to land at 400 knots, and then took a 2G turn into a hangar in what he assumed was Andrews Air Force Base. As if on cue, a regular-looking black Suburban pulled up, and Brian climbed in the vehicle. Brian saw the three FBI agents speaking with two other government types. After a brief conversation, the new agents climbed in the Suburban and sped out of the hangar with all the power the Chevy motor could give.

"Mr. Larson," said the lead agent as he shook Brian's hand. "I'm Agent John Womack with the Secret Service, and this is Agent Seid. You may not know it bud, but you and I will be close friends."

Brian stared at Agent Womack with a deer in the headlights look.

"You're to have the same security assigned as a senator, and I was the one who drew the shortest straw," laughed Agent Womack. "So like it or not, I'm your shadow until told otherwise by the boss."

"I'm almost afraid to ask, but, who's the boss?"

"We call him Liberty. You call him the President of the United States."

Chapter 16—That Old Feeling

Washington, D.C.

After the meeting ended, Glen and Jenny quickly grabbed their things and moved to the DOE lobby where a car was waiting, which was actually a first for Jenny. She had seen folks leaving the DOE in government cars, but she had never been that fortunate, or pompous.

Glen turned to Jenny and said, "Great job in there, Jenny. You're definitely the one for the job."

Glen's comments made her feel good. Glen didn't give out compliments easily, so this gave her a sense of relief. As they slowly cruised down Independence Avenue with all the traffic, Jenny was deep in thought and trying to breathe slowly to gain her composure. Her top-dollar education and solid career hadn't been enough to prepare her for a moment like this. To try and relax, she placed her thoughts on her horses, her younger days in Texas, the times of her life in college with her boyfriend, anything to help her calm down in the face of this kind of pressure.

God I miss him, thought Jenny. *He'd calm me down, know what to say.*

Jenny had taken brief note of the news of GeoGlobal's financial problems, but had been too busy to look into it. Jenny hoped Brian was okay, but on the other hand, she hoped his "mistress" burned in hell. Over the years, Jenny never had anything to do with GeoGlobal. She didn't buy their gas, visit their convenience stores, purchase their motor oil, you name it. Jenny in her twenties never understood Brian's obsession with GeoGlobal, and had grown to hate the company. Over time she realized the realities of a strong career, and the close relationships thus created. She had learned to forgive Brian, but she would always hate GeoGlobal.

Ironic actually; Jenny swore she'd never have a life like her mother's growing up, and would never spend time thinking of a long lost love. She had always dreamed of having a family with a father around but now, here she was in her late thirties; no love life, no family, and waiting on a man from her past to miraculously come back to her, just like her mom. Jenny sighed and gave a blank stare towards the Washington Mall. At this moment, she was a complete world away from Kilgore, Texas and her college days. Jenny had been in her daydream for quite a while when she came back to reality just as Glen completed his mobile phone call.

Jenny asked, "Who are we meeting at the White House?"

Glen said, "The President, Senators Matthews and Johnson, and a corporate guy they hope will take leadership of building the refinery. I'm looking at his resume here. It's really quite outstanding."

Jenny suddenly realized she'd be working with this person on a daily basis, and would probably have to deal with daily barrages of the demands and unnecessary drama associated with energy executives. Jenny summarized that this person was probably a pompous jerk. She knew many leaders in the industry, and most had the same type of personality. Oil and Gas leaders always seemed to carry an air of arrogance with them, and acted more powerful and knowledgeable than the average person or any government bureaucrat. Jenny was suddenly very interested in the resume Glen was reading.

Glen said, "Who knows how much he'll cost, but I think he might be the guy to build something like this. I've heard quite a bit about him, but mostly as an operational hot rod. I really didn't understand the depth of his complete oil and gas background."

"God!" Glen chuckled out loud, "Jim would kill for this information! Can he be any more transparent about being the ultimate power broker in the U.S.?"

"Who is it?"

"Jim Jackson?"

"No!" said Jenny, smiling. "The corporate guy with us in the meeting."

"Uh, Brian Larson from GeoGlobal Energy. I think I've met him before. It seems he started from a typical engineering role, roughneck kind of . . ."

Glen turned to look at Jenny, and didn't like what he saw. Jenny was sitting straight up in her seat grabbing her upper chest. She first turned pale, and then blushed bright red. Her other hand waved like crazy, but no words were coming out. This moment, the pressure, and now Brian caused Jenny's brain to snap.

"Pu . . . pull . . . I have to get . . . air!"

"Driver, pull over!" shouted Glen.

As soon as the car stopped, Jenny grabbed the door handle and jumped out. Glen sat in the car, stunned, not knowing how to handle this situation. He saw Jenny, walking down the sidewalk just overcome with emotion. As he watched her, she stopped on the sidewalk, grabbed her knees, and bent over as if she were going to throw up.

Glen's first reaction was to be pissed. After all, he was the one who put his neck on the line to keep Jenny through this time of crisis, and now his number one player was having a complete emotional meltdown when they needed her most.

Glen got control over himself, opened his door, and jogged over to Jenny.

"Jenny, I don't know what the hell the problem is, but . . ."

Then he saw her face. Jenny, this picture of beauty, smarts, strength, looking like a million dollars just moments ago, was completely distraught. Glen's fatherly instincts kicked in, and he simply gave her a hug. The two just stood there, in a hug for several minutes.

Finally, Glen said, "You want to talk about it?"

"Oh my God Glen, I'm so sorry. I just don't . . . I don't think I can go in there. Brian and I, we-"

"Look at me, Jenny. I can assume you and Brian had a relationship sometime in the past, and your emotions run deep here. But you have to put your passion somewhere else today. People are losing their jobs, their homes and their complete quality of life. I know it might not feel like it right now, but we're the luckiest people in the country, because we have the power to do something about this, and I have confidence in my team and you especially, to see us through it."

"I can't. I don't think I can completely focus . . ."

"Yes you can! Jenny, damn it. It's our moment. I don't care about your past, but I do care about your future. Nobody's more prepared than you. I need two brains in this meeting. These politicians are pretty good people, but I promise you, if we show any incompetence, they'll fire our entire team instantly. They understand this issue is greater than any one person or team. You and I represent the best in energy policy for the entire country. You have to do this for yourself, for me, for your team, everyone!"

Jenny felt her anger start to kick in. She couldn't believe she had let her emotions get to her this way. She knew Glen was right. This moment wasn't about her. Now Glen saw her this way, what a disaster.

Jenny wiped her face, leaving mascara and makeup smudges all over, and more importantly, she saw the concern in Glen.

"Glen, you're the closest thing I have to a family. I'm so sorry I acted this way. Brian was my first and only love, and I haven't seen him since college. With everything going on, the pressure, and the lack of sleep, everything. It won't happen again. I'm so sorry."

"You have to think of the upside; at least you didn't faint in the Oval Office when you saw Brian. Now, let's get you back to looking good. Our meeting is scheduled to start in about an hour."

Chapter 17—Presidential Resolve

White House—Washington, D.C.

President Rhea sat at his desk looking at the phone, getting more and more pissed by the minute. He had a scheduled 2:30 P.M. phone call with the president of Venezuela, and now it was 2:45 P.M. The senators convinced him to consider alternative methods of easing oil supply issues, rather than just the new refinery, and at least attempt a conversation with President Gamboa. He swallowed his pride and reluctantly agreed to a conversation.

Their first scheduled call was at 9:00 A.M. when President Gamboa's secretary informed him that he was busy, and needed to reschedule for later in the day. President Rhea, on the verge of blowing a gasket, simply let the secretary know that he'd be available at 2:30 P.M.

Now, here the President sat again, waiting for this socialist lunatic's call. He tried to study the detailed CIA evaluation of President Gamboa, attempting to get a handle on the personality and mental state of this individual. Gamboa's estimated IQ of 130 caught President Rhea a little off guard, not sure if he should resort to an intellectual conversation, or just keep it simple and confrontational.

The moment made the President reflect on a few things, and ponder how the position of the United States had fallen in the eyes of the world. This subtle gesture of the United States "waiting" on the President of Venezuela sent a very clear message, and President Rhea didn't like it at all. But the senators insisted the politically correct thing was to call the statesman and at least try to sell the merits of American buying power, regardless of the current economic environment. The President didn't like bowing down like this, but he considered the economic reality of his constituents, and decided his pride was a small price to pay for a chance at getting oil prices back to where they should be, regardless of the planned refinery.

The President's administrator slowly opened the door. "Mr. President, you have quite a list of people that have requested your call. Would you like me to connect you with one of them? Maybe fill the empty time?"

"No. I'll wait for Gamboa."

The administrator was long trained in reading the signs, and knew the President wasn't happy about his situation. "Sir, it's almost three o'clock. Maybe it's not too early for a drink. Want me to prepare one?"

The President gave a small smile towards the admin, "You know, that'd be great."

The administrator smiled and removed herself from the Oval Office. Almost as quickly as she left the room, she reappeared and said, "Mr. President, President Gamboa is on the line."

President Rhea took a deep breath and picked up the phone. "President Gamboa, thank you for taking the time to talk with me."

"President Rhea," was the only response.

President Rhea rolled his eyes, and rubbed his hand against his head. A socialist and fanatical mad-man versus a democratically elected and desperate President doesn't make for an elegant conversation. He just wanted to fight through this moment.

President Rhea said, "President Gamboa, first of all, I want to acknowledge your global position in this economic climate, and ask for your consideration in evaluating an alternate oil reserve proposal from the United States."

There was no response on the line. President Rhea was quiet for a few moments, waiting for a comment, but the line remained silent.

"President Gamboa, are you there?"

"Continue."

President Rhea rolled his eyes and continued, "As I'm sure you're aware, having the United States as a secondary customer for your reserves leaves us in a vulnerable position, and I hope to make you a proposal that would be considerably better than the offer from the People's Republic of China."

"Proposal? From the United States? You want me to deal with you? You have publically condemned my administration and our policies! You go on and on about our lack of human rights! Your country is the one that removed the Indians from their lands! And now, you want me to negotiate with the United States!"

The President stared at his phone; appalled that he'd been reduced to this conversation.

"Uh, President Gamboa, you're bringing up a history of our land that goes back one hundred and fifty years. Is there any way to discuss our current situation without discussing our history?"

"No, there's not! I won't negotiate with a country that imprisons their people, steals lands, invades foreign countries and has the blood of thousands of murdered children throughout the world on its hands! I won't be subservient to your country on any level . . ."

President Rhea sat back in his chair as the crazy bastard dove into a long rant about the evils of the United States. While President Rhea listened to the rambling diatribe, he realized President Gamboa was actually trying to look like a foolish idiot in the eyes of the President, giving an impression that negotiation wasn't an option. The more he listened to the man, the more he realized this was a planned speech. President Rhea was on-to him now. He obviously wasn't as naïve as his words, but his weakness was his ego, and that was easy to bring out.

Once Gamboa finished his speech, President Rhea scrambled to come up with a comment, and spoke in a slow voice, "President Gamboa, if my words personally offended you, then I apologize. If I was to retract the words, what would you have me say?"

The phone went silent for a few moments. President Rhea surmised that Gamboa felt like he was in a trap, and he was struggling in his mind about the opportunity. Gamboa knew if the United States made a formal apology to the Venezuelan government, then there would be a deal in the background. He decided to not go down that road.

Gamboa snapped back, "Your words are shallow. No one listens to you anymore! Any retraction would be useless!"

President Rhea grinned and then said, "Very well. Then I once again will ask the question. Would your government consider an alternative proposal from the United States?"

"The agreement is already done! My friends in China share a common goal in our governments. The U.S. is no longer our concern!"

President Rhea took a deep breath, and wanted to yell back, but thought better about it. Gamboa's childish rhetoric had quickly dissolved, and he could tell the real man was coming out. President Rhea decided to keep his cool.

"President Gamboa, your country is the fourth largest oil importer to the United States. We use over a million barrels of oil every day from your country. With our refining issues, we're now importing more than two hundred thousand barrels of refined oil as well. This volume contributes more than seventy million dollars each day to your country."

President Rhea paused for a moment. "How can you possibly say the United States isn't your concern?"

President Gamboa laughed, "Ah, you see the difference. You think of money. Our interest with China goes much deeper than money."

President Rhea knew exactly what Gamboa was implying. The United States had tried for decades to keep the western hemisphere from having a communist government. Somehow, Gamboa survived the political turmoil to stay in power, and now was dealing a major blow to democracy in Latin America. China not only brought an economic benefit; they brought intelligence and, more worrisome, a possible military presence.

President Rhea sighed, not really wanting to dig into a major world political discussion. "President Gamboa, China has petroleum agreements with Japan, Germany, India, South Korea, France, Italy and Taiwan. With the logistical realities of transporting your oil to China, we find your agreement to be financially and logically unrealistic. Considering the majority of China's exports are to the United States, we can predict a significant reduction in Chinese manufacturing. A twenty-five percent increase in petroleum usage in China over the next ten years won't happen. At best, your country might be able to export four hundred thousand barrels per day."

President Rhea paused for effect. "Can you really afford losing thirty to forty million dollars every day? As I understand, oil money is about all your country gets from the outside."

President Gamboa screamed, "I won't be lectured by you. We're much more than oil! Our country is building . . ."

President Rhea interrupted, "I'm not here to listen to this. We both need each other, and that's all I am saying. We need your oil at affordable prices, and you need the money in return."

"We're with China."

President Rhea lowered his voice. "President Gamboa. I want to be real clear. If your country ceases exporting oil to the United States, then we will take steps to impose an import tax on all your goods and commodities. Once we get on our feet, you'll be begging the United States to buy your oil and other goods for pennies on the dollar. Your decision will be a financial Armageddon to Venezuela. And I doubt there will be much sympathy from China."

President Rhea waited a few seconds before the final question: "Are you sure this is your decision?"

"We're with China. America can rot in hell," said a definitive President Gamboa.

The phone went silent as the President of Venezuela hung up on the President of the United States.

"That went well," thought the President sarcastically.

The President grabbed his drink, and then swung around in his chair to overlook the Washington Mall. The die was cast. Either America got back on top on her own, or generations of Americans would see their way of life dramatically change. The President was in a fight that would not only define his presidency, but shape the world order.

Chapter 18—Trepidation

White House—Washington, D.C.

Brian slumped down in the seat of the Suburban as his mind frantically wandered in confusion. *The President of the United States . . . Why would he want to talk to me? What did Gordon do this time? Why do I need a Secret Service escort?*

Brian had actually shaken the President's hand a few times during energy conferences, but nothing ever formal. The President would occasionally give speeches at conferences in his previous role as governor, but Brian left all the policy details to Mark Dye. Legal was always Brian's most hated subject. To Brian it was simple: either his lawyers got all the paperwork out of the way, or he found another lawyer.

As they pulled out of the base, two police motorbikes accelerated in front of the Suburban and gave them a priority escort to the Washington Mall area. The convoy was traveling at a high rate of speed up the Suitland Parkway, but he noticed a considerable difference with the cars on the freeway. In Texas, if the police escorted a vehicle, everyone pulled over to gawk at the happenings, hoping to discover the identity of the important person. However, in D.C., this was simply business as usual, and few if any people paid them any attention at all.

The motorcade exited from Freeway 395 and then turned onto 14th Street. Brian caught his first glance of the D.C. area proper. The Washington Monument was always a stunning sight, and Brian felt the hairs on the back of his neck begin to stand up. The motorcade suddenly made a left turn, and Brian saw it for the first time: the White House was coming into view, and the awesome power of this beautiful structure was overwhelming. The historical significance, matched with the mighty power of the American people, seemed to resonate from the building. And somehow, the pressure seemed firmly on his back.

The motorcade continued to the east gate. Here the police took a quick u-turn and stopped, but the Suburban continued straight through the gates. To Brian's surprise, the entrance actually turned right and under the White House. Brian had no idea there was a back entrance like this. The driveway came to a quick stop where there was real chaos, with people coming back in forth, but somehow it seemed under control.

Agent Womack turned to Brian, "Let's go, bud."

The beauty of the White House quickly faded to a sense of high security. Brian and the two agents quickly walked up to the security kiosk with two guards and one soldier behind a thick wall of glass. Two of the men were on computers with wireless microphones over their ears. The third man wore a camouflage military uniform, with an assault rifle held to his side and a finger at the ready.

Agent Womack took off his jacket, and removed his sizeable gun and holster. "Agent Womack—SSID 42987, here to see Liberty. Guest name Brian Larson, level five access requested by SS."

"Place your thumb and palm on the scanners below," said one of the men behind the glass.

Agent Womack placed his ID badge in a drawer that magically appeared from under the glass, and then miraculously put Brian's driver's license in the drawer as well.

Agent Womack had a grin on his face. "Damn, you didn't even know we had your wallet, did you?"

Brian made a quick move to his back pocket, which wasn't a good idea. Brian's hand was immediately grabbed.

The soldier said, "No fast movement, sir. Please keep your hands outside of any pockets."

Brian turned and saw a guard in military gear now standing right next to him. The man seemed to be seven feet tall, with a firm grip on his wrist.

Brian said, "Sorry, uhh . . . I didn't know my wallet was missing."

Agent Womack kept his head down with a grin on his face while he completed the paperwork. Once he was done he made a head gesture to Brian, letting him know it was time to go.

They walked towards the doors that were opened by two military color guards. Brian, Agent Womack and Agent Seid walked through the doors into a room that contained two standard looking metal detectors. There were another two security guards with metal detector wands, with an additional soldier standing behind the metal detectors.

As Brian walked through the metal detectors, a "Whoop!! Whoop!!" sound screeched. Brian saw it happening, but didn't have the skills or mental capacity to process it all. The security guard moved so fast that Brian put up no defense. Wham! Brian was slammed against the wall with the force of a blitzing linebacker. He tried to scream, but the breath had been knocked out of him. The soldier from outside was now about three feet from him, and the nozzle of his assault rifle was about two inches from his forehead.

"Whoa! Whoa!" yelled Agent Womack while holding both of his hands in the air. "What the hell is it? He's got nothing on him!"

The security guard was joined by the other guard, and he commenced to running his hands all over Brian, still pressed against the wall.

"It's an ankle bracelet, Agent Womack. You didn't notify us of it," said the soldier.

Agent Womack turned to glare at Agent Seid, who had a look of dread on his face. Secret Service agents aren't supposed to forget details, and Agent Seid had forgotten to remove the bracelet as instructed by Agent Womack.

Brian felt the pressure relieve from his midsection, and he slowly slid to the ground while his back was against the wall. He stared at the nozzle of the assault rifle as it followed his nose all the way to the ground. Maybe it was his imagination, but Brian swore the soldier had a small grin on his face.

The soldier slowly moved away from Brian and then made a shoulder move to wave over Agent Womack. Agent Womack walked over and pulled him to his feet.

"Protocol, Agent. We don't want to remind you again," said the soldier.

"Absolutely, our mistake," said Agent Womack, not really looking him in the eye but burning a hole through his junior agent.

As the soldier walked away, Agent Womack turned to Brian with a small grin. "Sorry Mr. Larson, we didn't put on the bracelet, and our brain-dead agent here completely forgot about it."

Son of a bitch, Brian thought to himself, just longing for Chase's couch again.

Brian was now a complete wreck. Suit all wrinkled, hair a mess, dirt on everything, no wallet, and he just got the shit beat out of him. This was going badly.

As Brian and Agent Womack were getting their things back on, Brian asked, "Uh . . . Can I have my wallet?"

"Negative," said Agent Womack as he worked to get his gun and holster in the perfect position. "Let's go."

Great, thought Brian. *This keeps getting better.*

Agent Womack walked at a high pace past an endless row of offices with Brian and the other agent close behind. The White House associates were impeccably dressed, fit and seemed to have a sense of purpose. As they walked down the hallway, Brian noticed nobody said a single word or a simple "hello" or "how are you." It appeared to Brian the culture of the staff at the White House was one of keeping your business to yourself.

As they reached the top of the stairs, Brian could tell they were on the first floor of the White House in the West Wing. Agent Womack turned towards the President's personal assistant, and she gave him a wave in towards the door.

This is it. Here I am by God, thought Brian.

Agent Womack knocked on the door and Brian heard the familiar voice of the President respond, "Come on in."

Agent Womack turned towards Brian with a knowing smile and said, "Good luck. I'll be right out here waiting for you. Just be yourself, the Prez is a good guy."

Brian gave a nod to say thanks. With that, Agent Womack opened the door. Brian looked into the Oval Office and saw President Rhea walking towards him. Brian entered through the door and held out his hand for a handshake with the President.

"Thanks so much for being here, Mr. Larson," said President Rhea. "Your country requires your services in an urgent matter. We'll do our best to make you feel comfortable."

Brian said, "Thank you. Anything I can do to help you would be my pleasure."

President Rhea said, "I appreciate that. Let me introduce you to some folks. First is Senator Matthews."

"Brian, great to have you here."

"Senator," said Brian.

"Senator Johnson," said the President.

"Hello, Mr. Larson. It's a pleasure meeting you. I've heard many great things about you."

"Thank you, Senator."

"Mr. Glen Abbott. Glen leads the Fossil Fuel Division for the Department of Energy," said the President.

"Mr. Larson. Good to formally meet you."

"Wow, pleasure to meet you. Your work with the DOE is great. I read almost everything you post. Your policies are rock solid."

"Thanks, Mr. Larson," said Glen.

The President continued, "And last but definitely not least . . . Where is she? Oh there she is, buried in her computer," laughed President Rhea.

"Dr. Liepert, come over here real quick and meet Mr. Larson. You'll be working hand in hand so better get the introduction off to a good start," said the enthusiastic President across the Oval Office.

Brian looked towards the long sofa situated in front of the President's desk and almost felt his legs give away. Jenny walked towards Brian with a look of fear and dread.

"Let me introduce Dr. Jennifer Liepert. She runs the O&G Supply group at the DOE."

"Hello Brian," said Jenny.

Brian held his hand out, but offered no response. Brian felt his blood pressure rising, his throat freezing; the tie around his neck started feeling way too tight. This situation, coupled with the lost love of his life standing in front of him, was too much. Brian cleared his throat and pulled his tie. He noticed Glen Abbott had a small grin.

"Uh . . . Great to meet everyone. It's an honor to be here," Brian said in the best voice he could give while trying to clear his throat.

Brian coughed and his face was bright red. His mind raced with thoughts of ways to get out of the conversation. He needed time to get his act together.

Brian scrambled and came up with the best he could, "Is it possible to grab a quick drink, maybe some water? I want to be at my best before we have any conversations, and my throat is really . . ."

"Uh, sure," said a skeptical President Rhea. "That's probably a good idea. I think our meeting will last several hours. I need to make a few calls anyway. Let's start in about forty-five minutes at 4:00 P.M. straight up."

"Thanks, I mean, thank you, Mr. President."

Now completely disoriented, Brian turned to exit the office, and his greatest fears were realized. The office really was an oval, and the door was disguised quite nicely. Brian started walking toward the wall, but couldn't find the exit. He started panicking. He heard the voices discussing other things in the background. He didn't ask anyone for help on anything, much less how to find a door in front of the President. Brian walked aimlessly against the wall for a few moments, and then heard the words.

"Mr. Larson," said the President, "the door's over there."

Brian thought he was going to die as he saw the President point to the complete opposite side of the room, and the most powerful people in the U.S. looked at him like he was an idiot. Jenny stood in a stunned silence, not knowing what to do. Brian eventually found the door, and turned to look at everyone once again, just to reaffirm his humiliation. Brian exited like a poor puppy.

"That's the best energy leader in the U.S.?" said President Rhea. "I don't think I want him managing a McDonalds. Les, Meredith, Glen, are you all sure this is the guy we want?"

Senator Matthews said, "Well, we might want to cut him some slack. I finally had a conversation with Mark Dye about an hour ago. Two days ago, Brian went to work thinking he was the next president of GeoGlobal, but then had the falling out with Gordon, which probably blew up any hopes and dreams for him. The next thing he knows he is standing in the Oval Office. He's probably just a little overwhelmed at the moment. As far as he knows, you're going to use any methods necessary to get information out of him about GeoGlobal, and he's probably nervous."

"Okay, maybe I should have a one on one with him to calm him down a bit."

Glen waited for Senator Matthews and the President to finish. "We have a little to add."

Glen gave a stare at Jenny who looked just as flustered. "Uh, Dr. Liepert and Brian were college sweethearts. They actually lived together in college and haven't seen or spoken to each other since."

Glen couldn't help but grin a bit, "So . . . with all that Senator Matthews explained, coupled with seeing Jenny as a part of the interrogation committee, he's probably in a full mental breakdown."

President Rhea pondered this for a second, and then the whole room broke out in laughter.

President Rhea said, "Oh man. Can you imagine what he's thinking? He thinks we're going to bust him for making GeoGlobal the next Enron, and then bust him for drinking as a minor in college to go along with other charges! Then we're going to have Jenny do all the torture to get even for anything he did to her with full vengeance."

Brian's head was spinning as he exited the Oval Office, *Jenny . . . Jenny . . . what in the hell is she doing here? Is this a setup? They're going to interrogate me about GeoGlobal to make sure they get all the inside scoop from me, then decide how to spin it to make sure I am the fall guy, then use Jenny to back up what an asshole I am. I hate to say it, but I need a lawyer.*

"That was fast. All this effort to get you here, and you're in there for two minutes," said Agent Womack, standing next to the wall with his arms folded across his rather large chest, looking at Brian like a pitiful idiot.

"Did they kick you out already? Damn boy, are you talking to yourself?"

Brian had given up any inclination of good manners, and just gave Agent Womack a kiss my ass look.

"I need some food and a drink. I'm about to pass out. I need the bathroom too."

Agent Womack stared at Brian for a moment, and then turned his head as he heard laughter erupting from the Oval Office. "Everything okay bud? You're a little worked up."

Brian put his head in his hands, wanting to be back at Chase's apartment. The door to the Oval Office opened quickly, and Agent Womack stood at full alert. President Rhea and Jenny came through and walked quickly towards Brian.

"Mr. Larson, we're piecing some things together here, and we owe you an explanation. Do you mind if we walk with you?"

Chapter 19—Pressure

Offices of Roy Ritchey—Arlington, Virginia

Jim Jackson was on the verge of vomiting. Jim was in way over his head, and no words were calming down Roy. At least he had the presence of mind to not make additional commitments he couldn't keep, as this would only create a bigger hole to climb out of.

Jim was reading Roy's behavior closely, taking full note of the aggressive body language. Roy's thinning hair slicked back, muscular build, arrogant attitude and constant frown made him an intimidating figure. His quick temper and no scruples were a recipe for a personality that could not be reasoned with. Jim's only thought was to find a way out of the meeting.

Roy's deep dark eyes were penetrating straight through Jim. "We paid you a lot of money to influence this project. Dr. Liepert has become quite bothersome. I thought you were going to take care of this problem, or is it something I should handle?"

Roy usually loved to see the other guy nervous in his presence, and took pride in exuding the aura of hate. But for this meeting, Roy wasn't playing any games.

Roy leaned forward in his chair with his elbows on the desk to get closer. "This won't give us the results you committed. Pipelines, fed-owned refinery. I think we made a serious mistake investing in your services. There you are, locked in a conference room for days with the DOE, and you bring me this shit."

"Mr. Ritchey, I hope you can see the value of this information. You're the only outsider that knows what's going on. There'll be at least ten additional pipelines built near San Antonio. That information gives you inside track to land in South Texas."

Roy raised his voice, on the verge of jumping out of his chair to punch Jim in the face. "I didn't pay you a million dollars to give me information! I paid you a million dollars to set the course!"

Roy decided to turn up the heat a little bit, and let Jim know his problem was bigger than just Roy. "My clients don't want this refinery at all, much less under government control. We paid you handsomely to give us information the world will know within the week. You're a total failure."

Roy let the message settle in a little bit. "You know, they tend to eliminate resources that don't perform, and this one won't just be my decision."

Roy leaned back in his chair, contemplating what to do with this guy. Roy was caught in a trap as Jim was the only mole he had inside the DOE leadership team. He really needed Jim, but couldn't let Jim know that was the case.

Roy was CEO, president, managing partner and end-all for a consulting company called OGMFR. Roy's firm was a little known company to the outside world, but one of the most influential in the oil and gas business. OGMFR was an acronym for Oil and Gas Management, Financials and Research. But his customers thought it stood for Oil and Gas Money for Roy. OGMFR had a long-standing reputation of being a shady company at best; however, if you wanted the inside track to the most lucrative contracts, you needed to pay OGMFR for their services. One way or another, Roy always had the best information. Most of the major original equipment manufacturers, exploration companies, architectural & engineering firms, and many oil and gas companies from all over the world would never acknowledge it, but they paid OGMFR handsomely to get inside information. OGMFR only had about twenty official employees, but had hundreds on the unofficial payroll. Jim Jackson was one of his unofficial employees.

Roy's business was growing, but he was looking for something more. His ultimate dream was to be of the social elite status, and he longed to be included in the club of influence and power; was determined to be on the list of power brokers and trend-setters. Roy had learned the hard way that being responsible, capable and knowledgeable really didn't mean a damn thing to the executives in the oil and gas business. The more he seemed to perform, the more his bosses were promoted, but he never seemed to be given credit.

Early in his career, Roy had risen to the level of Offshore Topside Manager for Pencer Petroleum, but was terminated when he belittled an executive at a company meeting. Although Roy was correct about the particular topic at hand, HR terminated him for insubordination; the constant grievances from Roy's direct reports made their decision an easy one. But to Roy, his only perspective was the appalling lack of appreciation. He had personally overseen the construction of dozens of off-shore platforms, making millions of dollars for Pencer, and was terminated for his efforts. With little money in his bank account, Roy made a solemn vow that he would no longer be at the mercy of ignorant people determined to hold him back, and would make it on his own.

After Roy's ouster from his job, he accidentally found a very lucrative business. One of his former vendors, who used to despise Roy, called him out of the blue and changed his life. The vendor, a turbine OEM, asked if he had heard any news on the next batch of platforms coming from Pencer Petroleum and their associated budgets. Roy being the opportunist said he did have the information, but they needed to pay him to find out more. The OEM set up Roy as a "consultant" and paid $25,000 for the information. Two months later, the OEM landed a $28 million dollar deal.

The OEM had quietly kept him on as a "consultant" and was now one of many companies that purchased his services. Roy's business had quietly grown to an insider trading house and he banked about $40 million a year for his "services." This was a perfect role for Roy, as he was in the know and made others pay dearly for the information. Roy had the benefit of not having any morals or scruples, and that only made his information gathering abilities better. Roy enjoyed driving his new Porsche, and he was going to keep it that way, one way or the other.

Most of Roy's "associates" were easy targets, as many worked 18 hour days on a crappy ship in the middle of the ocean, hoping their rig hit on the next large find. The crews working these ships mostly came from a criminal background, and were picked up from a gathering point near Morgan City, Louisiana. The crews were made of drifters who hoped to get a job for a six week assignment. The money was good and was usually blown on liquor, drugs or prostitution within the week, and then they slowly worked their way back to the gathering point, hoping to be selected for the next crew by one of the ship foremen. It was truly one of the last places on earth that resembled a cattle posse in the old west, and was a full throttle redneck society. All an "associate" needed to do was call Roy with good information, and they received a $500 cashier's check. It was that simple.

Roy's move into the big time was his dream coming true. One of Roy's "associates" worked for Deep Water Drilling, a large oil and gas exploration company. The associate called and gave him some very interesting news.

The associate said, "Hey man, don't know what's going on, but I think we hit some damn good pockets."

His associate continued in a deep southern accent, "Them engineers were spending long fucking hours in front of that damn computer, holding up our onshore time. They give a bunch of high fives and shit like that. On our last day, one of them mobile chopper landing platforms was brought in, and four different choppers came out there with all kinds of big wigs. And not them regular choppers, I'm talking the first class ride kind. If I was guessing, they hit a big fucking hole."

"Who flew in?"

"How much you got?"

"Five grand for information, ten grand if it is real."

"Pencer Petroleum."

"You'll have the money in the morning. Keep it up, keep it quiet, and keep me informed. Remember, the world won't miss your ass if I find out you're talking to anyone else. You got that?"

The phone was quiet on the other end, as his associate pondered telling Roy to kiss his ass, but thought otherwise as the rumors of Roy's methods might be true.

The associate finally said, "Yeah, I got it."

Roy immediately hit the phones to his "customers." By the end of the month, Roy had the other four major oil companies, A&E firms and OEMs calling, and paying him handsomely for information about the find in the gulf. Roy didn't actually have any concrete information, but he pieced the puzzle together by all the different phone calls from his associates.

The oil field wound up being the largest in the Gulf of Mexico, and Roy's reputation for being in the know was cemented. Pencer didn't have the capital to pay the phenomenal prices others were offering for the mineral rights, and they wound up breaking even at best for finding the best hole in the Gulf. Not only had Roy made about a million bucks, he put Pencer on their ass.

Pencer was now a paying customer, and Roy had found a way to get even. To make it a little sweeter, Pencer's first bit of information came at a little higher cost, in that no information was available as long as the executive that fired Roy was on their staff. Pencer got their information.

Over the years, OGMFR had found the real money with Wall Street investment houses trading in oil and gas, and his business had increasingly become back room deals. Roy now found himself at the brink of becoming seriously independently wealthy, and nothing was going to stop this. The world was working the way he planned it. Wall Street speculation money was growing, the media were buying inaccurate stories on the lack of inventory, oil futures were rising, the major gas companies were making record profits, and all his "customers" were winning major contracts.

However, Roy had recently cut a deal with a different type of client, and was offered an opportunity to join the multi-millionaire club. His new clients didn't appreciate it when things didn't go as planned, and had special methods of dealing with their disappointment. The news Jim brought was the worst possible, and he had to find a way to stop this refinery, at any cost.

After a long silence, Roy gave a dark stare to Jim, "Dr. Liepert and Mr. Abbott seem to be a serious thorn in our side, Mr. Jackson. I think the world would be a better place with them out of it."

When Jim agreed to work with Roy, he was only dreaming of his house in Maine and being recognized as one among the social elite. For the first time, Jim felt the realities of cutting the deal with the devil. Knowledge of murder wasn't what he signed up for. The smooth-talking consultant was now at a loss for words, and the world was landing on him.

"Mr. Ritchey, you can't possibly think of killing Jenny or Glen. I can't be a part of this, that . . . that's unimaginable."

Roy stood up and leaned over the desk, "Then kill the fucking refinery. It's them or the refinery."

"Advisor . . . the advisor!" said Jim, now suddenly not concerned about digging the bigger hole.

"What? What the hell are you saying?"

"Glen and Jenny went to the White House to meet the President and Senators today. They're meeting with a consultant . . . I assume some guy they are bringing in to build the refinery!"

"What's his name? Where's he from?"

"I don't know. They wouldn't tell me!"

"You have 48 hours. Either you tell me who it is, or we move on Dr. Liepert to start. And trust me, you go to any authorities, and you and your family will be out of the picture. Am I being at all unclear?"

Jim quickly left the offices of OGMFR. He walked around the corner of the building, and vomited uncontrollably.

Across the street from the OGMFR offices, a standard looking van with an "Industrial Plumbing Services" decal was parked among the other parked cars on the street. The two federal agents situated in the back of the van gave each other a concerned look.

The lead agent picked up the phone and said, "This is Agent Chambers, get me Agent Womack."

Chapter 20—Comprehension

White House—Washington, D.C.

Brian felt like he was in a surreal dream. He was actually walking with the President of the United States down a long hallway with his lost girlfriend next to him. Just six hours earlier, he was on Chase's couch watching Regis and Kelly for the first time, and now he was talking with the President.

As the three walked down the hallway with Agent Womack close behind, the President was stopped no less than five times by different folks asking all sorts of questions. They stopped for a few moments while the President spoke to his Chief of Staff. Brian caught Jenny out of the corner of his eye, and couldn't resist turning slightly to look at her. Although her looks had matured a little, she was still the most beautiful woman in the world in his eyes. Brian glanced down quickly and noticed she wasn't wearing a wedding ring.

She turned to look at him, and he could tell she was just as nervous. Brian reached out and grabbed one of her hands, and he saw her begin to breathe deeply. Brian stared at her, wanting to say something. As he was close to her, the old feeling came back. Her touch and smell took him back to a place long ago. One he missed like no other.

When they finally made it to the dining table in the upstairs residence of the White House, Brian started feeling much more relaxed. He gave the complete story to the President about his meeting with Chuck Gordon, and felt confident in telling the President he simply didn't want to go back to GeoGlobal. Brian made the connection that the DOE leadership must be worried about GeoGlobal, which was the reason Jenny and Glen Abbott were at the meetings.

Brian said, "Mr. President, the past few days taught me many things about my life. As much as I imagined GeoGlobal was my extended family, I learned that a business isn't a family. GeoGlobal has a ton of great people, but I don't think I can go back. A part of me wants to see GeoGlobal go down in flames, but the reality is my current disgust towards Chuck Gordon isn't a reflection on the company."

Jenny couldn't hold back a smile as she listened intently to Brian's story.

"Well, Brian," said the President, "that's fine, but GeoGlobal is a major contributor to our economy. You have some ideas on how we can get it back on its feet?"

"Yes sir, I do."

The President's administrator took notes on his recommendations, and Senator Matthews, Senator Johnson and Glen Abbott joined the conversation. Brian talked to the President as if they were good friends, and outlined a detailed plan restoring GeoGlobal back to its original position. Brian recommended disclosing the exact details of Chuck Gordon's meetings, including all the blackmail threats. He also recommended publicly releasing a document outlining the reinstatements for the recently fired leadership for the company, which included placing Mark Dye as interim president.

Brian said, "Mr. President, essentially I would let the world know that GeoGlobal has a great team, with great people and sound fundamentals. Telling the truth is never a bad policy. Mr. Gordon created the stir he wished to achieve, but the company leadership and its associates are well in control. As a personal note, I sure would like to see Gordon get in a world of trouble for causing all of this."

"Well Mr. Larson, it looks like you are the leader everyone around here has been talking about."

"Thank you, sir."

Brian found himself in an ironic situation. Just a few days earlier, his passion for becoming the most powerful businessman in the world completely consumed his thoughts. The events over the past couple of days made Brian face a hard reality that his drive for excellence in his career, at the end of the day, didn't matter. Brian had no doubt he could start another company, take the talent of his choice from GeoGlobal, and hurt them badly. But Brian knew deep in his heart that taking steps to hurt GeoGlobal would be placing his passion in the wrong place. He needed something much more.

Brian sensed a relaxation he hadn't felt in a long time. His internal drive to be the ultimate power energy businessman faded. Since he fulfilled his obligation to the White House and GeoGlobal, he thought about asking Jenny if he could hang out in Washington for a few days, formulating a way to rekindle their relationship. He'd love nothing more than to just hang out with her for a few days, weeks, months . . . No doubt he'd have to be in on many conferences with the team from GeoGlobal as it got back on its feet, but he could do that from almost anywhere. Brian could rent a car, spend some time in the Appalachian Mountains and take a very long vacation. If he was lucky, Jenny could join him. He couldn't keep his eyes off of her. Damn, he hoped she was single. Brian wondered if Jenny still rode her horse. Man, Brian was feeling like a kid again, thinking of asking a girl out on the first date.

Agent Womack walked to the table and interrupted, "Mr. President and Senators, may I have a moment with you?"

The four walked to the other end of the room and had a brief conversation. Brian contemplated how to get out of the company of the U.S. leadership to be with Jenny, but wasn't sure about the proper protocol. *Do I ask the President if I can leave? Surely the President is busy and needs to move on the other issues . . .*

The President and the Senators returned to the table; the President then excused the administrator and turned to Brian. "Mr. Larson, now that you've fulfilled your duties to GeoGlobal, let's talk about another type of duty. One you can complete for your country and become a wealthy man in the process. We need your services in matters of the highest importance."

Brian sat in his chair and stared at the President. His visions of getting together with his long lost love and his vacation seemed to become a distant dream at an incredible pace. This was not a turn he expected. His mind was screaming, *Run like hell*. But typically, U.S. citizens don't turn down the President when he asks for help.

"Okay." Somehow Brian knew that was a word he'd regret for a long time to come.

The President said, "Brian, first of all, we need your complete discretion on this subject, and ask for you to have an open mind. This conversation cannot leave this table."

"Yes sir. Absolutely."

"Brian, you're obviously aware of the dire economic situation in the United States, and energy's key role in contributing to our problems. Energy prices being where they are, coupled with our dependence on foreign oil supply that's now in danger, stand to destroy the very fabric of our society. This Administration doesn't intend to let the situation take its natural course. We plan on taking action."

"I assume you're talking about the new refinery. By the way, that's a great idea."

"Thank you. But very few people know the actual story," said the President as he slid his chair closer to Brian.

"Brian, the U.S. government is going to build it. We'll supply aviation fuel to the military and many of the commercial carriers, and it needs to come online within the year. It'll be the largest U.S. sponsored project going on at this moment, and will be funded by a U.S. Treasury bill, and will eventually be moved to a public company to get our money back once our energy supply is stable."

"Brian, we're asking that you lead this project. We'll give you an annual salary of $2 million, and offer you the presidency of the new company once it becomes publicly traded. Upon our initial public offering we'll make sure you have a large equity stake, and guaranteed contracts with the U.S. for a very long time. The only thing we ask in return is that Glen Abbott and Dr. Liepert are your counterparts, representing the people of the United States until the company becomes public."

Brian was stunned at the turn of events. In the past three days, Brian had gone from the heir-apparent president of GeoGlobal, to unemployed, to dreaming of starting a life with his long-lost love, to now . . . an opportunity to become the central focus of hope of saving the United States economy, and becoming one of the wealthiest men on the planet.

Brian wasn't sure how to answer. He felt the stares of everyone in the room. A million questions flooded his mind. Brian slowly turned his head and looked at Jenny.

"Uhh, Mr. President, I need some time to consider everything you've proposed. Can I have this evening to write down some thoughts and spend time with Dr. Liepert to discuss this opportunity?"

"No problem. However, I'd ask you to stay here in the White House where you'll have access to our services. Agent Womack will be close by as well if you need anything."

"President Rhea, I appreciate your concern, but I won't be a flight risk,"

Brian said in a light-hearted tone with his hands up. "I don't need to have someone follow me all the time. Plus, I'm still wearing the ankle bracelet. I feel like a criminal."

The President nodded his head and gave the "I hear what you're saying" look, but also the look of "you don't know the entire story."

The President said, "While you're considering things tonight, there are some other things you should consider."

"There're many people who don't want this refinery built. There's some intelligence that people are digging deep to discover the details of the refinery, and the names of those involved."

Brian felt his chest get tight and his breathing heavier. He'd never been in a situation where his very life could be in jeopardy, and even worse, Jenny's life could be in danger. Brian had seen many cases where environmental extremists became aggressive, and a couple of situations where he had a bodyguard while traveling in a foreign country. But this situation was much different.

"Which people do you mean?" asked Brian in a tone more of fear than curiosity.

The President considered this question for a moment. This was an important time during his interview of Brian. The President certainly had enough information to make Brian sprint for the nearest closet and go into eternal hiding. The President needed to be clear for his safety, but not scare him out of wanting the job.

"There're many forces here. First, we've got the oil and gas companies. Not to pick on you specifically; however, the lack of refineries has kept supplies limited, and creates a price increase. We have no threats from a domestic company, but let's say companies similar to GeoGlobal don't want prices to drop. Actually, we're concerned a domestic company will drag their feet when building a refinery, and that's why the government's building it.

"Secondly, China has a pretty big interest in crippling our economy. China wants the attention of all Third World societies, so as to become the dominant player. Their forecast of a 25 percent increase in petroleum usage isn't likely, but the media doesn't actually look for facts, and China knows this. If pricing drops, then their financial model with Venezuela will bomb. So China certainly doesn't want this refinery built."

Oh God, thought Brian, *I could become a target of a foreign state.*

"Third, there are other ways of harming us other than a direct war. Terrorist groups will take any action to stop our progress. Coincidentally enough, we recently stopped an attack on our natural gas supply, and let's just say that business is real ugly and complicated on several levels."

Brian understood what that meant, and wasn't prepared to think of things like this. Being the target of terrorists was bringing this situation to another level. Brian couldn't keep his eyes off Jenny.

The President looked at Glen Abbott before continuing, and then turned back to Brian. "However, these aren't the biggest threats.

Brian, let me ask you a question, is the price of oil worth $200 per barrel?"

"No. Absolutely not. These prices are inflated because the commodity traders create an atmosphere of fear. The price is where it is because O&G futures are driven up, so the calls make incredible margins for the traders."

"Exactly! And that brings us to our most critical threat. The people pouring money into these futures represent the social elite in the United States. These are the same people who created junk bonds in the 80s, the dot coms of the 90s, and the real estate balloon of the 2000s. You understand this kind of person I am speaking of?"

Brian somewhat nodded, not really understanding where the President was going.

"These investment bankers and trading houses have a unique ability to artificially create value. Oil and gas futures now have more than three trillion dollars invested, and this money being lost would severely undermine their plans. These folks have no problem taking steps to make sure this refinery isn't built."

Brian gave a stoic nod. The President was certainly correct in his analysis of the traders. Now Brian understood even more clearly why Jenny and Glen were at the meeting.

"Brian, this refinery represents more than just oil production. The price of energy, and our limited supply situation, have placed us in a position of vulnerability and created an atmosphere of fear for the average citizen. Seldom does a single factor affect the stability of a great economy like ours. Our enemies understand that any deterrent in building the refinery could rip our country apart. The battle line is clearly drawn. If our refinery is successful, then we win. If it's unsuccessful, then we chance losing it all."

The President stood and buttoned his suit jacket. "Mr. Larson, the United States government is prepared to build this refinery, with or without your assistance. We have two other candidates identified that could do the job nicely, and for certain would complete the job. However, you're the best person for this job. The people of our great country are calling upon you to help us in this endeavor. I hope your conclusion is a positive one tonight. Let's meet at nine thirty in the morning to discuss."

The President turned to look at everyone at the table. "Many historians compare the United States to the Roman Empire, and say our run as the dominant global power is destined to end. Many say this end is near, and a few are determined to take ownership of making that day happen. This refinery must be successful, and it's up to the people at this table to save the very core of America's future. America cannot fall."

Chapter 21—True Crime

Home of Gary Blackmon—Napa Valley, California

Roy Ritchey took his time driving north on the Silverado Trail that ran through the east side of Napa Valley. The highway passed many of the region's stunning vineyards and wineries. Roy smiled at the thought of this being one of the most "intoxicated" roads in the United States. Practically every car on the highway was carrying tourists who had done more than their fair share of wine tasting. It was about 5:00 P.M., and the cool air from San Francisco Bay felt refreshing. The Napa region had a distinctive character of old money for the select few, who were chosen to live a life celebrating one of nature's greatest fruits. Great wine, world-class foods, perfect weather, beautiful countryside, dirty money and no questions asked. Napa Valley attracted the masters of money, no matter how it was achieved. Roy longed to have enough capital to buy a major estate in this region. To Roy, Napa Valley represented everything he longed for in the world, and not a single gas well in sight.

Roy considered the risks of his new client. He'd heard rumors about the group, and completely understood the results of failing to accomplish their goals. The Impending Order was a rumor to most and the most secretive of secret societies. Many conspiracy theorists have long held a belief that the super wealthy take steps to control the banking, industry, media and political scenes. It was thought that members of this organization were leaders of many of the world's largest corporations. There were hundreds of online articles trying to connect specific names to the organization, but no definitive

101

proof. Their name was really one of folklore, a myth to most and a frustrating dead end to others.

About a year before the housing collapse, a ton of money went into energy trading well before the housing bubble, and Roy suddenly found himself a new client. The Impending Order intended to keep their investments safe, and Roy was one of their methods.

But if he did this right, he would become wealthy beyond his dreams. That motivation kept his mind in the right place. Pressure, intensity and a sole focus on accomplishing his goals while appearing very cool was the key. These men grew up in the world of privilege, and had become accustomed to high performance on a daily level. Only the chosen ones got to enter their world, and today was the most important meeting of his life. He knew they considered him a petty criminal, not nearly to their caliber or social status. Roy would prove today that he belonged in this group, and would be fully appreciated and compensated for his efforts.

Roy saw the sign for Eagle's Perch winery. The sign sat slightly angled to the southwest on the outside of a great gate. "Tastings by Appointment Only" was written in small letters, but this was a diversion, as this winery hadn't had a public tasting in years.

Roy slowly drove his car to the gate, and rolled down his window to pull up to a small microphone stand that was almost completely covered in ivy, and noticed the two different security cameras discreetly hidden on top of the gate. There was no button to push, so Roy sat in his rental car from the Oakland airport.

"May we help you, sir?" asked a pleasant male voice.

"Roy Ritchey here to see Gary Blackmon."

The gate promptly opened and Roy drove towards the grand house centrally located on the estate. The quarter mile road was made of fine gravel with a hard foundation, and had beautiful honeysuckle and yellow rose plants lining both sides of the driveway. Everything tended to be a light yellow color to align with the Chardonnay that was the signature wine.

As Roy pulled up the driveway, he saw the main estate up close. It was a graceful building, with seven columns running up all three stories. The house was made of large, multicolored rocks shipped in from various rivers running through central Italy. The top of the house had many handmade carvings of cement, representing several unique features of the estate, the local region and the old family money that owned this estate for years. The windows had shutters made out of a rough wood with different unique grapevines climbing on each one. The "backyard" of the estate was one of the small foothills that surrounded the valley.

However, Roy's breath was taken away when he got his first look at the open garage. The garage was situated to the right of the main house, and had the same look and feel. It had eight bays, and was completely empty except for the precious pieces of machinery located in every bay. Roy was suddenly embarrassed by his pitiful rental car, and quickly parked it.

Roy stopped for a moment to examine one of the exotic sports cars. He kneeled down and looked closely at every line of the Bugatti. He wanted to touch the car, but thought better of doing this. He dreamed of sitting behind the wheel of this fine machine, with everybody looking his way, thinking how lucky he was to be wealthy, and having the luxuries of life. Roy knew his day was close, and he would relish every single moment. Being in the club was at his fingertips.

"It's my favorite," said Gary Blackmon.

Roy quickly jumped to his feet, a little embarrassed he was caught gawking at the car like a teenage kid. "I'm admiring your collection, very impressive."

Roy walked towards Mr. Blackmon to shake his hand. It was the first time the two men had met face to face. Gary Blackmon looked to be in his late fifties. He was tall, with a slender build, thinning grey hair with a few black streaks. His look was that of a conservative man, wearing expensive khakis and a Ralph Lauren long sleeved button-down shirt as casual attire. He was wearing a Tag Heuer Formula 1 watch, which Roy thought was ideal for this man.

"Well, Mr. Ritchey, come with me."

The men walked in silence to the main house and entered through a massive door. They continued to the main gathering area of the house, where the floor was made of marble with two magnificent tasting bars loaded with exclusive wines from all over the world. This bar was a little different than most wineries, as there was liquor to be had if one chose to have a stronger drink.

The two men moved past the tasting area through a regular door until they reached the rear balcony of the house. To Roy's surprise, there were five other men already sitting at a large outdoor table, with three servants pouring drinks and laying table settings. The air was beginning to get a little cool, so everyone had on a blazer or pullover of some sort. Roy naturally felt out of place in the company of the men, but was happy he had chosen a dark blazer for his clothing.

Before Roy went any further, a security guard approached him with a wand.

"Sir, may I?"

Roy gave the typical groan of anyone about to get patted down for security. He just looked at the man and raised his arms. Directly in front of everyone, Roy received a complete pat down consistent with someone being arrested. The man's hands touch every part of his body, literally, and he searched Roy for better than a minute. He knew he was being checked for bugs and weapons as he was in the company of the wealthiest criminals in the world, but it didn't mean he had to like it. Roy sensed the looks of disdain from the powerful men. It was obvious to Roy that outsiders were generally not welcomed here.

Once the search was done, one of the servants came to Roy and asked what he would like to drink. Roy gave a quick glance at all the men at the table, and saw that they were drinking wine.

"I'll take the Chardonnay from Eagle's Perch's finest vintage."

"Absolutely," said the servant as he left to retrieve Roy's setting.

Gary said, "Roy, please have a seat where you like."

Roy observed the table and noticed the only empty seat was at the front of the table, with Mr. Blackmon at the other end. Roy picked up on the first lie, as Mr. Blackmon told him to take any seat he wanted. The Impending Order was subtle with their influences, and found a way of just making things happen. No need to say where your seat was, just understand you're at the head of the table because you're the one in the hot seat. Roy walked to his assigned spot, and the servers immediately made him a platter complete with grapes, cheese, bread and sausage.

Shortly after taking a seat, a whole bottle of Eagle's Perch 2004 Vintage Chardonnay appeared in a chilled ice bucket. The servant immediately poured him a sip to taste. All six men stared at Roy to see how he handled the moment, and see if he knew how to do a proper tasting. Roy wasn't falling into this trap of petty ritual. He was going to be judged upon his ability to deliver what these guys wanted, and wasn't about to let his wine knowledge change his well earned reputation.

"I'm sure the wine's excellent, just pour away."

The servant dutifully poured a full glass into an Eagle's Perch branded wine glass, and all the servants immediately disappeared. Roy swirled the wine a bit, and took a good drink. The wine was indeed excellent.

Gary said, "Mr. Ritchey, we appreciate you taking the time to come meet us. I believe we all have mutual goals in mind, and I think it's time for us to all align our thoughts. It's probably better not to mention anyone's full name, but let me do the high level introductions."

Roy nodded in agreement; probably the less he knew about these men, the better. But he was definitely interested in hearing the highlights.

"We represent financial trading, investing and banking. We take great pride in protecting our money, and growing it to its full potential. Over the past two years we've earned a nice income on energy, and therefore, make a nice living. We intend to keep it that way."

All the men gave a knowing grin. The man to Roy's immediate right shouted a "here-here," and toasted the table to continued exceptional returns. Roy was fascinated with the ultra wealthy. Here he was, at a table drinking wine with billionaires, attending a meeting that discussed destabilizing the oil and gas market, wreaking havoc for millions of Americans, and the men treated this moment like they were applauding the winners of a croquet tournament.

Gary said, "Our families and prospective businesses represent long lines of financial leadership. Several generations have trusted us to protect their well earned rewards, depending on us to keep the elite in their proper and rightful status."

Roy nodded again, understanding exactly what Mr. Blackmon was implying.

Gary said, "As you're aware, important trends don't happen by themselves. Our mutual efforts to destabilize the oil markets have worked nicely over the past few years; however, we seem to have the wrong man in the White House at the moment, and he's quite determined to bring energy costs down."

Gary never took his eyes off Roy. "And that's very bad news for our interests. With the downturn in housing planned years ago, we made a proactive move to energy. We now have a considerable amount of funds at stake with energy futures. Our primary objective is to make certain that energy futures look very frightful; therefore, you fit nicely into our plans. So, give us some good news."

All the men turned to Roy. This was the moment when there was no turning back. He was nervous for first time in a long time, and felt his skin chill a bit.

Roy cleared his throat and said, "Mr. Blackmon, I think we should be clear about my role. I agree that we have mutual interests, but I'm paid to give you important information early. The information won't always be good news, but it gives you time to make the appropriate decisions. If you expect me to always bring good news, then you'll likely be disappointed."

Gary and his table of conspirators didn't like this message. They were accustomed to giving subtle ideas about expectations, and then good news just happened. Roy's method caught them off guard.

"Very well, Mr. Ritchey. Then what news do you have?" said Gary in a slow and methodical voice, and with a much more ominous look.

Roy had nothing in writing, and all information was memorized to a tee. Roy decided to be as blunt as possible. "The government's going to build a refinery in San Antonio. It'll be one of the largest in the world. The refinery will focus on aviation fuel, and will be the primary provider for the U.S. Government. The refinery aims to boost competition to an already over supplied refined petroleum market."

Roy paused for a moment to get a glance at the group. He knew the term "over supplied" was a surprise to some of the men, when all you heard in the media was "under supplied." Because oil pricing was at such a high price, every refinery in the world was producing as fast as it could. There were better than 15 super-tankers loaded with high quality oil off the east coast of the United States, just looking for a buyer. The O&G traders had done a remarkable job of keeping this out of the news. Roy assumed they all had heard of the refinery, but not the details. Three of the men glared at Roy, not giving their hand into anything as of yet, but the other three moved around in their seats, not comfortable with this information.

Roy continued, "This move will increase competition. Plus, they're building it on an abandoned air force base, so there's little in the way of political roadblocks. If I was to assume a few things, the White House will launch an aggressive marketing campaign about the real oil supply situation, and sell the aviation fuel extremely cheap. My best estimate has oil dropping by more than fifty percent over the next three to six months."

The men gawked at Roy with their mouths open, and a slow panic took over the table. Roy wasn't sure of the total value of dollars these men were managing, but he was certain the only thing they heard was the price of oil dropping dramatically. All of the men were now obviously agitated.

Roy said, "To make things a little more interesting, the government plans on owning the refinery for the near future. The big five gas firms will have little say in limiting supply. In order to keep up with shareholder expectations, their volumes will increase, which lowers the commodity trading price even further. You guys say you're financial types, so I'm sure you understand that the oil traders will have to drop their pricing. All in all, we have a determined President that fully intends to eliminate the energy problem."

One of the men almost yelled at Roy, "How in the hell did you get the number fifty percent? With the limited supply in our reserves, how can anyone assume this number would ever drop this low?"

Roy now had the upper hand. If the men didn't respond, then they must know something he didn't. But their reaction told Roy he had the insider information, so they needed him.

Roy raised his voice equal to the temperament of the table, "If you remember correctly, the price of oil was about 80 bucks about a year ago. Now it's north of $200 a barrel."

Roy spoke with a sarcastic, almost arrogant tone. "Well, as I assume you're aware, this pricing actually has little to do with the business, and it's all based on futures. We've created hysteria with our media influence, but now they'll be forced to say the facts, especially with the President's media blitz coming up. And the fact is there's no oil shortage. There's more than enough petroleum; we just don't have the refining capability. If I was to guess, a nice number for crude oil to settle would be about ninety-five bucks a barrel, give or take a few dollars."

The table let out a collective gasp. The men ran the calculations in their minds. Most entered the energy game around $65 per barrel, and had all but consumed the rewards. Energy dropping that low would completely wipe out their fortunes. Two of the men start drinking their wine like beer, and another two gentlemen paced around with drinks in hand.

Gary gave a deep stare to Roy. "Mr. Ritchey, this information is completely unacceptable. We hired to you to influence the outcome, not to bring us this kind of information. I think you need to be reminded of the company you are in. We don't sit idly and watch our money dwindle away. Am I being clear?"

Roy's mind quickly drifted to his talk with Jim Jackson, remembering how he had the same comment.

"Yes sir."

Another one of the gentlemen pacing around quickly chimed in, concerned Mr. Blackmon was about to piss off, if not eliminate, the only real insider the group had access to. "Mr. Richey, we're impressed with this information. What steps do you recommend to make sure our interests are addressed properly?"

Roy was surprised by this question. He figured this group of men never got their hands dirty.

"Very simple. We kill the refinery."

Mr. Blackmon slowly nodded in agreement, "That's the news I'm looking for. Kill the damn refinery."

"I'm already working on that," said Roy in a smug tone, thinking he was way ahead of these guys.

Gary said, "Any major action must be approved by me first, so I can prepare for everything the future may hold. No actions without my approval. Understood?"

"Yes sir."

"Good. Your wire transfer hits the bank tomorrow. You gave a speech about good news vs. bad news, but we don't want another meeting like this. This table only accepts good news. The waiter will help you out."

Roy removed himself from the table, and quickly left the meeting. The men sat quietly until Roy was out of their sight.

One of the men said, "God damn it, Gary. I told you we should have shorted this thing. I say we do it immediately."

"We've been over this a million times. If we pull now, then we'll raise too many flags. We're way long on energy. We can only move our money when the market goes up. Moving our shares before the refinery announcement is too obvious considering we damn near cornered the energy market."

The man said, "You know we're taking a big risk here. Putting our hopes on a two-bit criminal doesn't feel very wise."

Gary said, "Look, we only need a few actions to push up energy a little further, then we can slowly move out. This guy has all the right connections to get us some movement in the right direction."

"He knows too much, Gary. New money doesn't get in the club. I want this loose end eliminated once things go our way."

Gary held up his wine glass. "Not to worry. Our club stays right where it is."

About two hundred yards away in the hills of the plantation, the two camouflaged agents recorded everything. The parabolic microphone picked up the voices nicely.

Chapter 22—Old Process in a New World

White House—Washington, D.C.

Kerosene. Brian couldn't get it off his mind since the President mentioned aviation fuel. He found it incredibly ironic that the future of the U.S. economy was based upon one of the oldest petroleum products.

Jenny was explaining the history of the fuel to Brian: "Somewhere around the mid 1800s, scientists found a way to extract a waxy liquid from a petroleum mixture they called asphalt. The liquid was named kerosene, which is the Greek word for wax."

Jenny and Brian had left the meeting with the President and walked to the upstairs area of the White House. Brian listened to Jenny, but thought about an entirely different subject. He really only imagined ways to bring up the subject of their past, and how she was all he'd thought about over the last few days, and really since they broke up. Brian watched her mannerisms, and found it touching how she tried to discuss anything other than their relationship.

Jenny continued discussing kerosene and how incredibly evolved the product had become with hundreds of different applications. She was somewhat of a petroleum historian, rooted back to her days in Kilgore. She frequently studied the history of different petroleum products to get a handle on mistakes others had made over the years.

Jenny continued, "And the rest is literally history. Kerosene was the most important commodity before electric lighting, and really kick-started the oil boom. A whole industry evolved to develop oil drilling and purification processes just for kerosene. It's fascinating how the fuel went from lighting lamps to driving the worldwide aviation industry."

Brian listened, but was caught in a haze. He glanced at Jenny's great figure, tried to take in the White House and comprehend what the President had just proposed, and did his best to keep up with her comments.

Brian decided to chime in, "I've been around it a little bit. It's an ideal product for the aviation industry. It's used instead of gasoline because of its high flashpoint. Commercial jet fuel is called Jet-A, and it's just processed kerosene."

They eventually made it to small dining room near a kitchen. As they walked into the room, no less than three people asked them if they needed anything.

Brian said, "A tall gin and tonic, whatever gin you have is great."

Jenny asked for a Chardonnay. Within minutes, both drinks were at the table. The waiter asked if they would like anything else, and Brian knew they literally meant anything.

Jenny said, "I'm fine. What about you?"

Brian thought for a second, and gave Jenny a knowing look. "You know what, a thin crust Pizza Hut sausage and jalapeño sounds awesome."

Jenny smiled and said that sounded great. In college, Sunday was date night, usually with a Pizza Hut pizza. Brian felt a huge relief, as Jenny's response was his first clue that she might be willing to forgive him, and at least discuss their relationship.

Brian noticed the waiter's reaction. He stared at Brian, obviously appalled that a pizza chain was selected over the five star chefs at his service. The waiter, ever gracious and accustomed to keeping his opinions to himself said, "Certainly, we'll make the arrangements."

After the waiter left the room, Brian took a deep sigh and got an anxious feeling. He should feel comfortable with her, but it had been so long. He thought he could tell her how he felt, but he really didn't know how she'd respond. He wasn't even sure if she had a relationship, maybe even a family. Jenny had seen him through his darkest days, during the time of his parents' death, and she knew the intimate details of his life, his childhood, just everything. But Jenny had become successful on her own, proving she was just fine without him.

The room became very quiet, and she stared at the wine glass in her hands. They sat at the table, and he sensed she was also at a loss for words. Brian decided to at least begin the conversation.

"Hey Jenny."

She slowly looked at him with a nervous expression. Her brown eyes were wide open, and he noticed her shoulders moved up and down while she breathed heavily.

Brian said, "This is the craziest moment of my life. I don't even know where to start, but I'm happy you're here. I've been thinking about you nonstop since Gordon fired me, and really every day since you and I broke up. A brick wall landed on me this week. I always knew I made the biggest mistake of my life losing you. I always thought we'd get back together, and then time caught up with me . . . . I just, I don't really know how to say it."

Jenny shook her head, and turned to stare at the wall. She wouldn't look him in the eyes.

Brian said, "Jenny, what are you thinking?"

"I can't do this again, Brian. You were the love of my life, and I already lost you once. I can't do it again."

"I know. I think we should just begin getting through this refinery and see where it goes. No good comes out of looking at the past."

Jenny's eyes were moist, and she gave him an exasperated look. "You're so arrogant. How can you say we can't look at the past? I totally gave myself to our relationship, and you left. You just left. After everything we went through, you just left."

"Come on Jenny, I didn't just leave. We both had good opportunities. You chose to move overseas."

Tears were now streaming down her face. "That's not fair. That's not fair. You know how much I put into my career and education, and you know I would have given it all up for us."

Brian knew she was right. Nobody had done more for Brian than Jenny, and he ran away from the relationship. Brian had made the mistake, and needed to acknowledge it.

"You're right. I ran away. I don't know what to say. After losing my parents, being so close to someone else scared me to death. I couldn't go through that again, Jenny. It was easier to run. To start over," said Brian in a defeated tone.

"I'm sorry. I'm sorry I hurt you so badly. I'm sorry I hurt us and ruined the best thing in my life. You were everything to me, and I ruined it. I don't know what will happen now, but I promise I will do everything I can to make it right."

Jenny heard the words. Jenny always knew Brian ran away, more scared of their relationship than being finished with it. She had never seen him like this. Brian, usually the vision of excitement and fun, was now at the bottom.

The room was once again quiet while they sat there. Both were caught in a trap of duty for their country vs. their personal relationship. Their country needed them, but they needed each other. Neither really knew what to say next.

Jenny said, "Brian, I think we both need each other. I can't commit to anything right now, but I'm happy you're here. I've been thinking about you too. Let's get through this refinery."

"Okay. But it sure is better with you here."

"Better for me too."

Brian let out a deep sigh of relief. Brian had lost his parents, lost Jenny and then lost GeoGlobal. Jenny was now miraculously in his life again, and he was going to make this work. She was the last thing of any real value in his life. Losing her for good would be devastating, and he wouldn't let that happen.

"So, what are the details?" asked Brian with a big smile, thrilled to have her with him.

Jenny had no problem remembering these details, as it was all she'd thought about for the past four months, other than Brian. "We're targeting 800,000 barrels per day. That . . . ."

While Jenny started talking, Brian was taking a drink of his gin, and choked on the first comment.

"Are you serious? A refinery of that size will take a damn army to build. There's no pipeline infrastructure for that much crude. The oil is damn sure in the ground to get, but getting it to the refinery . . . ." said Brian as he rubbed his hands on his temples.

Jenny gave him a stoic look. "I'm not an idiot. Nobody said this would be easy."

Brian picked his head up from his hands and gave her a "go to hell" look. He suddenly remembered how she could dig into his soul with a few quick words. Her "don't be a quitter" comment got to Brian's very core, and he knew she knew this better than anybody on the planet. Brian was about to start arguing and questioning her decisions, which he knew was her Achilles' heel. It was amazing how easy it was getting back to old routines with someone you know so well. But for now, Brian chose to take the high road and not say any snide comments, at least for the moment.

Brian started talking, essentially with his hands holding up his head by the cheeks, "If my math is correct, which is doubtful at the moment, the output is better than 15 percent of current U.S. refining capacity. That would definitely put a dent in oil commodity pricing."

Brian got a smile on his face, "Are you the one that came up with this scheme?"

"This is your payback for dumping me for your hydrocarbon mistress."

Brian gave out a moan.

Jenny said, "We're going to build on Kelly Air Force Base in San Antonio. Good infrastructure and minimal politics."

Brian nodded his head in agreement. It was the right spot. GeoGlobal had considered building a transfer station in San Antonio many times. But the politics of building new pipelines was too much, plus the price of oil stayed higher with limited production. Building on an air force base was a good idea, if there was enough space, good infrastructure and tons of concrete already laid on a solid foundation.

"First things first. We need the best process engineering firm," said Brian as he took a long drink from his drink. "Actually, to keep things less political, we should get an Architecture and Engineering firm that has a good process group. That way, we've got one throat to choke if the A&E gets behind schedule, plus they won't be able to point fingers at another engineering firm. I'll essentially have to be the project manager. I can keep them on schedule."

Brian thought out loud and talked in an exhausted tone while rubbing his eyes, "Because of the high capacity, the plant will operate continuously. We might consider a parallel batch processing unit for specialty fuels. It'll have to run at a steady state for long periods of time. A disruption at this refinery would have a huge impact. With this much capacity, process optimization and advanced process control is an absolute requirement. If Jet-A's the product, a hydro-cracking process system will be the primary design model."

Jenny smiled as Brian's leadership and engineering mode kicked into gear. Brian talked out loud, but really to himself to think through the situation.

"The problem is the big A&E firms don't have any great process guys on staff. They outsource nearly everything. They don't pay enough money. Hell, half the time you never know if the Professional Engineering stamps are real, or if they even really looked at the drawings. The good process engineers are at the process engineering firms. We really need a stud for this one."

Brian got a knowing smirk on this face, "I know who to call. Hands down the best process engineer for cracking processes on this planet. We'll have to hire him directly."

Then it hit Brian for the first time. He really didn't have his phone anymore! It had all his contact information from years in the industry.

Brian let out a groan, "Oh man, my old phone had all the contact numbers. God damned Gordon. Now I have to jump through all these hoops to get in touch with anyone."

Brian turned and yelled, "Agent Womack. I need a phone."

Magically, Agent Womack walked through the door. Brian couldn't help but think that from here on out, somebody would always listen in on every conversation.

Agent Womack said, "Here bud, this is a new phone that's secured, plus we can track it anywhere it goes. We already transferred all your numbers."

Brian looked at Agent Womack, "How'd you get all my numbers . . . never mind, I don't even want to know."

Agent Womack looked Brian right in the eye. "Okay bud, you need to understand we're monitoring every conversation. Just so you know, we'll investigate every single person you speak with about this project. We want this information limited, and we don't trust anyone. So, who do you want to call? I think I heard you say process guy or something like that."

Brian spoke in a frustrated tone, "Look, I'm going to call a guy I've worked with since college. We go way back. He's hands down the best process engineer I know. And trust me, I know a lot of process engineering folks. He has to be on my team for a project of this magnitude."

Agent Womack gave a skeptical look, not feeling very good about Brian calling anyone they hadn't researched. "Uh . . . I don't think so, Mr. Larson. I'd prefer you put a list of names together we can research before contacting anyone."

Brian said, "It's a deal, as long as I call this guy right now. He really should be involved with all the initial decisions of the refinery. Everything evolves from the process design. At least let me call him."

Agent Womack pondered the decision. "The first name on your list, huh?"

"You bet. I would prefer he be on the next flight to Washington," said a confident Brian.

"Okay," said Agent Womack. "Give him a shout. I have a direct link to your conversations into my ear, so I'll hear everything. I'll make some arrangements to get him on a plane as quick as possible. Go do your thing."

Agent Womack handed Brian a new smart phone, and excused himself from the room. Brian cussed for a few minutes while trying to master the new touch screen technology. He eventually found his contact list and dialed the number.

Brian waited for a voice to answer. "Manish, it's Brian Larson. Sorry to call out of the blue so late, but have I got a project for you . . ."

Just as Brian got off the phone, a piping hot pizza came through the door. Brian and Jenny devoured the food and shared stories of their lives. They talked until they passed out on the couch from exhaustion. They felt like they were back in college.

Manish mindlessly watched The History Channel, all the while consumed with the failed natural gas attack. His paranoia was driving him mad; he was certain he was being monitored by the government. He ran all the possibilities through his mind of what went wrong. How they discovered the meeting location, the torture his brothers had gone through; what should he do now? Manish kept eyeing his Qur'an, yet frustrated, he continued watching television instead of looking for guidance.

His cell phone rang, startling him out of his deep thoughts. A call this late was unusual unless he was in the middle of a major project startup. Manish glanced at the display of the phone, which said "BLOCKED." He decided to answer it, needing a diversion.

As Brian explained the initial plans for the refinery, a small smile slowly grew.

"Allah is great," Manish said to himself.

Chapter 23—Big Brother is Listening

White House—Washington, D.C.

Agent Womack and his team gathered information on the Impending Order, and now they added a man named Manish Gupta to their high priority list. Seldom in this line of business was the directive so clear and with so little politics. Agent Womack was amazed how quickly inter-department walls folded once an objective was so clearly stated. The President gave his team direct authority to keep this refinery on track, and keep the "detractors" from gaining any momentum. No bureaucrat in Washington dared to be on the list of "detractors."

Agent Womack and Director Beine of the Secret Service were visiting the Oval Office to discuss the unfolding events. In attendance were the Senators and the President. Agent Womack felt comfortable with the President and had all the details, so Director Beine was relieved when he offered to give the presentation.

Agent Womack said, "Well Mr. President, the economic events over the past few months have brought to light some interesting situations, and I must say your determination to create stability in the energy market has some powerful enemies nervous. This is good."

The President gave him a pretty stoic look. "Well, considering the Director is with you, I assume you're going to tell me some interesting news."

"Yes sir, you're correct."

"OK, lay it on me."

"The SEC's been watching an individual named Roy Richey for a few years. Mr. Ritchey is difficult to define as a criminal in many senses, more unethical than criminal. Kind of like securities or credit default swap trading on Wall Street, it's difficult to say what they do is illegal, just borderline unethical."

"Continue," said the puzzled President.

"Well, he makes a living by being a consultant. But he's really not a consultant. He's paid money for detailed insider information on capital energy projects. As an example, if a pipeline company is considering moving to a new market, Mr. Ritchey will make sure companies like technology providers, OEMs, and engineering firms have the inside track to the capital plans, but Mr. Ritchey has to be on your payroll if you want in on the deal. So let's say a new pipeline is going to be built in Kansas, the OEMs or engineering firms will be proactive in opening up local shops or purchasing a certain technology that will guarantee them the order, which shuts out the competition. It actually works the other way as well, in that the large oil companies will pay Mr. Ritchey to make sure certain things are leaked out to these companies so they can deliver on the expectations, or as a way to keep their competition out of their space. This is why many, if not most, energy related companies simply find it easier to keep Roy on their good side."

The politicians were interested by this bit of information, but didn't really know how to process it. Insider information on oil and gas capital projects was definitely not the route they expected this conversation to go.

Agent Womack continued, "Now the shady side of Mr. Ritchey is all the different moles he has all over the place. A company has real risk of being sabotaged if Roy finds out he's not in the know on major movements. He's made several companies wealthy, and has burned others badly. It's kind of a legal blackmail, if you will."

Agent Womack saw a very confused audience for sure. Director Beine pierced her eyes through him, wanting him to get to the heart of the conversation.

Agent Womack continued quickly to get to the point, "Over the past few days, we've done a more thorough investigation into Mr. Ritchey's background. The beauty of the oil and gas industry is, there are many people with a criminal record who have discovered a nice, legitimate living with a corporation of some sort, and they will give you any detail you want as long as their employers don't discover their acts as a young man. It's one of those things where roughnecks somehow wind up doing a major installation with a company as a temporary employee somewhere, do a good job and get offered permanent work. Fast-forward 15 years, and they live a suburban lifestyle somewhere with a wife and kids, and pray every day that nobody brings up their criminal past. We talked to several of Mr. Ritchey's former and current associates, and they all gave the exact same story on the way he operates."

"And this has to do with us, how?" asked Senator Matthews.

"Well, I'm trying to give you some background into this character. The problem is we can't say he's really doing anything illegal. He's not doing insider trading as he doesn't own any stock. There's nothing formally wrong with sharing information if you're paying for it, on both sides of the fence," said Agent Womack.

"And this has to do with us, how?" once again asked Senator Matthews in a serious tone, growing tired of Agent Womack's presentation.

Agent Womack said "Let me tell you how. I think you have a major problem when the Impending Order pays Mr. Ritchey over $100 million to kill your refinery, and you don't know who he has on the inside."

The President and Senator Matthews bolted up in their chairs with stunned looks on their faces. Senator Johnson stood up and paced around the room.

The President's mind contemplated many scenarios. Eventually, a President must trust somebody, but he couldn't help but be constantly paranoid about who was really on the wrong team. Old school money had a big interest in keeping the energy market unstable, and unreasonably priced. Many Washington insiders thought the Impending Order paid some employees in the government.

"Do you have any evidence to support this?" asked the President.

"We do. When you gave us authority to keep tabs on those involved with the refinery, we began with the basics of monitoring the key individuals. We looked for things such as unusual money transfers, criminal history and things like that. On our very first day of digging into this, we noticed one of the consultants with the Department of Energy, named Jim Jackson, had a substantial direct deposit of $250,000 four times over a four month period. We looked a little deeper, and Jim Jackson has been intimately involved with planning the new refinery. Apparently he's an eminent domain expert, and consulted with strategic oil and gas matters relating to the government."

Agent Womack noticed the group was doing their best to place the name. Agent Womack handed them a picture of Jim Jackson and, to everyone's relief, nobody recognized the name or the face.

"Since we don't have any real authority to get the details from the off-shore bank, we followed Mr. Jackson's movements. We were lucky to catch it when we did, because Mr. Jackson had a meeting with the DOE regarding the refinery, and then immediately drove to the offices of Mr. Ritchey. In our opinion this wasn't a coincidence, so I gave approval for an acoustic monitoring station."

The President and Senators couldn't believe their ears. All were tuned into this conversation as a sole focus.

Agent Womack took a deep sigh and delivered the news: "In this meeting, Mr. Jackson informed Mr. Ritchey of the details of the refinery. The conversation became very heated between the two gentlemen once Mr. Ritchey found out the refinery has been green-lighted, and he told Jim Jackson to take any step to kill the refinery."

The President lashed out, "Damn it! The one thing that I wanted kept quiet is the details of the refinery. Most people know we're up to something, but I specifically wanted this quiet. Damn it!"

"And here's where the news gets even worse. During the meeting, Mr. Ritchey told Mr. Jackson he intended to find a way to take out Dr. Liepert, as he thinks she's the key planner behind this thing. He said if Jim Jackson didn't figure out a way to eliminate the project, then he'd put a hit on her. Those weren't the exact words, but the implication's there. Mr. Jackson was also told to figure out who Brian Larson is, because all that Mr. Jackson knows is a key player was brought in to lead the building of the refinery. We have a feeling he'll take him out as well, if the opportunity presents itself."

Everyone's hearts sank on this news. The reality of the fight came to center stage, and lives were hanging in the balance. You could hear a pin drop in the room.

The President gave a look that only a President can give. At the end of the day, all the responsibility fell on his shoulders, and he above all understood this was no time for panic, it was time for leadership.

"Agent Womack, you mentioned The Impending Order. How do they come into this scenario?"

"Here's where the news gets better. I think we have some key players by the balls."

Chapter 24—Team Building

White House—Washington, D.C.

Brian couldn't get comfortable, and was wavering between alertness and slumber. Something told him to get up, but his body was resisting. He slowly opened his eyes, and it hit him, *Where am I?* His mind raced as his brain comprehended the events over the past 24 hours. He saw the ceiling's extraordinary detail and the hand carved trim. He heard a soft mumbling in the background and the aroma of breakfast was in the air. Brian slowly looked at the couch he was sleeping on, and there was a small quilt covering him. He looked at his watch and it said 9:36 A.M. Brian couldn't remember the last time he slept past 7:00 A.M., much less the last time he slept past 9:00 A.M. in the White House!

Brian was now more tuned in, and to his horror, he distinguished the voices more clearly in the background. And as fate had it, he heard Jenny speaking quietly with the President and the Senators. Brian was in full bore panic now as his mind considered the options. *What should I do? Should I get up? Should I pretend to be asleep? I've found a way to totally embarrass myself twice in one day.* With all the humility he could muster, Brian slowly removed the quilt and sat up on the couch.

"About time you woke your lazy ass!" said Agent Womack, sitting in a chair near the couch. "When Liberty says I can't let you out of my sight, I never figured it would mean sitting in a chair reading the Washington Post about seven times while you sleep. Well, look at the bright side; it's still only 6:45 in California."

Brian's stomach sank while he cussed loudly under his breath.

"You know, we do have beds in the White House," said Agent Womack. "But you know what; Liberty says you can have anything you want, so maybe we'll just bring in some cots to this room, maybe some marshmallows."

Son-of-a-bitch was all screamed in his head. What a way to start a morning.

"Morning, sunshine," said Jenny.

Brian felt a punch to his stomach. *Oh no! Tell me she didn't call me sunshine in front of the President.*

Jenny said, "Sorry about this. We decided to let you get a good sleep considering the day yesterday. But uh, we forgot to tell the President's staff to postpone the meeting. And uh, they all just walked in the room."

Brian slowly turned and saw several people having a discussion near the small dining table. Apparently they'd arrived for the 9:30 A.M. meeting as planned. There was Jenny, looking like a million dollars and dressed to the nines, surrounded by the President, the Senators and Glen Abbott.

With as much dignity as possible Brian said, "Uh, I really apologize for sleeping so late. I guess my body just went in lockdown for a few hours. Let me get cleaned up and we will begin working immediately."

Everyone had a good laugh about Brian sleeping so late, but all figured a fresh and alert Brian was better.

The President said, "Then I assume this means you accept the position."

Brian looked directly at the President as he attempted to get up from the couch and walk towards the table. "Yes sir. This project's too important. I'm not missing this ride. Dr. Liepert and I are fully committed to your program."

The President had a relieved smile on his face. "Great, Brian. Your country needs you, and we're happy to have you on board."

"Thank you, Mr. President," said Brian.

President Rhea said, "Now, first things first, before you get cleaned up. I understand you contacted someone about a strategic role for the refinery. And if I understand correctly, he's a foreign national."

Brian's was caught off guard by the President's immediate questioning of his decisions.

"Well, yes, I think," said a confused Brian. "I really never thought of Manish's background. I only know him as the best."

The President gave a knowing nod, "Look Brian, I above everyone else understand the importance of a team and working relationships. I'd be floundering in the wind without the help of the Senators and my Cabinet."

Brian knew a scolding was coming his way. Agent Womack suddenly moved into the conversation, and positioned himself directly next to Brian.

"You absolutely cannot contact key members of this project without going through proper security channels. You must understand that you have authority to hire whoever you want, build the plant how you want, I mean, whatever you need. But, you have to appreciate the depth our enemies will go to put our project in jeopardy. Just as we discussed yesterday."

The room was silent for a few moments. Brian didn't know how to handle the situation. There he was, dressed in a half-buttoned shirt, a 24-hour shadow on his face, no shoes, standing in front of the most powerful people in the United States, and getting a scolding from the President. All of this within one minute of accepting his new position.

The President looked at Brian while speaking. "Agent Womack, do you have any information yet?"

"Very little. Manish Gupta is an Indian national who's been in the U.S. for about 15 years. He has a Ph.D. in Petroleum Engineering, and has been with a few engineering companies over the years. He has a few patents to his name. This seem right, Brian?"

"Yeah. Yeah. That's right. That's Manish. He and I go way back to building a plant in Kuwait. I think he has a family in India."

Agent Womack said, "He does. He sends the vast majority of his salary to them. But, uh . . . that's not what concerns me."

All eyes turned to Agent Womack.

"He has almost no electronic signature. NSA can't find anything, which is highly unusual. He never uses a credit card. Never uses his cell phone to call anyone other than something to do with work. In today's world of electronic media and financials, we find this highly unusual. To an outsider, it looks like he works during the day, and then disappears for the other hours. It's odd."

"Look," said Brian while holding his hand up, trying to change the perceptions of the highly skeptical people in the room. "I get it. I'll never contact anyone again without going through Agent Womack. I was just excited to get rolling last night. But on a personal note, I'll vouch for Manish. Manish is very committed to work, so it doesn't surprise me he has a simple life."

"When's he going to get here?" asked the President.

"He is on a government plane as we speak," said Agent Womack. "He should be here within the hour. We'll give him a basic interrogation when he gets here. I'll keep an eye on him."

The President said, "Okay, I think we've covered this enough. Brian, for your team, we've set up a conference room for you in the basement. We've established full data services so e-mail, Internet and data servers are at your disposal. Plus, Glen and Jenny have a full team of 300 folks at the DOE who'll drop what they are doing at the drop of a hat in support of your goals. Agent Womack has direct access to me at anytime, so just let him know if you need me for anything. My only formal request is a daily briefing on your progress."

The President held his hand out for a handshake. "Brian, welcome aboard. Look me in the eye, and let me know this will be a success."

Brian shook the President's hand and confidently said, "Mr. President, you have my word."

With that, the President and Senators excused themselves. Suddenly, a White House staffer showed up and informed Brian that all his new clothes and toiletries were ready to go in the bedroom down the hall.

About 30 minutes later, a refreshed Brian showed up in a nice suit, and caused Jenny to catch her breath. Brian and Jenny gave each other a knowing look. It was time to start rolling.

Chapter 25—Engineering Talent

Apartment of Manish Gupta—Houston, Texas

Manish's mind was running at a thousand thoughts a minute. He was reminiscing from his low point at the coffee shop, and back to this euphoric feeling. Ever since his brothers were raided and murdered, he was even more careful about whom he called, his online activity, his associations and conversations. Manish couldn't be sure if the government had already done a background check on him before Brian called, but was now certain every detail of his life would be investigated. Brian let him know so much during their conversation. But they wouldn't find anything on him. Manish only went online through aliases, and logged into chat rooms through multiple network hops and secured VPN tunnels. Tracing the IP address of any computer he used would only lead to a dead end, or maybe some obscure PC where there were no cameras with historical records.

Manish couldn't sleep at all last evening, and was completely infatuated with the opportunity to fulfill his life's mission. His first order of business was to resign from his current employer. He worked for Trade Winds Engineering which primarily focused on upstream processes, the production and delivery of crude oil and natural gas to a downstream source such as a refinery. As usual with engineering firms, he had about three different bosses, most of whom weren't actually responsible for anything. Being in the know was much more important than being accountable.

Trade Winds' latest business opportunity was process control designs for deep water oil platforms. For these platforms, advanced process engineers were a coveted commodity. Their systems partially refined the oil on the platform, which eliminated the need for primary refining onshore. The patented technology that Manish designed had made multi-millions of dollars for the company, but Manish never got a dime of royalties, a fact that wasn't missed by him. Although there were thousands of educated chemical and petroleum engineers in the world, only a handful truly understood how refinery processes worked, and this made Manish the prized possession of Trade Winds. It always made him sick that he was guaranteed to work on projects by the sales reps, and this sales tool always closed the deal. Manish constantly felt he was being used but not getting paid his value. Being a pawn in the game added to Manish's passion towards hating companies that only focused on the dollar.

Trade Winds was on contract by Flagstone Petroleum, a major Architecture and Engineering firm, to design 10 new platforms off the east coast of Mexico that would eventually be sold to PEMEX, Mexico's state-owned petroleum company. This single order created enough revenue to have the Trade Winds board of directors considering an initial public offering, and had the managers and equity owners giddy and planning on early retirement.

Manish called Trade Winds at 6:00 A.M., which was the typical time most engineering companies' management teams got rolling. The engineering manager almost hyperventilated as Manish gave his resignation speech. As the key associate for their $250 million order at 43 percent labor margins, the man wasn't necessarily worried about Manish; rather that he would surely be blamed for losing him. He offered Manish a $25,000 raise on the spot. He had no authority to offer this raise, but this at least gave him an out that he tried to keep Manish.

Within 30 minutes of hanging up on the begging manager, Manish received another call from Trade Winds, which he didn't pick up. It was the CEO and founder of the company offering Manish an equity position in the company via voice mail, and guaranteeing him a $300,000 salary if he stayed. Trade Winds had a large backlog of orders, and they quickly realized that Manish's knowledge was mostly intellectual property in his mind. Without Manish, Trade Winds would lose many of the orders and likely would have to delay the completion of existing orders. Manish's resignation was the worst possible news for Trade Winds, and panic was setting in throughout the company. But no worry to Manish, he would be gone from Houston in about 30 minutes. As far as he was concerned, the arrogant company could burn in hell, and he smiled at the thought of them going down in flames. They might have a patent, but too bad for them that nobody else actually knew how it worked.

A few minutes later the CEO left another voice mail, threatening to sue Manish if he took his designs to anybody else. The ever-cool Manish thought about this for a moment, and decided to have some fun. Manish called the CEO and told him he would consider his offer for an upfront payment of five million dollars and required his decision within five minutes. The stunned CEO stuttered with his thoughts, and rambled about extortion, blackmail, ethics, integrity, lawyers . . .

Manish simply said, "Okay, I then resign. I might have considered staying, but your threat of legal action is concerning. I've made the right decision to leave your company. Thank you for the opportunity to work with Trade Winds, and I wish you future success."

Manish hung up the phone, leaving the clueless CEO with the thought that he contributed to Manish's departure. Manish's phone continued ringing constantly, which he ignored. Manish had serious thoughts on his mind, but he did find a moment to laugh at their situation.

Manish's next call was to his family in India, which was 10 hours ahead of the time in Houston. He informed his wife of his new assignment for the government, and that he would give her his contact information once he was settled. His wife immediately reminded Manish of his family obligations, and dropped a subtle hint about appreciating his marrying into a better family. Her high caste classification was always foremost on her mind, and it highly annoyed Manish. Money seemed to be the only thing anyone worried about, and his family only added to his feeling of being used for money.

After hanging up the phone, Manish reflected on his life choices and the many lies he carried with him. Every time he spoke with his family he pretended to be someone he wasn't, and it left a hollow feeling in his stomach. To his family, he was a beacon of work, family and faith in their Hindu religion. In reality, he was a completely different person.

Like many engineering types from India, Manish lived as a bachelor in an average apartment in Houston. The majority of his considerable $165,000 a year salary was sent to his family in Pune, where he had a wife and two children who lived with his wife's parents. He only saw his family once a year when he took his annual three week trip home. When he visited, he was greeted with indifference by his in-laws and his wife, but others lauded him as a hero. His wealth, wisdom and looks made him a pillar of the community, and a prototype of supporting the vision of bringing money back to India. Manish was considered a proud example of the Indian education system by contributing to equalizing the world's wealth among nations. Manish's salary afforded his family a good living, and both of his children attended the finest schools. It was only with these expectations that Manish was allowed to "marry up."

Remembering back to his time growing up, he reflected on the subtle decisions that brought him to this point. Manish was born into a poor family, and was raised in a marginal structure at best, similar to the other family dwellings intermingled throughout his hometown. However, at a very early age, Manish showed not only superior intellect but also interpersonal skills that made him excel through the politics associated with the thousands of potential students, and he was always the favorite student of the teachers throughout his education. He was eventually offered a student visa, and was selected to attend the University of Houston Department Of Engineering, where he focused on Chemical and Bio-molecular engineering with a minor in Petroleum Engineering. Manish continued his education through a PH.D. in Petroleum Engineering. He wrote a thesis on hydro-cracking, which is the process of breaking down complex organic molecules into simpler molecules by the breaking of carbon bonds.

Manish's first job after school was at GeoGlobal Energy. His initial assignment was among the herd of new engineers with the company, and he was assigned to help in the design and planning of a new refinery producing 350,000 barrels a day in Kuwait. Manish's team was led by an up and coming project manager named Brian Larson. Brian immediately recognized Manish's talents, and they became teammates in building one of the most efficient refineries in the history of GeoGlobal. Brian and Manish spent hours upon hours together for three years developing the refinery, and built a relationship that one can only get during the most stressful of times. The refinery was completed ahead of schedule under Brian's supervision and Manish's talent, and became one of the most profitable refineries for the entire company.

During the project, Manish took note of the dramatic differences in the social classes of the country. The Indian caste system always felt unfair to Manish, and he was highly attuned to social inequities. He observed firsthand the millions of dollars being spent on the refinery, and saw the same amount of money being paid to the Kuwaiti government. The rebuilding of Kuwait after the war promised to deliver social justice by American politicians, but just the opposite occurred. Even at Manish's hotel, an entire shanty town was just adjacent to the entrance. Instead of feeling proud of his efforts, Manish had feelings of being used for his services, and wondered if his career choices were for the betterment of mankind, or simply betterment of the privileged.

About three months prior to the project completion, Manish witnessed how GeoGlobal simply released most of the day workers from their services, and saw the look on the men's faces, knowing they would go to their families with no pay for the day, and for a long time to come. These men had dedicated more than two years of twelve hour days, sometimes in 115° temperatures, to building the infrastructure of the facility. The more Manish watched this disparity, the more he wanted out of the business and the more he hated capitalism. Manish's singular focus on being one of the premier engineering talents in the world subsided, and a deeper feeling for human rights took hold.

Manish certainly wasn't unfamiliar with poverty. Growing up in Pune taught him how to be a survivor, but he really never considered what poverty really meant. To Manish it was just how things were, and he couldn't remember ever having a feeling of wanting to be wealthy; he just wanted to beat the competition. Since Manish was essentially handheld throughout his early years of higher education, he'd never paused to think about the huge difference between the truly poor and the truly wealthy. Manish was now in his late twenties, and was beginning to think the world had a deeper purpose for him. He just needed to find what this purpose was supposed to be.

One night, while sitting alone in his hotel room, Manish decided to take a walk down the streets and attempt to get to know the people and the culture better. Although the language barrier from Indo-Aryan to English to Arabic was pretty large, Manish had learned how to have a basic conversation over the past few years. Manish left his four star hotel and walked through the many small shelters littered throughout the area. While walking through the streets, he heard laughter coming from one of the small huts. He walked towards the laughter and was delighted to see a family having a seemingly good time. They were laughing and talking about their days and what they were going to do tomorrow, and what their hopes and dreams were. The father made each of his children name the best part of their day, and what things they had planned for tomorrow. As Manish listened in, he couldn't believe how truly happy this family seemed and how their minimal existence was the least of their worries.

One of the children noticed Manish, and then the rest of the family looked up and immediately quit talking.

"مساء الخير," said Manish.

"Good evening to you," said the father in pretty plain English with an Arabic accent as he walked to the entrance of his shelter.

"People often think they know Arabic, but usually don't, so we find it easier to just use English. How may we help you?" asked the father.

"No help needed. I was walking around this evening, hoping to meet some of the families in the area, and get to know the people a little better. I've been here for a few years working on the refinery. My name is Manish and I . . . ."

"I know who you are. We've been working in the same area of the refinery for the past two years, but I doubt you remember seeing me. I'm usually assigned to the steel hanging group, and involved with the installation of your designs. I must say, you have an excellent engineering talent."

The comment hit Manish like a ton of rocks. Manish had become so wrapped up in himself and the refinery that he didn't even bother to take time for basic courtesy. Not just lack of courtesy, but blatant arrogance towards others. Here was this man, being so polite, who seemed so satisfied and content with his life, had probably only gotten home a few minutes earlier from a 10 mile walk. The man seemed so well spoken and so knowledgeable, and was living in a scant structure without any obvious material items. Manish stared towards the ground for a moment, frozen in his thoughts.

Then the father said, "Manish, it seems that something is troubling you. Can I be of help?"

Being the introverted, quiet type of personality, Manish wasn't very good in these types of conversations. In his entire life, he couldn't think of a time when someone genuinely asked him this question. Manish felt very much at ease with this man.

Manish said, "I don't know who I am anymore. There seems to be something missing. My life's work isn't satisfying, and I'm contributing to something that I've grown to despise. I sometimes wonder what it's for."

"Manish, the answer to eternal happiness is simple, and the choice is yours to make."

The father paused to put his hand on Manish's shoulder, "Command the good and forbid the evil."

He walked into his shelter briefly, and then returned with a book, and slowly handed it to Manish. The book had a simple Qur'an title on the front. Manish stared at the book, not knowing how to respond. Religion was something that Manish hadn't spent much time contemplating, or how religion affected his destiny. Like most children of India, Hinduism was his assigned religion, and he'd never been exposed to Islam, Christianity or any other religion for that matter. For Manish, the only thing he worshipped was his constant appetite for engineering and science knowledge, and he had devoted very little time to religion. Now Manish, alone in a distant country, far removed from his family, was finding a sense of comfort and security he hadn't felt.

The father sensed Manish was a lost soul, and spent the next two months with him every night, discussing in detail the teachings of Islam. The more Manish became rooted in non-materialistic items, the more he found a burning hatred for capitalism, the raping of minerals from this land and the short-sightedness of big-money oil companies.

During the remainder of this time in Kuwait, Manish was slowly adopted by imams with more radical Islamic views. The more extreme the perspectives, the deeper Manish became committed to taking steps to destroy American oil. Manish knew his experience, intellect and political capabilities could get him into some key situations to make a difference, and he just needed to wait for the right time and the right moment to dedicate his final act to Allah. Upon completion of the Kuwait refinery project, Manish made solemn vows to his new brothers to continue their mission. They would stay in contact via the Internet and new encryption tools they had discovered.

For GeoGlobal, they were celebrating their final week in Kuwait. During a party commemorating the completion of the project, Brian noticed Manish sat by himself and simply drank water. Brian had observed a considerable change in Manish's demeanor over the past few months, and decided to talk with him.

"You know, if I designed one the best refining processes in the world only two years out of college, I'd be thinking of taking a class on negotiating salary raises," said Brian in a joking tone as he walked up to Manish.

Manish gave a smile back. Although he had grown to hate GeoGlobal and what it stood for, Manish couldn't help but have a soft spot in his heart for Brian. Brian was everything people wanted in a leader, and Manish knew today wasn't only celebrating the successful project, but was celebrating good friends in Brian's mind. He might be an infidel, but Manish liked him. Plus, Brian could be a great asset for the future.

Brian asked, "So, have you been told where you're going next? I bet it's the new gas plants in Louisiana."

"No Brian, I think I'll be leaving GeoGlobal."

"Oh man, you've got to be kidding. We did such a great job here. You know how much we need you on our team. It just wouldn't be the same with you gone."

Brian paused for a moment. "You know, Manish, it seems to me that you've been a little distracted for the past few months, a little more to yourself. Is everything Okay?"

Knowing Brian the way he did, it did warm Manish's heart that Brian took time to notice how he was doing. Brian had a real talent for knowing people's personalities, and making them feel good about themselves.

"Everything's fine. Just tired I guess. I would rather work in a smaller company that only focused on process engineering. I don't think I am cut out for dealing with the managers in Houston who only worry about utilization, overhead and payrolls. I want to work for a company that focuses on good process designs, with minimal politics."

Manish paused for a moment, and then put down his drink for a direct conversation with Brian. "Brian, are you satisfied with our work here?"

Brian gave a puzzled look at Manish, "Well, yes. Great project, on time, on budget, meeting all performance expectations. We have a great team and great friendships. I'm very proud of our work. Why do you ask?"

Manish considered digging deeper into the conversation, but thought better of it. He knew Brian had no perspective to appreciate his real concerns and changing opinions towards capitalism.

"No reason really. I guess I'm just a little disappointed all this is ending. Brian, I really have enjoyed working with you. Perhaps we'll get to work together again some day."

"You know, those managers are going to be pissed when I get back to Houston. But to hell with them, I'm going to miss working with you as well."

Brian and Manish became long time working partners, and had stayed in touch through the years. Brian chose the GeoGlobal management path, whereas Manish chose the technical path with smaller engineering firms, and plenty of flexibility to make other plans.

Manish's life had become one of contradictions and alienation, and he really was a lonely soul. If his family knew about his conversion to Islam, he would quickly be expelled and no longer allowed back in the community. He would lose his wife, family and all he was known for as a hero. If Brian and the government only knew about his real interest, he would be placed in prison for his contributions to international terrorist groups.

Manish arose from his daydream. The government plane would be at Hobby airport at 7:30 A.M. sharp, and he had everything ready to go. He packed for a long trip, and couldn't care less about anything else left in the apartment. He hoped to never see this place again.

The team of Brian, Jenny and Glen moved to their conference room. As they walked through the White House, Brian sensed the White House staff now understood their importance. Yesterday's indifference to his presence turned to nods and pleasantries. As they entered the conference room, Brian was very excited to see Manish sitting at the table next to Agent Womack.

"Manish!" said Brian. "Man, it's great you're here! Thanks so much for coming."

"Oh, you're welcome," said an equally excited Manish. "When the great Brian Larson calls to say this is the ultimate project, I just had to be here. Trade Winds' a little upset, but they'll get over it."

"Ah, I know those guys. People always seem to figure it out. PEMEX will just have to wait a little longer to get oil from their new field. But I got to tell you, I'd hate to be in their shoes!"

Manish and Brian laughed and continued to exchange pleasantries. Brian took time to introduce everyone to Manish, including Jenny.

Manish gave a puzzled stare as he shook Jenny's hand. "Dr. Liepert, you look familiar. I can place your face, but I don't remember meeting you."

Then it came to Manish: "Oh I know. Brian was talking about you constantly in Kuwait. He had a picture of you . . ."

Brian jumped in immediately, "Uh . . . that was a long time ago. Jenny and I are just now really getting to work together again. Uh . . ."

Jenny asked, "What did he say? Was it good?"

"Was it good? For the first six months on the project, I knew I'd show up to work and Brian would be gone. I mean, he constantly . . ."

"Okay, okay, we get it," said Brian with a blushing laugh. "Let's get rolling here."

Agent Womack said, "We have security detail assigned to your team. I'll be around often, but there's also an additional team of agents that'll be coming and going. For now, I need to take care of some things. The other agents are right outside the door. Brian, I'll check in later. You have my number on your phone. Call me any time for any reason."

Agent Womack gave a nod to the team and excused himself from the room.

Manish said, "Man, ever since I got on the plane, I've had nothing but constant questions from these guys. They're serious about security."

Brian said, "Yeah, I appreciate you being here, but you should know, we're all essentially under house arrest for the next year."

Manish waved him off, "No worries. I think I passed their test. They had a ton of questions about my money transfers to India. I bet my wife is being interrogated at this very moment! As far as being locked in the project, all I do is work anyway. No problem with me."

Brian said, "Alright then, welcome aboard."

Manish asked, "So, what are the metrics?"

While Jenny gave the details of the refinery, Brian was watching Manish's response closely. This was the first time he had heard these numbers or statistics.

Manish turned to the team and said, "Cool."

Brian had the right team.

Chapter 26—Tightening the Grip

Secret Service Headquarters—Washington, D.C

Agent Womack watched Director Amanda Beine read the draft of the Gary Blackmon arrest warrant. Her body language said everything he needed to know. She shook her head back and forth with a serious frown on her face.

She suddenly took off her reading glasses and said, "Agent Womack, your approach to this is seriously misguided. Taking down Gary Blackmon right now would put us in an incredibly challenging legal position. Not to mention the media circus and stock market ramifications. You have to get something more concrete."

Agent Womack couldn't believe her words. He had spent hours drafting one of the most important documents of his career, and she wouldn't accept it. After their meeting with the President, he felt this was surely the route they should take. He wasn't expecting this kind of pushback.

Director Beine said, "This investigation is too important for us to make any mistakes. It'd become an absolute nightmare for our agency and put the President in a horrible political position. If our actions aren't rock solid, the media and our political enemies would spin this, saying we're bypassing the rights of Americans in order to get even with Wall Street and the banking community."

"That's not my concern. You heard the President yourself, we're directed to take any action to protect this refinery, and the easiest thing is to arrest him. Let the chips fall where they may."

"Surely you're not that naïve. This is absolutely your concern! Plus, that's not what he said."

"That's exactly what he said. Were we not in the same meeting?"

"A politician is never that direct, Agent Womack. He asked us if we're sure about our data, and told us to take steps to defend this project. No President's going to give us specific orders to ignore fundamental American freedoms in arresting our citizens!"

Director Beine pointed directly at Agent Womack, "Be very careful making that kind of leap on a politician's words, Agent Womack. If this thing isn't done right, trust me, you won't get a shred of White House support."

"Come on, you heard it yourself, Gary Blackmon told Roy Ritchey to kill the refinery. It can't be any more direct than that!"

"Kill the radio."

"What do you mean? What? Kill what radio?"

"I said kill the radio. Obviously that means I want you to put Motorola out of business, eliminate all our communications and put all our agents in jeopardy. Saying kill the radio obviously means murdering Secret Service agents."

Agent Womack rolled his eyes, not believing his Director was acting like this. Typically, she was the aggressive one in taking down criminals, and looked for reasons to take action, not reasons to take a step backwards.

Director Beine said, "Look, I said kill the radio. In a court of law, I would simply say the music was too loud, and that's why I wanted to kill the radio. I just wanted someone to turn it off. Do you get my point?"

Agent Womack nodded his head and looked out the window. This situation was not one he was accustomed to. Usually the FBI would be involved with domestic terrorism issues. His daily job dealt with direct threats to the President, and was a much clearer line for him.

Agent Beine stood up from her desk and moved to a chair next to Agent Womack. "Listen, I'm sorry for losing my cool, but we can't mess this up. We must have definitive proof of a direct threat on the refinery, or on the President. I've listened to the tapes a hundred times, and have discussed this with our top attorney for hours on end. Gary Blackmon definitely has an interest in stopping the refinery, but as of this moment, he hasn't done anything illegal. He can use hundreds of different methods to protect his money, and hiring a consultant to evaluate the situation just isn't against the law. He's one step removed as of this moment. However . . . ."

Agent Womack looked directly into her eyes with full attention while Director Beine continued, "Mr. Blackmon did make one critical mistake. He told Mr. Ritchey to inform him of any direct action, and specifically said he had to give approval for any moves. As far as I'm concerned, and our attorney is concerned, we have authority under the Patriot Act to track his every movement closely, as we do suspect him of conspiring to commit murder and possibly domestic terrorism."

"OK, then I get to keep close tabs on him, correct?"

"Use all available resources."

"How about Roy Ritchey?"

"Once again, use all available resources."

Agent Womack understood what that meant: permission for full monitoring using any method they chose, including entrapment. For Agent Womack, now that he had these bastards in his sights, he would find a way to take them down.

"What's the latest on Manish Gupta?" asked Director Beine.

Agent Womack shook his head, "I can't find anything. His routine seems so standard; it just can't be right. He works about fifty hours a week, takes his monthly paycheck to a bank, deposits all of it except for a few thousand dollars for himself, and then pays cash for everything. We've talked to his apartment landlord, visited businesses around his apartment; we spoke to his closest relationships in Houston and even searched his apartment."

Agent Womack continued speaking, but really thinking out loud, "He wires the rest of the money to his home bank in India. He rides his bicycle or uses public transportation to get around. He doesn't have any close friends. It seems so bizarre that a modern day engineer has this simple of a lifestyle. When I spoke with him, he essentially gave me the same story. He just works, and then goes to the library to check out books. He said he enjoys a simple lifestyle because work is crazy enough for him. He keeps to himself, and then calls his wife and family once a week. That seems to be it on the surface."

Director Beine gave a stoic look at Agent Womack. "That sure fits the pattern."

"It sure as hell does, and it's driving me crazy. Being that Manish spent some time in Kuwait with GeoGlobal; I thought it'd be a good idea to ask the CIA if they had any information on him. They did have some information, typical of any foreign national who spends considerable time overseas. But they didn't have any flags on him, and didn't put him on any watch list."

Agent Womack stood up and walked around a bit while thinking. "They did mention a hit that the CIA had a few months ago. NSA picked up an encrypted message board out of North Dakota of all places. The message posted information for a terrorist gathering in Lebanon. Apparently, using Internet service providers in the U.S. is better than overseas, as NSA isn't allowed to trace anything in the U.S. But they caught a break, because they can at least monitor the board if someone from outside the U.S. accesses the data. NSA got the information they needed, but didn't follow the originator of the data, other than the source IP address with the connection."

"So they got to view the board, but couldn't trace it because the information was posted by someone in the U.S. The devil is with us."

"Yep. They can't go any further. But, there might be an interesting coincidence, or maybe a connection. The people they took down in the raid had one thing in common. Most were Kuwaiti nationals, including a few who worked on a refinery in Kuwait as day laborers."

Agent Womack turned to stare directly at Director Beine. "It's the same refinery that Manish and Brian Larson worked on together. Manish and the terrorists were at the same plant at the same time."

Director Beine gave a concerned look. "I would guess there's another link in this connection."

"There is. The source of the message board originated in Houston, Texas, and that's as much as they know."

"Like I said, use any method necessary, Agent Womack."

Chapter 27—Refining

The 1812 Hotel—Washington, D.C.

Manish was completely obsessed with the refinery and his good fortune. He knew why the government wanted kerosene without having been told the political purposes. They wanted well-understood processes as the basis for the refinery, keeping theoretical engineering out of the way. He knew they had no intentions of making this refinery a research and development project. Volume and speed were the requirements here, not innovation. But more importantly to Manish, his designs had little chance of going through any major engineering design reviews. His designs would be final.

After his initial meeting at the White House, Manish asked for one week of work, which Brian understood as "don't bother me and I'll get this done." Manish had ultra strict orders to not use the hotel Internet. Instead, he was given a highly encrypted cellular modem that connected to a local tower the NSA had established in Washington for direct content filtering when connected to the Internet. He knew the NSA was watching every keystroke on his computer and thoroughly analyzing each file. He was quite impressed at the 18 megabit per second downloads from the modem, but was annoyed that the cellular carriers so adamantly denied this kind of service to everyone. To Manish, this was another case of bureaucratic companies gaining a monopoly, and then sticking the everyday user with old technology and no other choice.

Manish was given a room at The 1812, a luxury hotel just two blocks from the White House. The name 1812 was a loose reference to the war of 1812. After the British burned the White House during the war, a temporary housing area was built for government leaders, and eventually a permanent hotel was built on the site. It's a place where the elite leaders of the country would stay during their visits to Washington, and the pompous attitude had remained to this day.

Everything about the hotel made Manish nauseous. The staff exuded an air of unearned arrogance, and treated him as a lower class person. The fact that every United States President had stayed here somehow gave the staff an illusion that everyone else wasn't to be respected. Manish felt a personal satisfaction that the conceited staff was actually hosting the man who would truly change their lives, but simply didn't have all the pageantry that came with large delegations. Manish reflected on the hundreds of different global leaders who had stayed in this hotel and the steps they took over the past decades to grow American imperialism, or negotiated more money at the cost of sacred lands and people's rights in foreign countries. This hotel only reinforced his conviction that this materialistic lifestyle must come to an end.

Manish was solely focused on work, and didn't even bother calling his family. He did manage to transfer a considerable amount of his personal funds to their bank in India. Manish was disgusted but not surprised at the difficulty getting money to his family. It seemed that every step he took was watched, and then everything needed approvals. It was only on Agent Womack's authorization that he was allowed to complete the money transfer. He knew he was being watched and monitored closely, but had no doubt the bureaucrats would have no idea what he was doing, even if they had hidden cameras in the room.

His only real request was an extensive collection of flip charts, an easel, masking tape and pens. Manish had practically wallpapered his room with the fundamentals of the plant piping and instrumentation drawings that showed the process flow for refining raw petroleum into kerosene. Once he was comfortable with each stage of the process he drew on paper, he sat at the computer and drew out the process details using his AutoCAD P&ID software. Manish was working as much as 20 hours a day and, all by himself, completing work equal to those of most expensive engineering firms armed with teams of mechanical designers.

Although he wasn't told of the political reasons kerosene was selected as the primary fuel, he knew better than anyone how to make this plant pump out kerosene like Niagara Falls pumped water. Manish smiled at the thought of this process, and couldn't believe his fortune. The fast track refinery freed him to completely design the major infrastructure of the factory, and its high volume allowed him to design a devastating sulphur cloud, one that had enough chemicals and deadly vapors to make San Antonio uninhabitable. All the extra crude oil going to the new refinery would inhibit the distribution to other plants, making his man-made disaster all the more devastating. Even better yet, Manish would hand select engineers who were much more incompetent, who wouldn't ask questions and would follow orders.

Making kerosene was a relatively simple process, compared to the advanced oil refining he usually dealt with. The first step was distillation, which would more or less boil the oil. He couldn't focus an explosion on this area, since the builders would instantly recognize deviations from that well-known process. The construction companies building the refinery might know these fundamentals too well, and be suspicious of the process control methods if they weren't within nominal heating ranges. Manish could create a large explosion with the boilers, but that would likely only delay the process, not kill it for good.

Manish studied his drawings closely, knowing the real magic in refining was catalytic cracking, and this was where he had the advantage. Once the oil had been distilled into its kerosene fraction, further processing was necessary to create pure kerosene required for Jet-A fuel. Most any chemical engineer out of college thought they understood cracking processes, but Manish was certain nobody would catch on to his real intentions. Because of the massive volume required of the refinery, most would consider his designs necessary. The detailed and intricate processes required incredibly high volumes, run-off processes, high temperatures and high pressures that weren't the norm in the industry. So any special design considerations would simply be considered another one of his brilliant ideas. The cracker unit required for this refinery was definitely not something taught in universities.

The constant worry of a vapor release was the primary concern for refineries. Because of the presence of high efficiency heaters, the real possibility existed for a vapor fire, which could cause a massive explosion, not to mention the chemical release of phenol, ammonia, hydrogen sulfide and other materials. Floating vapor gas would cause a major explosion, not unlike the huge explosion at the refinery in Texas City, or the methane gas explosion at the Pennsylvania coal mine.

To safeguard against these types of accidents, extensive and highly sophisticated safety shutdown systems were integrated with the process control system for the catalytic cracking unit, which triggered an immediate shutdown of all petroleum flow and any looped process valve.

These typically work well . . . unless designed by Manish.

Chapter 28—Marketing

White House—Washington D.C.

"Ken and Barbie. Americans will love this story! I'll get some photos leaked to obscure paparazzi to get the ball rolling. Then the entertainment media groups will pay a ton of money for the photos, and then the big networks will scramble for the story. That's how we'll start. Make the rumor the story, finally exploding to the front page. I bet there's a million web hits on the first day. We'll get going on the viral marketing as well."

Brian and Jenny stared at this strange man while he studied them both up and down. Bill Pence was a senior associate for Congressional Communications. CC was a consulting firm, or some said marketing firm, that focused on government relations and public affairs. Most of their clients were global corporations that required representation to Congress during a crisis, or a strong marketing push to land large government contracts. But this time, instead of making presentations to government bureaucrats, Bill was actually prepping the government for a marketing campaign.

Bill Pence was tasked to head up one of the most visible marketing campaigns of all time, and he was now infatuated with spinning this story to have a romantic side, a real life struggle. Bill would make certain the masses were on the side of the U.S. succeeding, and would leverage all the social media it took in today's world.

Bill's look was the definition of the pink mafia. He only wore high dollar suits created by the fringe designers from the UK. His hair was groomed daily by his personal salon, with the slightest hint of blond highlights. He made it his business to have very close, even sometimes intimate, relationships with many high level entertainment executives, federal government insiders and corporate elite. No matter what the news, good or bad, Bill had the connections to make it front page worthy or, even more valuable, to make sure it was not on the front page. Bill's appearance, mannerisms, dialect and interactions with people sometimes made his presentations to an all male board of directors very interesting. But no matter to Bill, they paid him handsomely.

CC selected Bill to lead this campaign because of the intense media interaction required. The government wanted to launch an educational campaign about oil reserves, pricing and how the federal government was going to stabilize energy pricing. The government needed much more than a boring bureaucrat talking to Sunday morning talk shows with a Nielson rating of 0.1. The campaign would be one of showcasing the federal government in control, angling to beat the competition with a sense of excitement. American ingenuity, creativity, money and spirit would put the Chinese back where they belonged, and squash any hopes of oil future traders and their fear tactics.

Brian and Jenny were standing in the middle of the White House media briefing room, and Bill was pacing around them back and forth. He had spent the past two hours going through the details of their careers, their love life, their backgrounds and any other personal questions he wanted answered.

"Who the hell decorates this damn room? God, it looks like a 1970s funeral parlor in here," said Bill. "Nobody's better at making the government boring than themselves. One thing's for sure, neither of you will be talking to the press from any of these rooms."

Brian and Jenny didn't know what to say. They only knew the Press Secretary informed them that a consultant would run the media show. Now here they were, talking with this strange man. And for Jenny, she never even considered talking in front of a camera, much less to millions of people. Brian sensed she was very uneasy about this situation.

Bill stopped directly in front of Jenny, and gave a deep stare into her cleavage. "Jenny, what's your bra size?"

"Excuse me!" said Jenny.

"Hey, that's enough," shouted Brian.

Bill snapped, "No it's not. We're not in a situation where the leaders of this program can simply sit in the back seat and let things just go on as they have in the past. We're going to be proactive, and create a personal story to go with this refinery. You both represent a human side to this mess, and by God, it'll be told. Do you think it's an accident that Brittney's seen clubbing with 20 different guys before the release of an album and tour? Hell no. My Ken and Barbie finding their passion together for a singular cause will be told for decades to come. Your personal appearance gets us ratings and your story is romantic. You'll both do whatever it takes to make you a celebrity couple."

Brian looked at Bill with disgust, walked directly up to him and put his finger right in the middle of his chest.

Brian said, "I don't give a shit about your story. If I hear you talk to Dr. Liepert like that again, I'm going to rip that fucking pink tie right off your neck, then use it to hang you by your balls out the nearest window."

Bill's serious look turned to a small grin. "Oh, I like you. You're America's next Indiana Jones."

Bill stepped away with a huge smile on his face, and then turned to leave the briefing room. Bill shouted back, "I'm getting this going. You both need to stay in shape. Lots of cameras on you for the next year."

The door closed behind him, leaving Jenny and Brian all to themselves.

"Oh man, what have we gotten ourselves into?" said Brian as he took a seat in one of the many chairs in the room. "You know, there was a time when I'd dream of being this guy. The guy everyone depended upon to make everything okay. I don't know if I want this anymore."

Jenny slowly walked over and sat right next to him. She then leaned into his shoulder. Brian suddenly had a completely different feeling, as this was the first time Jenny had even been inclined to get this close.

Jenny said, "We'll be alright. We'll get through this together. We can't stop now."

Brian said, "We? Do you mean we as Mr. Larson and Dr. Liepert leading the refinery? Or we as Brian and Jenny the couple?"

Jenny didn't say anything, and Brian's mind was spinning. The refinery didn't really mean anything if she wouldn't take him back. If that was the case, then Brian had no desire to continue doing this. The only person he was interested in impressing was Jenny, and he really needed to know what she was thinking.

Brian said, "Because I really screwed things up, and I only want you back. I mean, I'll do anything you want on this refinery, but I need to know it's worthwhile for you. I . . . I don't want to work the 12-hour days, knowing that you need me to be someone else . . . ."

"Shut up, Brian," said Jenny, looking him right in the eyes. "You still don't know how to read the signs, do you?"

She leaned in and gave him a kiss, and then leaned back into his shoulder.

Jenny said, "God, it's a wonder we ever had a first date."

Chapter 29—Not Going as Planned

Offices of Roy Ritchey—Arlington, Virginia

Very seldom did anything catch Roy off guard, but this surely did. Roy was reading a web page that discussed the secret planning of the new refinery, and posted obscure photos of Brian Larson and Dr. Liepert having a conversation while walking on the White House lawn.

The lead story on the web page was titled, "Breaking Story—The Government's Hope of a Stable Future." In it, Brian Larson was named as the leader of the development of the refinery, and Dr. Jenny Liepert as Chief Liaison to the refinery for the federal government. The web posting discussed Brian's long history in the oil and gas field, and Dr. Liepert's background in energy and finance.

The story also discussed rumors of an affair, and had a link to a few different gossip websites. One of the websites had a huge headline, "Houston's Most Eligible Bachelor Finds His Long Lost Love!" In it was a picture of Brian and Jenny in a close up picture when they were young, cheek-to-cheek, standing on the sideline during a Texas A&M football game. The story discussed how Brian was a multi-millionaire and had a long trail of lovers in his wake, and that Jenny was smitten with excitement about their renewed relationship.

Just to make matters worse for Roy, there was another link to the business page, showing the price of oil futures dropping by five percent on tomorrow's trading on the news of the refinery. He immediately knew this was bad. He had failed to deliver the name of the person leading the refinery, and now, not only was it in the open, these bullshit news sites run by a few interns had more information than he did. Roy had heard rumors of the Impending Order's influence on the media, and assumed they now had even more information than what was being posted.

Roy scrambled through the contacts organizer on his computer, and sorted all his moles at GeoGlobal. Roy had to get as much information on this man as he could, as quickly as possible. He was flustered, behind the eight ball, out of the loop and struggling to catch up. Not having this information ahead of time would be embarrassing for any client, but especially the Impending Order. Considering the amount of money he just deposited over five foreign banks, he knew his time was limited. Roy assumed he had less than 72 hours to put a detailed plan together, or a hit would be out on him. Roy already knew too much, and now that he wasn't delivering, the Impending Order would find the world much safer without him in it.

Roy thought of Jim Jackson, his idiot Ivy League DOE mole. "I'm going to kill that motherfucker."

Roy's cell phone rang and startled him out of his raging trance. He stared at the word "UNKNOWN" that was displayed on his phone. His number was unlisted and received few if any calls. Roy considered not answering, but assumed it must be somebody at one of the foreign banks; the blocked number was likely a phone line from outside the United States.

He answered as he usually did, "Roy."

"We need to talk. Immediately."

Roy instantly recognized the voice of Gary Blackmon. Roy was stunned. If Blackmon could get this number, then they surely knew more about him than he thought.

Roy, not wanting to sound intimidated, simply said, "Okay. But I have a lot on my plate. Another trip to the West Coast would take two days out of my work."

"No need." The phone quickly hung up, and he heard the front door of his office open. Roy's office consisted of a few administrative staff and one accountant to handle the legitimate books.

Roy heard his receptionist say, "May I help you?" in a guarded tone. The receptionist's primary job was to answer the phone appropriately, and to make sure that nobody came through the door that wasn't supposed to be there.

"Here to see Roy Ritchey."

The receptionist replied in a conceited tone, "You don't have an appointment, and without an appointment, there's no meeting with Mr. Ritchey. We don't allow people to come off the streets unannounced . . ."

Gary Blackmon said, "Enough. I don't have time for this. You'll get him immediately. He's expecting us."

Roy heard the voices and began to panic. He looked at his window, and thought he could sneak through to get away from the situation. He just sat in a stunned silence, not sure what to do next. He assumed that Gary must be here for a hit, but he wouldn't do this himself. Why in the world wouldn't he just call? Roy could hear the footsteps of his receptionist coming towards his office. Roy glanced at his closet; maybe he could pretend he wasn't there. He was breathing heavily as the door opened.

"Roy, there's two guys here to see you. I tried to tell them you weren't available, but they seem to know different," said the receptionist.

Roy stared at her. He never considered two men. Maybe the hit was on after all.

"They don't seem very happy, and one won't even look me in the eye. These look like pretty bad people. Do you want me to try and get them to go away?" said the concerned receptionist.

Roy took a deep breath and regained his composure. "No. Have them come on back here."

The receptionist knew this was a bad situation, but wasn't really sure what to do about it. Over the years she pieced things together about Roy's business, and knew he dealt in some situations that were pretty intense. He had some clients who wouldn't think twice about taking matters in their own hands. She hoped these men weren't some of those people.

Roy said, "Go on and get them. Then you and everyone else go on an extended lunch. Everyone leaves immediately."

The receptionist paused for a moment. To her, their office affair had grown into a relationship in her mind, and she was scared at this situation. Roy had never told everyone to leave like this. After a few moments she gave a quick nod, and then walked back to the front of the office. Roy quickly reached into his office drawer, pulled out the Glock, and slid it into his blazer pocket. He heard the men coming down the hall. There was a quick knock on the door and both men entered, not waiting for Roy to invite them in.

Gary Blackmon's appearance was considerably different. He was wearing a high dollar charcoal suit with white pinstripes, a red and black tie with yellow highlights that resembled a mural painting, and a pocket handkerchief to match. Gary was dressed for high-level business, and was more intimidating than at their first meeting. His gray hair was greased back in a slick fashion, and now appeared blacker with gray highlights.

The man with Gary was younger and more intimidating looking. He was a steely thin man, wearing a deep black suit with a navy blue dress shirt underneath. Roy could see the veins running through his neck, and had no doubt he had a well-trained body underneath. The young man had coal black eyebrows and eyelashes, and his light blue eyes sat deep in his eye sockets. The man never took his eyes off Roy.

Roy never left his seat as Gary shut the door. He came to Roy's desk, and quickly threw a file on Brian Larson across his desk. Gary took a seat with the bodyguard standing immediately to his left. The bodyguard's arms were folded across his chest with his right hand tucked slightly under the front of his blazer. Roy caught this fact, certain that he could grab his weapon in a matter of seconds.

Gary said, "I thought I would save you some time in your research. It seems you're not as connected as advertised."

Roy offered no response, so Gary continued, "I've been thinking quite a bit about our situation, and it occurs to me that although you have an interesting background, you're totally unfamiliar with things of high urgency, or the speed that comes with these matters."

Roy thought about his next comments. Part of Roy wanted to argue the case, and use his intimidating tone to get his way. After all, he had delivered the information hitting the news days earlier than anybody else. The other part of Roy wanted to lay out a detailed plan to Gary, but he didn't have one in place. The other part of Roy wanted to run away as fast as he could.

Roy leaned forward. "I remember your last direction distinctly. You want me to kill the refinery. That plan, Mr. Blackmon, hasn't changed. It's obvious this news got leaked to the press to let the public know things are being put in place, just like I told you it would. It makes no difference."

"The hell it doesn't!"

As Gary's voice rose, the young man took a small step towards Roy's desk. Roy knew the man would make a move to protect Gary. Roy was certain this was the best security money could buy.

Gary said, "Since you can't do research yourself, we have everything you need to know. Brian Larson has no immediately family, and has plenty of money in the bank. Jenny Liepert has no immediately family, and only rides her horses on the weekend. Both of them have a sole focus on building this refinery, and won't be stopped. To make this a little better, both of them are practically celebrities in their circles, so there are a million people willing to take their places if they become martyrs for this refinery. So Roy, you tell me, how in the hell are you going to kill the refinery?"

"Mr. Blackmon, respectfully, you know very little about the energy business. I've made a living knowing the engineering companies, land companies, traders and the oil companies themselves. I'll get on the inside, one way or another," Roy said convincingly.

"Plus, we still haven't put option one in place yet. It occurs to me that Dr. Liepert out of the picture will essentially put Mr. Larson out of the game as well. My insider is setting that up, and I'll take care of that personally. We'll put a number of distracting actions in place, and in that, I guarantee you'll get the results you are looking for," said Roy.

Gary said, "One week, Roy. We need definitive action in one week. Don't worry about contacting me, we'll find you."

Gary and his bodyguard then walked out of the office. Roy sat back in his chair and let out a huge sigh of relief. He had dodged a bullet, literally, but knew that was all the rope he'd be given. As Roy tried to compose himself, he noticed something hanging on the door knob of his office door, still rocking back and forth from the men leaving. It looked like a lanyard of some sort, with a badge hanging off the end.

"That's odd," thought Roy, not remembering anything being placed there previously. He stared with curiosity at the item, and slowly got out of his chair and moved closer. The closer Roy got, the more panicked he felt. Roy grabbed the item and gazed at it in stunned silence.

"Oh shit," said Roy under his breath. The item was a unique identification card for the Tropical Bank of Belize. The card was complete with Roy's picture, ID number and RFID tag on the back. Roy scrambled for his wallet and pulled out the exact same card. As he held the two cards together, he realized even deeper whom he was dealing with. Roy supposedly owned one of only two of these cards in the world, allowing only himself and the principle of the bank to have access to his financial accounts. The Impending Order obviously had insiders at the bank, and had access to the money he put in the offshore account.

As Roy stood in the doorway of his office staring at the card, he caught a glimpse of a shadow down the hallway. Roy looked up and tensed with fright. Gary's bodyguard stood in the hallway near the front desk, staring directly at him. He was in the stance just like in Roy's office, with both hands folded over his chest and one hand slightly placed under his blazer.

Both men stared at each other for a few moments. The signs were clear; the man could pull the trigger to end Roy's life any time he wanted. The bodyguard slowly walked out the front door.

Roy pieced it together. They had his office location, phone number and bank access. They had assigned a hit man. They had everything. There was nowhere to hide. Roy must complete this job and somehow get the hell out of Dodge.

Roy moved to his desk and picked up the phone to call Jim Jackson.

"We're meeting. Today."

Chapter 30—Press Conference

White House Lawn—Washington D.C.

Bill Pence was in a complete frenzy with too much drama. He barked orders back and forth to the entire White House staff, the President and Press Secretary included, directing the exact scenario that would play out today. The White House was hosting the first major press conference about the refinery, and it was being staged on the White House lawn, with shots of the Washington monument in the background. Definitely not in the White House briefing room, just as promised. Bill was extraordinarily careful to guard the details of the press conference, as he understood the more the rumors flew, the more the media would want to be a part of this. Getting a ticket to this conference was harder than the Super Bowl 50-yard line.

The press conference was the first major step to the President's promise of economic reform, and all media types wanted to be part of it. Rumors of Brian and Jenny were going crazy, with sleazy gossip of ex-boyfriends, girlfriends, old friends done wrong, etc., all over the morning talk shows and the web. The media couldn't wait for the first good pictures of Brian and Jenny, and all prayed this was the topic of the day. The more juice they had in the story, the more advertising revenue they generated. The Press Secretary had word that more than 50 news outlets were making this conference a priority, and all the majors were broadcasting the event live. The typical stuffy White House correspondents were quickly replaced by their ace on-air staffs.

Bill Pence shouted orders: "The President walks out first, followed closely by Brian and Jenny. After they get to their positions, only then will the Senators and Mr. Abbott follow."

The President said, "Now wait a minute, the Senators represent the people of the United States, and they should enter when I enter the . . ."

Bill immediately cut him off, "No sir. There's time for pomp and circumstance, but right now, Brian and Jenny are the stars, with the President leading the way. On the 6:30 news I only want the shot of you, Jenny and Brian. This is our story. You'll have every one of the major media outlets screaming for an interview with Brian and Jenny, as they are the ones implementing your idea, not some lame bureaucrat. Brian's your man of action and that, Mr. President, is exactly who you want standing next to you during the conference."

The President held his tongue and lowered his head. Here he was, surrounded by bureaucrats, people he depended on every day, all pissed to the boiling point by this man and his quick dismissal of their service. But the President knew he was right, so he just let him roll.

Brian wore a suit that cost the taxpayers way too much money, but Bill wouldn't have it any other way. He was in a dark suit, and had changed his tie no less than five times. Every time he changed his tie the wardrobe consultant would ask Bill his opinion, and je would just say "no." Finally, they settled on a red power tie with a hint of a checked pattern. Brian looked good as usual, and couldn't wait to get this show over with.

Jenny, on the other hand, was about to pass out from the pressure. She couldn't believe she had been cast into the spotlight this way, and had the paparazzi scrambling to get her picture. She discreetly peeked at the web site articles about her over the past few days, and was stunned at how much detail people had about her life, and how people she hadn't spoken to in 10 years talked about her like she was their best friend. There were pictures she didn't remember taking, some looked okay, and some were not so flattering. She even found an article about an "old boyfriend" with whom she had never even held hands.

Jenny was dressed in a long black skirt and a white shirt with an oversized collar, and a very tight fitting blazer. Bill insisted that she have her hair long, and wear the Coach tortoise shell style reading glasses. As Jenny walked into the room, every man about passed out at how beautiful she looked. She was every bit the powerful woman who was too sexy for an average Washington bureaucrat. Even Bill had to pause to take note of her looks. Bill thought to himself, *Ken and Barbie baby. Ken and Barbie.*

One of the White House staffers came to Bill and whispered in his ear. Bill immediately shouted, "Okay, they're ready. Remember; just give short answers to their questions. There's plenty of time for talk later. Don't give out anything that will undermine your control over the situation."

Thank God, thought Jenny. Speaking at all might give her a cardiac arrest right there on the spot.

As coached, they walked down the southern outdoor corridor of the White House. From there, they moved through the lawn and directly in the middle of the media. Even in full daylight, the lights were unbelievable. Brian and Jenny heard the constant snapping of cameras, and felt the weight of the world on their shoulders. Somehow, they were totally aware that more than 100 million Americans would hear their words and see their faces by the end of the day. The President walked through the media with the look of confidence they were accustomed to seeing on TV, and Brian and Jenny did their best to give equally confident smiles.

They walked up to the small stage that had been set up for the event, and the President immediately moved to the microphone with the Presidential seal. Brian moved to the President's left and Jenny walked to his right. Jenny and Brian then got their first good look at the media event unfolding before them. They could see the first ten rows, about twenty people across, all standing and taking notes. The first rows of reporters simply had a notepad and a pen.

Standing behind them seemed to be an endless line of cameras and photographers.

The President leaned into Brian, "I whisper in your ear here to pretend to tell you a joke. This is a good picture, so laugh like I said something funny."

Brian let out a quick smile and the best small laugh he could muster. The President then leaned over to Jenny, and did the same thing. There all three of them stood with smiles on their faces.

The President waited for the Senators and Glen Abbott. Once they took their positions, the President said, "I gave the American people a promise that a new refinery would be critical to our economic future. A new refinery increases our capacity to refine our own oil, show American ingenuity, American speed, and proves to the world we'll fight for our future. I'm here today to announce the leadership of our refinery, and to give a few details about the expectations of this considerable project.

"On our darkest days over the past few months, we were close to letting others define our identity. But we fight back. This refinery gives us more freedom than we can possibly imagine, and allows us to decrease our dependence on other countries. As an example, President Gamboa doesn't want our business right now. But that's fine. By this time next year, we'll be watching his country have a 20 percent hit to their economy, and he'll see America once again stand on top of the industrial world. The great people of Venezuela will then clearly understand the mistake he's made."

The reporters wrote fanatically, and Brian and Jenny were stunned. They were standing next to the President during this moment, now squarely in the middle of an international business movement not seen since World War II. The President was clearly pissed about the circumstances, and he wouldn't let this moment pass without punching back with a full swing. When the United States got a cold, then Latin America got the flu. The President was determined to give Venezuela pneumonia with America holding all the antibiotics.

"Additionally, later today, the Department of Energy, led by Glen Abbott, is launching a new website that articulates the details of the real oil issue in America. This madness of inflated energy costs is grossly exaggerated, and without merit. The irrational speculation by the oil and gas traders must stop. Once completed, energy prices will be where they need to be."

The line had been drawn, and the media were going crazy. The President in a few short paragraphs had called out Venezuela and the titans of Wall Street. The President's legacy was now defined by the price of energy, and Brian and Jenny were in the dead middle of it.

The President continued his speech, giving the details of the refinery locations, output, and timeline. Each word of his speech mesmerized the entire media corps, and Brian and Jenny knew this was total news to all in attendance.

Once the details of the refinery were finished, the President turned to Brian, "As for the leader of the refinery, I would like to introduce Brian Larson."

Brian gave a nod towards the media, and listened to the President's words. He watched them write notes as they stared at him. His dreams of being in the spotlight were for real now, and he didn't like it. He took a quick glance at Jenny, and gave her a smile. Brian knew she was on the verge of a panic attack, and he was really much more worried about her.

The President then turned to Jenny, "As for our government liaison, I would like to introduce Dr. Jennifer Liepert."

As the President spoke of Jenny, she took deep breaths, and heard the sounds of the cameras clicking her direction. She gave a look towards Brian. He had a proud smile, and gave her an "it will be alright" look. She found strength in him being there, and quickly turned to the President and the media with a confident smile.

The President said, "These two outstanding individuals, coupled with the DOE leadership of Glen Abbott and the political support of myself and Senators Matthews and Johnson, will no doubt deliver a project that will become a beacon of success. I'm reminded of President Teddy Roosevelt, and the building of the Panama Canal.

Many folks said it was an impossible project, and we saw the result. With this project, I look forward to watching the oil hitting the tank farm, and watching the price of oil drop to where it needs to be for Main Street America. Okay, we're open for questions."

The journalists shouted out like kindergartners wanting to answer the teacher's question. Jenny and Brian were at full alert. Jenny gave a quick look to Brian. She wanted very badly to go stand next to him.

The President acknowledged the first reporter who quickly stood up. "Thank you, Mr. President. This question is for Dr. Liepert."

Jenny felt her knees start to buckle, as the entire crowd went silent. The reporter asked, "Dr. Liepert, as the government leader of the refinery, I find your choice of Texas a very interesting one. With all the political power from Texas, did you find you really had any choice for the refinery location? It occurs to me that unemployment is not nearly as bad in that state as compared to other states, and they need the influx of money much more desperately. Why exactly did you choose Texas?"

Jenny was silent. She wasn't prepared for a political question. The others on the podium tensed up, as they pondered jumping in and answering the question. Glen Abbott saw his career flash in front of his eyes.

After a few moments, Jenny said, "I'm sure you're not aware because it takes considerable research and an oil and gas background to understand, but the DOE's been considering using Kelly Air Force Base for a long time. Kelly gives us an industrial infrastructure, and close proximity to the crude oil. All things considered, Kelly is the only location that meets all the required criteria. Kelly Air Force Base is a technical choice, not a political one."

The President and the others were so excited they nearly jumped over to carry Jenny off on their shoulders. Not only did she answer shortly, she showed the confidence that this was the government's decision, and a decision that had long been considered. It showed that Jenny was in control, had planned this out, and could chastise a reporter. The reporter sat back down, and started writing in her notepad. Her perfect trap question to the weakest link backfired miserably, and showed that she hadn't really done her homework.

They answered a few more questions, and then retired back to the White House. When Jenny and Brian found a spot to themselves, they gave each other a huge hug, and Brian spun her around.

"I did it, I did it," said an exuberant Jenny.

Brian said, "You did. Man, I'm so proud of you! I nearly shouted out "'That's my girl!'"

Chapter 31—Setting the Stage

Law Firm of Blanchard and Blanchard—Arlington, Virginia

The law firm of Blanchard and Blanchard boomed with business. The premier law firm in Washington D.C. for eminent domain issues constantly received calls from smaller firms all over Texas. Small time lawyers that represented car crashes, work injuries and divorces suddenly represented landowners. With the new pipeline infrastructure required for the refinery, landowners from Corpus Christi to Victoria, back to Houston, all the way to Austin, were looking for the best law firm to represent their interests. The small firms in Texas had no problem handing their clients over to Blanchard and Blanchard, for a considerable percentage of the final settlement of course.

Jim Jackson's insider status within the DOE made him a superstar at the firm, and certainly gave them influence on the pipeline routes, or at least that was what they told their clients during contract negotiations. Blanchard and Blanchard charged unreasonable fees for any work they did for their clients, plus a set percentage for any future settlements. Positions like these were what law firms dreamt about. Not only did they bill at full rates for their time, they enjoyed the riches of the final prize. Jim was on the fast track to partnership, and his equity position would make him very wealthy.

Although Jim should be euphoric, he sat alone in his office staring at his monitor, absolutely scared to death. His firm had a modern ambiance with all the offices having windows that allowed everyone to see inside. His door was locked, and no less than five people had come by during the past thirty minutes. When the door wouldn't open, everyone gazed into the window and gave a quick knock. Every time, Jim looked up with a fake smile and gestured he was busy. He was in no mood, position or state of mind to discuss any matters on any legal topic.

Jim had just gotten off the phone with Roy Ritchey who insisted on a meeting in a few hours. Jim knew this meeting was about a hit on Dr. Liepert, and it was a shallow feeling like he'd never felt. He moved his trash can close by, as his upset stomach kicked in again.

Jim's desk phone wouldn't stop ringing. The display on the phone said "Receptionist." He didn't have anyone scheduled for a visit, so he ignored the calls. A few moments later, he once again heard the familiar knocking on his office window. He looked up and saw the receptionist, looking animated. Jim waved her off and pointed at his computer, pretending he was working on something. She knocked again, with even more animation on her face. Jim gave a wince and walked to the door.

Jim said, "Look Debbie, I'm really busy with a lot on my plate. Whoever it is, just have them reschedule. Plus I have to leave here in about an hour anyway."

The receptionist tried to cut him off. Once he quit speaking she said, "Yes Mr. Jackson, I completely understand, and I'm so sorry to interrupt you. But there are . . ."

"Debbie!" snapped Jim. "I don't give a damn who it is. I hate to act like this, but I have no time right now. You've been here for five years. Come on, you know how things are done."

"Yes, yes Mr. Jackson. I do, but, but . . . I need to speak with you. I think this is really important," said Debbie in a low tone while looking around the office.

Jim stared at Debbie. He knew something must be wrong. Jim had her step inside his office, and he shut the door behind them.

Debbie spoke in a low tone while looking out the window of the office to make sure nobody saw them, "Mr. Jackson, situations like these are really sensitive, so just let me know how you want to handle this. There are two men and a woman in the lobby here to see you. They're very insistent on talking to you immediately, but I don't want to make a big scene. I was hoping just to escort them to the conference room like regular clients. I think that would be best as it would look normal."

"Who are they?"

"It's the Secret Service."

Jim felt his abdomen suck into his body as the air left his chest. He started feeling dizzy and small stars came into his vision. He slumped over, and put his hand on the office window to stabilize himself as the world began to spin under him.

"Oh my God, oh my God!"

Debbie wanted to run away so nobody would see this situation while she was in his office. The rumors would be crazy.

"Mr. Jackson, you need to sit down!"

With all the energy he could muster, Jim stumbled to his desk and took his chair. Debbie quickly exited the office and walked to the break room to grab a couple of sodas and a few paper towels. She kept as cool as possible, saying hellos to everyone she met in the hallway. Debbie casually walked back to Jim's office, and handed him a drink and the towels. Debbie then took a seat in the chair by his desk.

Jim grabbed the drink and chugged it down and rubbed the towels across his face. "This is it. My life's over."

Debbie pretended to ignore his comments and said, "Mr. Jackson, I think it'd be best if I escorted the visitors to the main conference room. Since most associates use the other door to enter and leave, I believe that'd be best in case an uncomfortable situation occurs."

Jim leaned back in his chair, constantly rubbing his hands on his face, "Fine."

"Okay," said Debbie as she got out of her chair.

Debbie walked back to the reception area. All three agents were still standing and not looking pleased about being delayed, but didn't speak a word.

"Please come with me. We're going to the main conference room," said Debbie in her most professional voice.

Debbie walked them through the large wooden door to the law firm offices, and took an immediate right to the conference room. Right on cue, the first agent sat closest to the exit. The other two walked to the far end of the table, and both took a seat towards the end across from each other, leaving the very end of the large table open for Jim Jackson's interrogation. After Debbie left the room, Agent Womack quickly dropped to his knees and swooped under Jim's chair. He pushed in the lever that locked the chair in place, not letting it recline anymore. This was a small mental game the government used when questioning people. The agents had a nice, relaxed, reclined style, while the person in the hot seat was isolated to one position.

After a few minutes, the door slowly opened and Jim Jackson slowly walked into the room. He looked like death warmed over, and his body had a complete slump to it. Jim thought about calling his personal lawyer first, but knew this wasn't a subject to be buried in paperwork, delays or motions. Jim was in a bad situation and the Secret Service had unique ways of dealing with legal tactics. Both agents at the end of the table stood up and walked towards him. Jim lost it and shook uncontrollably. He stopped in his tracks about half way down the table.

This is it. They're going to arrest me right here, Jim said to himself. *What am I going to tell my kids? Their life is ruined. Their dad is being indicted on the planned murder of a high-ranking Washington official. What will my wife do? What would my father think of me? Where are they going to get money to live?* Jim was humiliated, embarrassed and scared beyond the point of thinking normally anymore.

Agent Womack walked straight up to Jim with his hand out, "Mr. Jackson, my name is Agent Womack, with the United States Secret Service. This is Deputy Director Beine, also with the Secret Service. We have several items to discuss with you. Please have a seat up here with us."

The agent at the front of the room was never introduced; he quickly walked to the door to close it, and stood directly in front of it so nobody else could walk in on their conversation.

Jim slowly moved towards his chair, and thought maybe this wouldn't be the end of his life after all. An internal feeling of euphoria took over, as it seemed he might make it another day.

Agent Womack and Director Beine took their seats, and started rocking slowly and steadily. Jim took his seat, and put his elbows on the table. The Secret Service psychological evaluations took over, and they both summarized they had here a broken man, and more importantly, they had a man they could work with.

Agent Womack said, "Mr. Jackson, we understand you have a meeting to attend here this afternoon. Is that an accurate statement?"

Jim looked down at the table and nodded his head. Jim decided he'd work with these people; at least they gave him a possible option other than the dire ones he faced.

"What's the nature of the meeting?" asked Director Beine.

Jim's mind flooded with thoughts. Jim's legal background taught him how to ask leading questions, the questions that caught someone in a lie with no way out except with other lies. Jim assumed they already had the answers, so he wasn't about to begin telling false statement to these people.

"I'm not exactly sure. I made a deal with someone who I shouldn't have, and now I'm caught in a situation that's out of my control," said Jim in a low, despondent voice.

The agents didn't respond. They wanted their key witness to do all the talking. They knew this man was in a bad situation, but nonetheless, it was his situation. He accepted bribes to pass information. He might be scared, but he was still a man without scruples. If Jim was looking for a hug from this group, he was sorely mistaken.

"What's the nature of the meeting, Mr. Jackson?" asked Director Beine once again, a little colder and more stern.

"A man named Roy Ritchey approached me about three years ago. He knew a lot about the work we did here at Blanchard and Blanchard, and how we often had the early insights into new oil and gas infrastructures because of all the land concerns and eminent domain issues that surround the business. The deal was relatively mild; he kept me on retainer for information about the projects."

Jim gave an exhausted look, actually hearing the words of the kind of person he had become. Jim spoke in a quiet but matter of fact tone.

"He wanted to know what company was funding the projects, the location, the petrochemical being produced, things like that. Most of the information I gave him was public knowledge, just buried somewhere in paperwork. It's really simple, I'd meet him at a coffee shop and we'd talk for a few minutes, and he'd slide me an envelope."

Jim continued, "So, here a few weeks ago, Glen Abbott called me about a top priority project. Once I got inside, I worked with the DOE on legal issues with the property, and all the politics that surrounded the land deals. All the typical things associated with building such a huge refinery. Once I got a full grasp on the scope, urgency, and speed of this thing, I decided to give Roy a call."

Jim shook his head, hoping the agents would be sympathetic, "I, I just had visions, visions of financial freedom. I made a huge mistake by going to Roy for more money, because I sold him on the idea of giving me a million dollars, and I would influence the project the ways he wanted. I really never had that power, but since I was on the leadership team for the planned refinery, he bought my story. I really screwed up."

Again, the agents were silent. Jim continued to get everything off his chest. "So, last week, I went back to him with details on the refinery. Where it was going to be built, timeframe, and all the information most anybody would want, and a full week before it hit the press. The information I gave him was worth at least ten million, and probably a whole lot more. Jesus, the land between San Antonio and Corpus Christi was going for about a grand an acre, and now its north of twenty-five grand an acre."

"He reacted in a way I wasn't expecting. He really went off the deep end. He screamed at me about delaying the refinery, finding a different location, manipulating the system, you name it. Anything I could do to delay or kill the refinery. Mr. Ritchey usually acts real cool, not easily flustered and very quiet. He's really lost his grip on things. I got a feeling he's under a lot of pressure."

Jim took a deep sigh. "So then, he got a really bad look on his face, and told me we're going to put a move in on Dr. Liepert. His exact words, I think, were it's either her or the refinery. I understood that to mean stop the project, or eliminate an important factor behind it. I believe he intends to kill her."

"So," Jim said in a dire tone while turning to Director Beine, "I haven't heard from Roy since that meeting. Then today, out of the blue, he called and said he wanted to meet. I'm not sure exactly what the conversation will be, but I know it's not good. That's everything I know right now."

Director Beine never took her eyes off Jim. The room was silent for about one minute, another psychological move by the Secret Service. People wanted to talk, you just needed to put on the pressure, and silence was usually the best pressure you could apply. During their pause, Jim started shaking again, sure his arrest was imminent. Saying the words out loud emphasized even more what a bad situation he was in, and how much of a scumbag he had become.

Agent Womack said, "Well Mr. Jackson, we're pleased you chose to be honest."

Jim stared at Agent Womack, frightened at what was on the other end of this conversation.

"Your insider trading has placed you in the middle of one of the largest financial crime organizations on the planet. You started a cascade of actions to try and stop the refinery."

Agent Womack paused, "And to eliminate anyone who gets in the way, including you."

Agent Womack sensed Jim was on the verge of vomiting. He decided to go for the jugular, just to make sure this man totally comprehended the situation.

"We have authority to arrest you right now, on direct orders from the President himself, and put you away for a very long time. You're facing charges of bribery, collusion, accomplice to a planned murder, stealing government information and domestic terrorism. All of these add up to actions detrimental to the United States, and actions consistent with a traitor."

"So answer me this, Mr. Jackson," said Director Beine, "When you watch the news and they show a major arrest for spies in the United States, or accomplices to murders for innocent victims, or inside traders with financial scams, do you see yourself as the same type of individual?"

Jim put his head down and said, "No."

Agent Womack moved his chair forward and put his elbows on the table. "You know, man, white collar criminals always think the same. Every time I've booked someone like you, they always perceive themselves in the same way. 'I didn't think I was hurting anyone; I didn't know my actions would cause these types of problems; I just wanted a little more money.' You understand where I'm coming from?"

Jim wanted to answer, but all he heard was "booked, traitor, criminal and murderer." Jim stammered out the words: "I've made a mistake. Just please let me help you in any way to get some shred of my life back."

Agent Womack gave a quick look to Director Beine, and then turned back to Jim, essentially putting his mouth directly to his ear. "Fucking right you're going to help us."

Chapter 32—Team Building

White House—Washington D.C.

The small project planning conference room in the White House was packed full of people. Today was the selection of the Architecture and Engineering firm, the company that would lead the effort in building the refinery. The selection of the proper company was critical, and Brian needed to get this one right. The project lifecycle for building a new refinery typically took two to three years of planning and design, then another two to three years for construction and startup. For this team, they only had a year for a working refinery. Brian's team simply didn't have the time to go through all the steps usually required for this type of project.

Brian invited the two companies to the meeting today, both with the capability of building a refinery from the ground up. Both companies had significant track records of building major industrial projects all over the world, and both were fierce competitors. Brian's process for the selection was simple, unlike the unbelievable bullshit most procurement groups usually go through. Brian would lead a presentation to the companies together in one room, and then Manish would give a preliminary overview of the plant processes. The companies would individually come back and give their own presentations on how to tackle the refinery. Brian wasn't looking for sophisticated PowerPoint slides; he was looking for the company that fully embraced this challenge and ran with the program. Both the companies understood oil and gas refining; all they needed to know was the production basics.

All Systems and Colt Engineering had very different approaches to capital projects. If there was such a thing as polar opposites in the A&E business, then All Systems was the absolute inverse to Colt Engineering. The difference in the two companies was obvious just by their appearance. All Systems had their president, vice president of engineering and chief financial officer present. All three men were dressed in nice suits, trendy bifocal glasses and similar IBM style haircuts. They were ready with their engineering grid notepads with All System logos, and their smart phones on the table.

Colt Engineering only had two associates at the meeting, their president and capital projects manager. Their president wore a suit, but their manager had on starched blue jeans, a white button down shirt, blue blazer and tan steel-toed cowboy boots. About the only thing missing was his hard hat. Neither one had a notepad or a smart phone.

Upon entering the room, both companies gave contentious handshakes as a formality, but essentially just stared at each other. Definitely no business cards were passed, and no Christmas cards would be sent. The team from All Systems looked upon Colt Engineering with disgust, struggling to comprehend how these cowboys could even be considered in the same league as their company. Colt Engineering looked upon All Systems with the same disgust, wondering why any company would be so stupid as to spend millions more on pinheads who forgot what a construction site looked like, much less building a plant at double the price for the exact same results.

Attending the meeting on the government's behalf were Brian, Manish, Jenny, Glen Abbott and a few DOE team members. Overall there were 12 people in the room, which felt pretty cramped. The room had a standard DLP projector hanging from the ceiling, and a pull-down screen that hid the white board behind it.

Brian kicked off the presentation, "Okay. We're looking for an A&E firm to take complete hold of this factory, and run with it until we're pumping 800,000 barrels a day. I understand that building a refinery from the ground up, after the design phase, takes two to three years. You have one."

The gentlemen from All Systems dropped their mouths in sync, while the guys from Colt Engineering sat there, unfazed. This didn't go unnoticed by Brian. Since this news was already announced, Brian was immediately concerned with All Systems' reaction.

Brian gave his presentation for about another 10 minutes. From there, Manish outlined the process flow. The team from All Systems wrote notes as quickly as they could, while the gentlemen from Colt continued to sit there.

Once Manish was finished, Brian said, "Okay, questions?"

The All Systems VP of engineering immediately said, "You selected Kelly Air Force Base as the location. Depending on many factors, different pavement specifications are established. Most Air Force facilities use extensive soil samples to determine the aggregate material grade, and based upon the relative load of the planned aircraft, determine pavement guidelines as stated by the Department of Defense, or by Federal Aviation Administration Standards for Asphalt and Cement. Typically, for heavy-duty aircraft, the pavement thickness varies from as little as twelve inches to four feet. Have you established the cement load capacity for the required equipment, as this is a major consideration given your timeframe?"

The executives from All Systems nodded their heads enthusiastically, thinking they had already discovered a major hurdle for the project to overcome.

Brian gave a glassy-eyed stare at the VP, "Uh, no. We haven't considered that factor."

After a few moments of silence, the president from Colt said, "We've already thought about that. The first thing we'll do is lay a four foot, triple rebar reinforced slab down on the whole thing. It should only take a couple of weeks. That's SOP for us so we don't have to worry about foundation concerns. Hell, we could start today if you want us to."

The All Systems team shot a quick glance at the Colt Engineering team, then immediately looked back down at their notes. Brian gave a quick acknowledgement to the Colt president, doing his best not to have a big grin on his face.

The All Systems VP spoke up once again, "Manish, these are higher volumes and pressures than most anyone has attempted for a refinery. I don't think there are valves, instruments, manifolds or reactors available for this application. It's going to take an incredible level of effort for design, testing, manufacturing and commissioning. Just curious, what are your thoughts on all the custom equipment required?"

Manish said, "Well, from my background, most pipe builders, welders and metal hangers generally just follow the specifications. There are plenty of water agencies that push through this kind of volume, so I'm pretty sure we can get the valves and instrumentation."

"Well, not in a caustic environment and Class I Division I safety classification," snapped back the VP. "The corrosion factor for such pressures and volumes is exponentially higher. I can't imagine finding any quality manufacturers to provide us workable equipment in such a short timeframe."

The room went silent again. Brian sensed that All Systems just didn't get it. The government wanted to hear the reason this could be successful, not the reasons it couldn't.

The president of Colt said, "Manish, are you putting your PE stamps on these designs?"

"Yes, I will put my personal Professional Engineering stamp on all the drawings."

"Then that's good enough for us. We assume the process works," said the Colt president, giving an arrogant grin to the All Systems team.

He continued, "No need to worry about vendors making equipment. With the money behind this thing, we'll have five vendors lined up to build the skids within the week. They'll guarantee their work, or they don't get their money. We know how to squeeze 'em hard."

The president of All Systems quickly realized he was in the middle of a commercial situation. The score was Colt Engineering 2, All Systems 0. He saw the leaders of the refinery all nodding their heads in agreement with Colt, feeling much, much better about their tone as compared to All Systems.

The president of All Systems quickly said, "Wait a second. I had the understanding that we can ask questions, then come back and present in a few hours. We're just trying to get some major topics on the table here. So far, both of these issues are surmountable, we just want to highlight a few things."

Brian said, "That's correct. You're coming back around 1:00 this afternoon for a more detailed evaluation, without Colt in the room. Okay, are there more issues to discuss before we break up?"

The vice president of All Systems spoke up again, "Yes, on the risers, we need to . . ."

"No, no. We don't have any more questions," interrupted the president of All Systems quickly, stunned at the total lack of commercial presence of his VP.

Brian said, "Very well, let's break up and we'll meet All Systems at 1:00, and then we will meet Colt at 3:00."

All Systems quickly exited the room with Colt Engineering following. On the way out the door, the president of Colt turned to Brian. "Actually Brian, we don't need any more time. We can discuss things right now."

Brian said, "Okay, but you do have a full understanding of what's at stake here?"

"You bet."

"OK, come on back in here."

They returned to their seats as the president of Colt Engineering stood at the front of the room. He paused for several moments, looking at the carpet while everyone was silent. He moved his arms in front of his body, and one of his hands gripped his other wrist.

He looked up at the government team in the room. "As our company has grown, I usually look at all our projects as, well, just that, projects. But getting a call from Brian really got me to thinking;

we've evolved to a point where we can make a real difference. I'm not a very humble man, 35 years in the business will do that to you; however, I must say, I'm very humbled and honored to have the chance to help out on this project."

The Colt president wasn't looking at anyone, or looking for "you're welcomes." The room sensed this man was truly proud to be here.

"During my whole career, it seems I've been told constantly that all these capital projects were of the 'highest priority', with absolute dire consequences for being late on delivery, no matter what the application. I can't tell you how many times CEOs have called me, essentially threatening me if our group was late on delivery. Frankly, I've grown numb to those words. And then Brian Larson gives me a call. And what does he say? You guessed it, 'this project is the highest priority.'"

The room smiled, entranced by this man's speech. Brian grinned at the thought of the conversation from a few days ago.

The president of Colt said, "We can talk here all day long about technical details, but we have the skins on the wall for the largest of projects. We understand your sense of urgency. We'll meet your schedule, beat your budget and deliver you a working refinery as ordered. We ask for your business."

Jenny said, "We want full audits on your books."

"Done."

Manish said, "I want to be recognized as technical leader on all process, controls, instrumentation and electrical."

"Wouldn't want it any other way. Save me a hassle."

Manish asked, "What is your construction method?"

"Skid based. Interconnect piping, plumbing and wiring."

Brian said, "We want to use American labor, OEMs and vendors."

"Okay on the vendors, okay on the OEMs, okay on construction, no way on the engineering."

"Why not?"

"Manpower's not available."

"All Systems says it is."

"They're also going to tell you three years. You want one year, so the answer is India."

The room was quiet for a moment as they considered this decision. The President and Senators wanted U.S. labor on everything. However, Colt was correct in their comments. Over the past decade, American engineering talent had become more and more scarce. The largest engineering pools were now overseas.

"If I give you the fundamental drawings, when can you start the details?" asked Manish.

"Four hundred engineers are ready to go out of India. The approximate numbers are forty-five process, twenty electrical, thirty mechanical, forty programmers, thirty SCADA, twenty-five networking, ten information systems, ten civil and a couple hundred designers and drafters. I'll have my Indian ops center up to speed by the end of the day, and have about fifteen project leaders starting this Monday."

"I'll do the cause and effect drawings," said Manish.

Damn thought Manish, making his first mistake. The president of Colt looked at his counterpart with a puzzled face. The cause and effect diagrams were the basis for the entire control system programming, and the sole guideline for developing a parallel safety system. Manish asked for the safety of the plant to be put solely in his hands.

Brian turned to Manish with a surprised expression. Safety systems were usually automatically generated, leaving little room for errors that could cause an explosion or caustic reactions from the different chemicals.

"Once your process is detailed, why don't you just let the auto generation code take care of that?" asked Brian.

Manish answered the best that he could, "Well, I should've said I want supervision over the final set. There's more than 20,000 inputs and outputs on this project, so I can't build the whole set. The problem with today's software packages is they're conservative because of safety concerns. I want to make sure the code guidelines in the software don't override the actual process requirements. It's more of a final tweak of the diagram prior to code development, because if the pressures aren't right, then we'll never get the cracking points and temperatures needed. I'm just trying to think ahead to keep us on schedule."

The president of Colt said, "Well, that's no problem. You have to sign off on it as the PE anyway, so you have final say."

Brian said, "With no offense to your manager of capital projects here, all the project managers report directly to me, not him. We have daily meetings, and other meetings to discuss specific details, even the most mundane tasks. I'll be the lead project manager on this project. I need all the project managers to meet me in San Antonio on Monday."

After a small pause, "Okay."

Brian asked, "Are you sure you can commit to this one?"

"I can," said the president of Colt.

Brian rose to his feet and went to shake his hand. "Let's go with Dr. Liepert and meet the procurement agent. Congratulations."

Brian left Colt and Jenny with the government procurement officer and laughed at the thought of all the paperwork he was about to go through. He walked back down the hallway of the White House basement until he found All Systems. They had their heads buried in some document and were arguing with one another. No doubt the VP gave all the "oh my God" arguments he could, and the president and CFO were talking him off the ledge.

"Gentlemen," said Brian as he knocked on the open door. The men immediately quit talking and looked up at Brian.

Brian took a deep sigh, "Look. We're going with Colt."

The three men took a collective sigh, two of which were upset, and one was relieved.

Brian said, "Guys, I know all of you personally, and you've never let me down. But realistically, this isn't a deep engineering project. As a matter of fact, it's much more of a construction project with totally unrealistic time schedules. We have no intentions of making this a research project. We all know there're only two companies on this planet that can even accomplish this project, and the more I think about it, it just fits Colt Engineering better than All Systems."

The president of All Systems got a sick feeling in his stomach. This single project was larger than the entire revenue of his company from the last fiscal year. With the economy tanking, a small feeling of anxiety started coming over him.

Brian said, "However, I'm the project manager for this refinery. As PM, I'll insist that every OEM and vendor have to get approvals from All Systems for all disciplines. As long as you commit to not delaying the process, that should be good for at least 40 engineers at $175 per hour. If it takes a year to complete, then that's a $15 million labor order. Plus, we'll make you the preferred contractor for any future projects at the facility, which is in the range of $10 million to $30 million a year. I don't know much about the engineering services business, but I've got to think that's a damn good labor order and long-term commitment. Let me put up the skeleton, then you guys can give it the muscle to run for a very long time."

The team had smiles on their faces, and really felt more relief than anything. Labor was where you made the profit, and this was a really good order. Brian shook hands with the team, and excused himself. He felt good about his choice to go with Colt Engineering. One thing Brian learned a long time ago was to not second guess a decision unless there was a reason.

As Brian walked back to his living area, he got a nagging feeling. Manish's comments on the safety system were odd. He couldn't remember ever putting a safety system into a single person's oversight on any project. Brian shook off this thought, assuming Manish was overburdened with too many details, and trying to take over ownership of another item for the sake of speed. Brian decided that Manish needed some quality help, someone that Manish could trust for the different critical areas of the plant. Brian turned around and walked back to find the president of Colt. His first major chore was to find the best electrical controls engineer to work closely with Manish.

Brian was certain Manish would appreciate finding another great engineer for the project.

Chapter 33—Influence

Washington Mall—Washington, D.C.

"Okay, here's how this thing's going to go," said Agent Womack.

Agent Womack turned around and looked in the back seat to speak to Jim. "We're following Roy right now. He parked on Ohio Drive right by the Potomac, and is walking towards the memorial."

Jim Jackson acknowledged him and then looked out the window. His body constantly shook now, way beyond nervous. Agent Womack noticed his shaking, and even saw his teeth chattering. Agent Womack had to make a decision. In one way, having Jim this nervous made this meeting look more realistic; on the other hand, somebody this nervous might completely lose his cool, putting the whole thing at risk.

Agent Womack asked, "Can you hear the agents in your earpiece?"

Jim gave another head nod while looking out the window, shaking uncontrollably. Agent Womack decided Jim's being nervous added to the moment, so he let it be instead of giving him a Valium. Agent Womack felt for the man, but no matter, he got himself into the situation and he had to deal with it. Every word Jim uttered during this meeting would be monitored, so they would just deal with any unforeseen circumstances should they occur, or if Jim said something he shouldn't.

Agent Womack said, "Alright, like we discussed, go forward with your meeting. You won't see us, but we're there, so you can calm down a bit. Your earpiece is hidden well, so he won't notice it. Just try to stay a few feet away from him. Here in a minute, you'll get out of the car and jump in the taxi that's parked behind us."

Jim made a quick turn to look out the back window of the government SUV. There was a standard looking minivan taxi parked right behind them. He shook his head, not quite believing he was in the middle of this whole mess. His hole kept getting deeper.

Agent Womack said, "The taxi driver's one of our agents. He'll pull you up to the memorial and let you out. He'll stay there and pick you up when the meeting is over. He's one of many agents armed around the area, so if Roy tries to pull anything, we'll be on him instantly."

Agent Womack said, "Let's recap the plan one more time."

Jim took a deep breath and said, "I'm going to meet Roy as planned, and let him do the talking. I'll give him a few details to keep him thinking I'm still on the inside. If he mentions anything about taking out Jenny or Brian, I'll let him know that the government is watching everyone closely, and that getting to them would be like getting to the President. I'll add more detail if I need to."

"That's right," said Agent Womack. "We want him to keep moving forward with his plans, but scare him just enough to consider other alternatives. We need him to track a longer term plan."

Jim asked Agent Womack with an anxious curiosity, "Why do you want him to keep going at all? Why, why not just . . ."

Agent Womack raised his hand to cut him off, "Don't worry about any of that. Just have the meeting, and do your best to keep him moving forward with his plans. If he asks you for any insider information, let him know you'll get it to him."

Jim shook his head, not wanting to hear the words. "Agent Womack, he paid me a lot of money to influence the refinery. He asked me to kill the whole damn thing. If I don't get him some good details or actions to try and stop it, then he'll go off the handle. I have to give him something."

Agent Womack considered this for a moment. Jim was right, he should give Roy something. If Roy further disappointed the

Impending Order, the government's best link to taking down the organization would be in jeopardy.

Agent Womack asked, "Do you have any thoughts?"

Jim said, "If you're here to protect me, then I'm a little more confident in telling Roy some half truths, just enough to let him think something's going on. You will protect me, right?"

Agent Womack said, "We'll protect you. Just don't screw this up. You're in enough hot water already. Okay, let's go."

Jim took a deep breath, put his hand on the door handle and exited the SUV. He walked directly to the taxi as instructed and hopped into the minivan. Jim was shocked at the detail. The taxi had all the carpet and seat stains one would expect of an urban taxi, and the smell that accompanied them. The driver was of Middle Eastern descent, wearing an old Member's Only jacket and sitting on a wooden bead seat cover. The dash had the rate meter just like one would expect to see, complete with a GPS device and a permanently mounted cell phone with instant talk features.

The driver never started a conversation as he put the minivan in drive and headed towards the Jefferson Memorial. They drove down Daniel French Drive and took a quick right onto Independence Avenue, and then another left to Ohio Drive. Jim saw the Jefferson Memorial coming up on the south side of the tidal basin, and felt the familiar knot growing in his stomach. Jim constantly took deep breaths as he struggled to get his nerves under control.

As the taxi approached the memorial, Jim heard Agent Womack in his ear, "Jim, you got me?"

"Uh, yeah, I hear you. Can you hear me?" asked Jim.

"We got you loud and clear. Your earpiece doubles as a mike and a speaker. I might be talking to you through the piece, trying to direct his or your thoughts a bit. Just do your best to fight through it if I speak into your ear. You copy that?" asked Agent Womack.

Jim tried to comprehend it all. At first it seemed like the Secret Service was a way out of his situation. Now it seemed he was a pawn in an impossible chess game, having to placate both Roy and the Secret Service. Jim had a bad feeling he was doing all these things for the Secret Service, and then they would come back on him for a long-term prison sentence, minus five years for his help. On the other hand, he had given Roy enough information to make him a millionaire several times over, and now Roy wanted him dead. Being caught in the middle of two evils was only making the nightmare worse, with a serious lack of appreciation coming from both sides of the equation.

"Jim, do you copy?" once again asked Agent Womack in a more stern tone.

"I got it," said a curt Jim.

As they entered the Jefferson Memorial, the taxi quickly stopped in front of the main visitor entrance. The driver turned to Jim and said, "The fare is twelve dollars for the ride, the meter will keep running while I wait."

The driver pointed towards a small remote parking lot. "I'll be parked right over there."

For a moment, the thought crossed his mind that this might not be an agent, but then thought again, as he gave no directions to the driver; he had to be an agent. Jim looked to where the driver said he would be parked, double checking where his only visible security blanket would be.

Jim sat in his seat for a few moments, too scared to move. The driver turned to Jim, "We're here. I'll be waiting for you over there. The meter's running. You know what I mean?"

Agent Womack spoke up in Jim's ear, "Jim, Roy's waiting on you. Snap out of it, and get this thing rolling. You're fine, we're watching everything."

Jim built up his self confidence, and then took another deep breath. He grabbed the door handle, slid the door open and jumped out of the car.

"Okay, he's standing near the water in front of the memorial," said Agent Womack.

For some reason, it hit Jim. He'd finally had enough. He was tired of being scared, and quickly focused his anger in one area, and that was Roy Ritchey. He picked up his pace along the oval sidewalk that rounded the memorial. As Jim came near the waterfront, he quickly found him. Roy was dressed in dark blue jeans, with cowboy boots and a bomber style jacket. He was staring across the water as Jim approached.

Here it comes, thought Jim. *Something's going to happen one way or another out of this conversation.*

"Mr. Ritchey," said Jim.

"Well," said Roy.

"Well what?" snapped Jim.

Roy turned to look at him, giving him a piercing glare, "Thought I was pretty fucking clear on my request from our last meeting."

Roy turned back to look at the water. "We followed up on your wife today. She's probably at the gym right now, doing one of those workout programs. You know, the kind that turns an average body into a smoking hot one for a few thousand bucks. I'd sure hate to see her get attacked in an unfortunate mugging on the way out tonight."

Jim's cocky attitude quickly turned to one of dread, not prepared for the words. Jim felt the panic growing in his body.

"She's not there, Jim!" said Agent Womack. "He's lying to you. We have her covered. Just stay cool; this guy's a lying bastard, just trying to manipulate your thoughts. Stay on point, Jim."

Agent Womack let out a sigh, as this was a lie. He had no idea where Jim's wife was at the moment, but decided to take a gamble. Agent Womack long ago learned to listen to his instinct, and he knew Roy was lying. He quickly called one of his agents and told him to get to Jim's wife as a priority, and find out where she was as soon as possible.

Jim glared at Roy and said, "I'm tired, Roy. I'm tired. You say another goddamned comment like that, and I sprint to the nearest cop. I'll gladly hand myself in, go to prison and give up my life to get out of this. I'm tired."

"Well, you can get out of this, if you give me what I need," said Roy in a cool voice. "What can you tell me? Oh, and cut out the attitude. No way in hell you're turning yourself in. Don't think you're the prison type."

After a brief pause, Roy turned and said, "Give me what I need, Jim, and it'll all go away."

Jim said, "Alright. First of all, Jenny and Brian are off-limits. I'd give some insight to their whereabouts if I could, but they're covered. And I mean totally covered. The President has assigned top level to them both. Even if you could get to them, there's no way of knowing when or where they are going to be. I mean, I only have meetings with Jenny or Glen on a conference call, with secured lines and no indications of where they are. I don't have anything to offer there. But so you know, even if I did, I wouldn't give you the information. I can't be a part of that."

"I choose what you're a part of!" said a suddenly animated Roy. "You've no idea what you're dealing with! I don't give a shit about how you feel."

Jim fired back, "Oh I think you do! I think you care a lot about how I feel, and even more about what I know. When I say I'm tired, I mean it! I'm done with it all. I know your type. You get what you want out of intimidation and scare tactics. That's it, you're cut off. If you want more information, it's going to cost you a lot more money than a million bucks!"

The words surprised Roy. He wasn't prepared for this strong of a push back from Jim.

Jim said, "Hell, the Secret Service has been all over me. They've been all over everyone. They probably have a bug up everyone's ass who is involved with this thing. If you're going to stop this refinery, then you better take a step back and think of something a lot bigger than putting a hit on somebody. No single action is going to stop this."

"Easy, cowboy," said Agent Womack. "Quit talking for a minute and see where this thing goes."

Roy felt the anger boiling. It took every shred of willpower to not reach over and grab this bastard by the throat, and rip it right off of his neck. Roy struggled to gather his thoughts. He needed

Jim, regardless of the cost. He needed insider information, and this situation was quickly getting out of his control. Roy was used to dealing with people with little or no ethics, not the educated family type that actually had something to live for. Now this motherfucker wanted more money. Roy's mind drifted in and out from point to point, not sure how to handle the situation.

Roy looked at Jim. "Give me what I need before this gets real ugly."

Jim said, "Alright Roy. Brian Larson's going through a selection process on two different architectural and engineering firms for the refinery. One is called All Systems, and the other one is called Colt Engineering."

Roy caught his first break. He knew both companies well, and more importantly, he knew the primary OEMs that supplied equipment to the refinery. He had a shred of hope he could pull something off there.

Jim said, "There's another thing that might be of some interest to you. There's going to be some serious pushback on major construction in south Texas. This area is covered in historical locations and highly protected aquifers. I know it doesn't sound like much, but the Corps of Engineers tried for years to build a lake through the rolling hills of that region. It was held up in court for years until the Corps just gave up. This thing has some teeth, and I'm certain some funding to the right law firm could really make things difficult for the government. I doubt it will stop the project, but it definitely could hold up things for a long time. This is good news to you, Roy. As I said, you need to think bigger."

Roy stared at the ground, pondering this comment.

Jim said, "No more threats. I'm done with them. I gave you insight to the refinery, names, places and more than enough information to make ten times the money you paid me. If you want more, then give me more money. If you make any more threats on my family, then I go to the feds. I'm done."

"Walk away Jim. Just walk away," said Agent Womack.

Jim took a step backwards and slowly walked towards his taxi. He felt relieved, thinking he had at least gotten out of the conversation. The further Jim moved away from Roy, the more he wanted to sprint.

Suddenly, Jim's shoulder was pulled backwards, and his body was whipped around. Roy grabbed Jim's chin and moved their faces within an inch of each other.

Roy screamed at Jim as loudly as he could, "That's not enough, motherfucker! I want more! I need to know where Larson and Liepert are! I need to know their exact location! We're going to kill this refinery, and you're going to help us! I don't give a shit about a fucking lawsuit! Give me what I need! Now!"

Jim struggled as hard as he could, and managed to separate himself. As Jim pushed away, he tripped and fell backwards. He quickly rolled over to his knees, trying to prepare for the next attack from Roy. Then Jim felt something like a rock hit the back side of his left shoulder, causing him to fall face first into the ground. The pain was the most intense he had ever felt, and then the world went black.

As Roy reached down to pull him up, blood shot out of Jim's body, covering him with red spackles all over his face and jacket.

The agents heard Jim scream through their microphones, and then it went silent.

"What happened?" yelled Agent Womack.

"He's down, do we move in?" said one of the agents stationed at the memorial.

"What do you mean he's down?" asked Agent Womack. "Did Ritchey push him down?"

The agent said in an excited but quiet tone, "Ah . . . I'm not sure, sir. Ritchey's just looking at Mr. Jackson, standing right over his body. He looks shocked, and I think blood's all over him. He doesn't appear to be holding a weapon."

There was a pause in the agent's transmission. Everyone listening to the communications was on edge, not sure what to do next.

The agent continued in a matter of fact voice, "He's been shot, Agent Womack, and I don't think Ritchey did it. Do we move in?"

Roy looked down at Jim, and heard him screaming in pain, and then silence. He saw the blood flowing out of Jim's body to the grass below. He gazed down on his own clothes, and then ran his hand slowly across his face. Roy cringed as he felt Jim's blood smearing all over him. Roy whipped around as he heard the first screams. He saw a man and a woman look directly towards him while they pointed their fingers in his direction. Roy backed away from Jim's body.

Roy was stunned and confused. How did Jim get shot? Roy didn't even have his gun on him. He quickly put it together. It was the Impending Order, closing any possible links. Roy continued to back away from the body, and then did a dead sprint around the water's edge, singularly focused on getting to his car. He'd been set up.

Agent Womack's mind scrambled, and quickly summarized that Jim had been hit by someone else. It was the Impending Order, closing the loose ends on Roy Ritchey. Agent Womack couldn't let his cover be compromised. He assumed that if they were watching Roy and Jim, then they were watching for others as well. He still needed the Impending Order to be unaware of their presence. Agent Womack made a snap decision.

"Negative. Don't blow your cover! Do not move in. Just follow the crowds of other people as they try to see what happened. Is the memorial security team moving in yet?" asked Agent Womack.

"Yes, sir. Memorial security team moving in right now!" said the agent in an excited tone.

"Everybody stay calm. Don't blow your cover. Slowly move away from your locations and head back," said Agent Womack.

After Agent Womack gave the last order, he hit the mute button on his microphone and cussed out loud while hitting the dash. He'd promised this man he would protect him, which he did not. And just as importantly, his direct link to managing Roy Ritchey's thoughts was now gone.

Gary Blackmon sat in his car with his bodyguard. They were watching Roy's office while waiting on word from the sniper. Gary reviewed the detailed files of Jim Jackson on his smart phone, getting a handle on how Roy had gathered his information. Jim was definitely in the know in terms of the initial refinery plans, but was no longer needed. The refinery plans were now in the hands of Brian Larson, and Jim Jackson had no more influence.

Gary's phone rang. He quickly pressed the answer button, "Go ahead."

"It's done. Target's down," said the sniper.

"And his accomplice?" asked Gary.

"Ran away from the scene," said the sniper.

"Any unusual security personnel seem present? Did anyone follow him?" asked Gary.

"No. Just the normal security staff. It appeared the other man wasn't followed. I'm out. You know how to find me," said the sniper as he hung up the phone.

Gary put down his phone and turned to his bodyguard. "Go inside and put the pictures on his desk. Stay in hiding."

Gary's bodyguard stepped out of the car, and casually walked across the street to Roy's office. Gary shook his head, not enjoying these situations and how ugly they got sometimes. The Impending Order's investments were in serious jeopardy, and he needed ideas. Many strings had to be pulled to influence this project properly. Gary returned to his phone and opened the Brian Larson file.

Chapter 34—Engineering

Plaza Hotel—San Antonio, Texas

Udaya Suthar had been on an airplane for the past 24 hours in his travels from India, but it only felt like a few minutes. He had an uneasy feeling, but didn't really know why. As he looked out the window of the 777 on descent into San Antonio, he somehow knew this project was going to be the most difficult of his career, and he had a bad feeling about it.

As Electrical Engineering Team Leader for Illuminate Services, Udaya was often a part of large scale projects, and usually led the electrical control system integration. Illuminate Services claimed to have more than thirty thousand engineers on staff, but as everyone understood, that number was actually any number it needed to be for the sales team to get an order. To the general manager types, Udaya was generally seen as one of the many hordes of engineers that swooped into a project, got it running, and then quickly left the project site with the same expediency. But to people who actually sold and delivered electrical control systems for a living, Udaya was considered one of the premier engineers on the planet.

Based out of India, Illuminate boasted itself as one of the world's largest outsourced engineering organizations. The company was essentially made up of about a hundred engineering leaders similar to Udaya across different engineering disciplines, and then had an endless line of associates through their HR department to fill the holes as required.

Udaya's job for this project was to lead the automation and instrumentation engineering of the project, and to be responsible for the ultimate delivery of the industrial computer, safety and visualization systems. This wasn't unusual for Udaya, as his deep knowledge of large systems generally made him the best man for high visibility projects. Systems such as these required the best engineers to translate the requirements to a resource pool of engineers in India, who then developed thousands of AutoCAD drawings, computer codes, graphics and algorithms for a successful project. The system was then tested thoroughly and implemented by the local engineering team at the plant.

As Udaya left his family in India, he fully expected to be gone for at least a year. His bosses let him know that under no circumstances would he be able to take any time off to return home for vacations or personal time. His family was accustomed to his extended travel, but this trip was especially difficult considering he had so little time to get things in order. Life as an outsourced engineer was very difficult, as your skill sets were appreciated, but always abused.

This project developed faster than Udaya had ever seen. Certainly he had been involved with many different global projects during his career, but he had never been interviewed for a major project one day, only to find himself flying to an assignment on the next, being told to ignore any prior responsibilities or commitments.

Udaya was on the plane with about 20 other associates from Illuminate, all with different engineering disciplines, and none of them were looking forward to working with Colt Engineering. Illuminate had worked with Colt many times before, and everyone knew that no excuses were to be given for anything, at any time. An Illuminate associate who raised a concern to Colt was lucky to be on the job for more than a few hours. Given the magnitude and scope of this project, most felt this would be the most difficult of their career, and they would be lucky if they survived with their jobs intact.

Upon learning he was assigned to this project, Udaya had a call from the president of Colt Engineering and the president of Illuminate, which was extraordinarily rare for any associate. Udaya had never even spoken to either man before this call, and this caused all kinds of red flags in his mind. The president of Colt Engineering explained that a man named Brian Larson had specifically requested the best electrical controls engineer for the project, so Udaya was the automatic choice.

"Udaya," said the president of Colt.

"Yes sir," said Udaya.

"I want to be totally clear. Mr. Larson gave a direct order that you're to do whatever a man named Manish Gupta requests. Understood?"

"Yes sir," said Udaya as he wrote the name down quickly.

The president of Colt continued, "Mr. Larson made it crystal clear that Manish is the absolute end-all decision maker on the plant automation and instrumentation system, and as far as you're concerned, Manish is your direct boss and decision maker during the entire duration of the refinery. No questions are to be asked."

Udaya listened to the man speak, but thought how odd this situation was. System engineering leadership was seldom if ever a one man job, and usually comprised of a complete review team. The man went on to explain that right after the initial project kickoff meeting, Udaya was to have a breakout meeting with Manish to discuss the high level process drawings he had developed for the refinery, and anything Manish requested was Udaya's only concern.

The team from Illuminate arrived in San Antonio late on Sunday evening, in time for a planned Monday 9:00 A.M. kickoff meeting with the refinery leadership. Udaya was quite surprised to see his living accommodations for the initial stages of the project. They were staying at the Plaza Hotel in San Antonio, which was essentially the project headquarters for the time being. Usually his company rented the cheapest apartment possible, and housed them for an extended period of time with about five other guys, and a few dollars a day for food expenses. Their living quarters were always an interesting biology experiment by the time they moved out.

The following morning, Udaya and his team were meeting in the large foyer of a ballroom type facility, typical of those found in large hotels. As Udaya walked through the lobby towards the ballrooms, he noticed a considerable number of media gathering outside the front door of the hotel.

"That's odd," thought Udaya.

He noticed another associate from Illuminate hanging out in one of the massive lounge chairs, and Udaya walked up to him to discuss the commotion outside. "What's going on? Why are reporters here?"

The other associate took a brief look outside, and then turned back to Udaya. "They're here for us. They're covering the kickoff of the refinery."

Udaya stared out the front door of the lobby and studied the commotion outside.

The Illuminate associate said, "Udaya, you know this is the biggest project of our careers?"

"Yes," said Udaya as he stared out of the lobby windows.

The Illuminate associate said, "I sure hope it goes okay, or we might not be offered a ticket back home. I just saw Brian Larson and his entourage come through here after discussions with the reporters. I recognized him from all the Internet reports about the refinery."

"Brian Larson's here?" said a surprised Udaya. "I can't imagine someone at that high of a level even bothering with the details."

"Me either," said the other associate with a concerned look on his face. "I've been on semi-conductor and pharmaceutical startups all over the world, and I never so much as met a plant manager."

Udaya said, "Well, I guess we better get going. No way am I being late for the first meeting."

Udaya and his associate walked towards the ballrooms, and met up with other associates from Illuminate. The large foyer had all the coffee, snacks and pastries that one could want, and seemed to be rather quiet with a sense of apprehension. Each person attending the meeting stood in line to receive a badge and lanyard. The official-looking badge had their names, company and responsibilities printed on the front. As Udaya scanned the room, he noticed security cameras were everywhere. Upon a second glance, he saw at least one security type person standing at every door, complete with a wire in his ear, just standing there while observing the crowd. It was obvious that security was very high, making the anxiety even more intense.

While Udaya received his lanyard, he was informed to go to the double door towards the end of the foyer. As Udaya came to the doors, a tough looking agent gave him a glance-over, and then opened the door without saying a word. Inside the room were essentially 10 lines of security columns running down the length of the ballroom. The columns were made of tall rows of curtains, each with a short line of people formed in front of the entrance of each one. The entrance to each security column had a standard looking metal detector in place, with signs on the top of the scanners reading A-C, the next line read D-F, etc. Udaya quickly found the S row, and dutifully stood in line with the others. The room was eerily quiet, and nobody was saying a word other than the security agents. Upon finally reaching the metal detector, Udaya was asked to hand over his computer bag and to empty all clothes pockets, with the pockets showing if possible. After walking through the metal detector, Udaya suddenly realized it was a full body scanner, and he could see an outline image of himself on a large flat screen. A security agent then walked up to Udaya, and patted him down unlike anything ever seen at an airport.

The agent gave a thumb up to the security leader, and then said "looks okay" while handing Udaya's computer bag back to him. Udaya was told to walk down the aisle of curtains to the next station. Here two agents were sitting at a desk with a typical computer monitor and three additional security devices. Udaya once again noticed the additional security cameras.

"Please put your bag on the floor, and place your toes on the white line and look at the camera," boomed a voice from behind the computer. It almost sounded like the agent yelled because everything was so quiet. Udaya quickly did as instructed.

"Thank you. Now please have a seat at the table and place both palms on the scanner, and all ten finger tips on the scanners as well," continued the security agent.

Once Udaya was done the agent said, "Thank you. Now look into the retinal scanner."

Udaya looked up from the table where he had his palms, and saw a device similar to a set of binoculars. Udaya leaned over and stared into the device. It had a bright white light, almost burning his eyes.

After a few moments of looking into the light, the agent said, "Thank you. Please remove yourself from the retinal scanner and state your name."

Udaya removed his head from the device, seeing stars everywhere as his eyes adjusted. Udaya finally said, "Uh, Udaya Suthar."

"Say it again in a louder voice. Don't add any extra words," ordered the agent in a firm tone.

"Udaya Suthar."

"Again please."

"Udaya Suthar!"

"Thank you. Now please hand me your badge," said the agent while holding out his hand.

The agent quickly inserted Udaya's badge into a machine. He heard the machine making a crunching noise. A few moments later, the agent handed his badge back. The badge now had his name, picture and RFID tag etched into the plastic, along with the original information.

The security agent looked straight at Udaya, and spoke in the strict tone of a police officer, "Okay Mr. Suthar. This badge is your main security identification card. It must be shown at all times outside of any clothing. If you don't have this badge on you, then you'll be immediately escorted off any premises dealing with the refinery. No questions asked. There're many security features associated with this project. Sometimes your badge and fingerprints will be used, sometimes your badge and voice, and possibly your badge and a retinal scanner for the most secure areas. Never, ever lose sight of this card. If it's lost, you must report it immediately."

The agent then pointed towards the two large doors behind his security system. "Now exit through these doors, and immediately enter the other set of double doors down the foyer to your right. Have a nice day."

As Udaya exited the room, he suddenly realized this was a United States government project, and they had everything. Passport number, voice, fingerprints and eye signature. Trying to hide anywhere in the world was fruitless. Udaya cussed to himself under his breath, as this process only added to the bad feeling with the whole situation.

Upon entering the ballroom, Udaya found other counterparts from Illuminate sitting at a spot near the front of the room, and took a seat close to them. The huge room was full of long tables, each covered with white linens, and a hotel notepad and pen located in front of each seat. The team from Illuminate essentially took up two complete rows, and was situated to the left of the standard podium located at the front of the room with a huge screen for presentations behind the stage. Every person immediately booted up his or her notebook computer, hoping to find the strongest Wi-Fi signal to connect to the Internet and their e-mail systems. But to everyone's disappointment, there were no Wi-Fi signals available. One gentleman behind them complained out loud how they confiscated his cellular PC card when going through security. Other than that, most people kept to themselves as the knots in their stomachs got a little more intense, kind of like this was the first day of school.

Right at the scheduled 9:00 A.M. start, a serious looking gentleman took the podium. Instead of a lot of rah-rah type talk with fancy PowerPoint presentations on the large screen, he simply said, "Welcome to the kickoff meeting for the refinery. Before we begin, we have to take additional security steps. First thing, please turn off your notebook computers and hand them to the team at the end of your row. Please place a sheet of paper with your name and login password between the screen and the keyboards. We'll be moving these computers to a secure room here at the hotel, and you'll be able to perform activities on your personal PC in the evening. However, first we will run a detailed scan of your PC, load monitoring software, and only allow you to use these through a secured connection. Your PCs will be available by this evening, but can only be used in our secure room."

The men and women in the room stared at each other in a stunned silence. Their PC was the last semblance of home. All their personal information, pictures, schedules, calendars, finances, contact list . . . everything was loaded on these hard drives. For Udaya, his immediate thought was the intellectual property. One of the key advantages of years of engineering experience was drawing upon applications which had been successful in the past. His computer contained thousands of documents including control system code, drawings, instrumentation, key contacts and reference documents from numerous systems over many years. All this information gave him the ability to do applications quickly, and to re-use his well-earned information. His PC was a key tool to doing things more efficiently. Losing his PC was like losing a security blanket, and most all of the others in the room felt the exact same way. Having access to your PC for a few minutes in the evening simply wouldn't cut it.

The man sitting behind Udaya who had his cell modem confiscated said, "I think I speak for the rest of the people in the room . . ."

The man at the podium cut him off, "Not an option. If you don't like it, then leave."

The man and three others immediately stood up and exited the room as quickly as possible. All the others, however, slowly wrote their names and passwords on a piece of paper and shut down their computers, albeit with very uneasy feelings. Handing over your single most important tool for your job and connection home to a total stranger didn't feel right at all.

The same gentleman approached the podium, and everyone glanced at their cell phones, sure this was the next item to be confiscated. The man said, "Now, we're going to call out your name, and will tell you what table to go to in the back of the room. Please go to the correct table, as each person's PC is specifically designed for your role within the refinery."

Everybody quickly looked to the back of the room, and saw several table setups with large letters. In the background, large rolling carts with new notebook computers were being moved into the room.

The man at the podium continued, "Once we call your name and give you a table number, please approach the table and receive your new PC."

Certainly this made the audience feel better about the situation. At least the cell phones weren't being taken away. As the man called off each person's name and table number, they left their seats and went to their assigned table.

"Udaya Suthar, Illuminate, table A," said the man just like the many others he called.

Udaya made his way to the back of the room. He noticed everyone was a little more polite, and saw several people greeting each other and having conversations, which was great for Udaya. Long-term relationships were the one thing he truly loved about this business, and he always enjoyed keeping in contact with his customers or partners long after a project was completed.

As Udaya slowly worked his way to the front of the line, he simply said, "Udaya Suthar." The lady filled out information on her computer, and then handed him a new PC box. The PC actually excited Udaya, as this computer had the horsepower required for the software he would use on this application, unlike the cheap one his company provided.

As Udaya left the table, someone called his name. He turned and saw two men standing there, one of whom he immediately recognized from all the media coverage over the past few weeks; the other he was sure to be Manish Gupta.

Brian Larson held out his hand. "Hi Udaya, Brian Larson. It's good to meet you, and welcome to our team. We've heard a lot about you and your previous experience, very impressive."

Udaya, always humble and friendly, shook Brian's hand with a small bow, "Thank you, Mr. Larson."

Manish then extended his hand with a more serious look, that typical of those in the engineering space, "Namaste, Udaya. Manish Gupta."

"Hello Mr. Gupta. Pleased to be working with you," said Udaya with another small bow.

Manish said, "The kickoff meeting gets the new associates up to speed on the refinery, and the logistics of getting around in a secured environment. But, Mr. Larson has arranged for you to get started immediately. So come with me to another room, and let's start discussing our plans. I'll fill you in on the logistical details later."

Udaya remembered his direct orders from his bosses and never hesitated. "Yes sir. I'll get my things and be right back."

After Udaya returned with his backpack and new computer box, he and Manish left the room just as Brian took the podium. While he and Manish took a large escalator to the second level, Udaya once again noticed the level of security. There were people in nice suits and wearing ear pieces all over the place, and at least one stationed at every door. Manish made no attempt at a conversation and Udaya did the same. His thoughts of being in a trap with no way out were reinforced.

As they walked, Manish's mind raced as well. He managed to get Udaya's resume from Brian and reviewed his extensive background. Udaya was considered the preeminent electrical engineer out of India, which was an amazing level of respect. Manish fully appreciated the effort it took to be a highly regarded engineer in India, but to be considered the best industrial controls engineer was a title very seldom acknowledged to anyone. Manish had no intentions of hiring someone of this caliber for his team, but Udaya came to Manish as a gift from Brian of sorts. In Brian's mind, the best talent he could find for Manish would only be a positive, as Manish's plate was already overloaded. Manish thought it best to not befriend Udaya, as this was not typical cultural procedure for Indians. Plus, the less Udaya felt comfortable about digging into the process, the better.

Udaya and Manish approached a room that once again had an agent at the door. Manish gave a quick nod to the man while doing a badge and fingerprint scan. The room was about 1500 square feet, and was completely covered in E size process drawings. The center of the room had a large table with seven or eight large computer monitors with AutoCAD process drawings displayed. This room really startled Udaya, as he grasped the scope of the project they were embarking on and the level of its importance. Never in his career had he seen such money and speed being applied to a project.

"Put down your things, and I'll give you a few minutes to take a look," said Manish.

Udaya understood this to mean, "Start studying and then I'll give you a test to see if you're as good as they say." Although you would never hear him say it, Udaya was every bit as talented a controls engineer as Manish was a process engineer, and this put Udaya in an awkward situation. Battles between electrical control engineers and process engineers were legendary, and Udaya had many battle scars from previous applications. Electrical control engineers are often burdened with "overcoming" the lack of process designs from process engineers, so Udaya chose to walk this line carefully.

Udaya assumed the reason Colt Engineering and Brian Larson insisted on him was his track record of designing many sophisticated control systems over the years, all of them running to this day. The control system was the eyes and the ears of the entire refinery, and provided the intelligence, operator interface, programming and data to give plant operations the tools they needed to run a refinery to its maximum potential. Without a best of class control system, even the best-designed plants were a disaster. Udaya prayed this design was quality enough to avoid any unnecessary confrontations with his new boss.

Udaya scanned the drawings on the wall, and quickly found the beginning of the process. Often in engineering, you either have "it," or you don't. Udaya had whatever "it" was in the engineering space, and could grasp even the most remote of ideas or applications across any engineering discipline. Udaya had a unique ability to "pretend" he was a molecule, and could visualize himself within the process. He walked through each drawing, understanding how a petroleum molecule would travel through the equipment, and be modified to ultimately become Jet-A fuel.

Udaya was immersed in the drawings. He stepped through the incoming feeders and manifolds, he thought through the raw petroleum storage tanks, pumps, boilers and risers. He studied the refined petroleum transfer, and then imagined the cracker unit reaction; he saw the filters, and the completed product tank farm. He reviewed the custody transfer processes and ultimately the completed refinery.

Udaya was in deep thought when Manish walked up behind him. "What are your initial thoughts?"

A startled Udaya quickly realized he had been reviewing the drawings for more than an hour. Udaya had many, many red flags running through his mind, but thought better of bringing up any issues or concerns.

A nervous Udaya got his thoughts together. "Well, if you just avoid the large volumes, it seems like a pretty straightforward process. I've seen many more difficult. There are probably some instrumentation issues getting large devices in a caustic environment, but nothing that can't be overcome."

"Okay," said Manish, getting the exact answer he expected, but disappointed that Udaya didn't offer more information.

After a long pause, Udaya finally yielded: "Ah, overall, I'll have to understand the physical layout a little bit better, but I believe we're looking at two major distributed control system panels, with about sixty remote control stations. I'd guess about twenty thousand discrete points and about six thousand analog points. Overall, we'll install a system that has worked for us many times, but we have the luxury of working with all the right components, and do not have to deal with purchasing agents telling us to buy cheaper parts."

Manish and Udaya let out a quick laugh, obviously both in the same camp when it came to bureaucratic purchasing policies. But Manish was doing anything but laughing on the inside. Udaya had nailed the control system fundamentals without a single word of input from Manish. Remembering back to Udaya's profile, Manish recalled that Udaya designed some of the most complex control systems in the world, including a few nuclear plants and linear accelerators. A concerned feeling began to take over Manish, as the possibility of Udaya understanding his intentions was very high.

Manish maintained his cool, and spoke in a noticeably happy tone, "Very good, those are my thoughts exactly. What about the SIS?"

This question caused Udaya's heart to skip a beat, as he didn't like what he reviewed at all.

"Well," said Udaya, "For the Safety Instrumented System, it seems you have a few processes considerably out of standard operating guidelines. Our tool sets are tied in pretty closely to the standards, so we'll have to build in some overrides, with your supervision of course."

"Excellent," said Manish. "I appreciate your concern here, but trust me, we need these operational points to get the results we all hope to achieve."

Udaya nodded his head in hesitant agreement, thinking to himself these "designs" were definitely not only intended to refine petroleum.

Manish said, "Go ahead and get your computer set up and let me show you the software we've loaded on the machines. This room's going to be your home for a long time."

Chapter 35—Desperation

Offices of Roy Ritchey—Arlington, Virginia

Roy watched his rearview mirror as much as the road ahead. He took every back road he could to his office, certain he was being followed. The turn of events shocked Roy, and had him frazzled and looking for answers. Roy was a mess, and couldn't manage to rub all the blood from his face and hands, which now dried up all over him. The alpha male attitude that Roy had was gone, and he was scared. His deal with the Impending Order was something he should've never agreed to, and now he was out of his league. Roy now had no influence on the project's outcome, his money was in jeopardy and his life was too.

Think . . . Think . . . . was all he continually told himself. He struggled to come up with any action plan. Jim gave him a break in mentioning Colt Engineering, as they had the cheapest engineers and project managers, and they could be bought. Some of the OEMs could probably be bought . . . Roy tried to think. This thing moved so fast. *How can I kill the refinery? Think . . . . Think . . . .*

Roy slowly pulled into his office parking lot. He noticed none of his regular employees were there. This raised flags in his mind. He suddenly remembered he told everyone to leave the office earlier in the day. His paranoia had taken complete control.

"Get a hold on yourself!" shouted Roy. "Think . . . Think . . ."

Roy entered his office and immediately went to the bathroom. He looked in the mirror and saw the blood all over his face and clothes. He turned on the hot water full blast, and pressed the nozzle on the foam soap at a furious pace. He frantically scrubbed all the blood off of him. He had a disgusted feeling, and could sense Jim's blood residue digging into his skin. The thought of Jim's body fluids soaking into his body made him irrational, and he dug his fingernails so deep in his skin that he almost drew blood from his own body.

Roy discarded his clothes, as the thought of any part of Jim being near him made him sick to his stomach. Roy looked back to the mirror and examined his naked body thoroughly. It seemed all the blood had been removed, and then Roy truly saw himself in the mirror. Here he was, naked in his low rent office, no future, and his dreams of a winery in the valley were gone.

The longer Roy stared at himself, the more disgusted he became. The dark and evil flame in his soul returned, and he wouldn't sit by idly and watch all he had worked for be cast away. He became angry to his soul that he had lost control, and let anybody push him into a corner. He continued staring at the mirror, looking deep into his own eyes. He daydreamed, completely focused on the situation. He pieced it together, his office visit earlier and now the hit on Jim. He was still alive. They needed him.

The Impending Order needs me . . . The motherfuckers need me, said Roy to himself. He suddenly felt the confidence building, and could sense the true reality of the situation. Roy was now a more focused man.

Roy wrapped a towel around his torso, left the bathroom and headed to his office. He had a suit hanging in his closet that he kept for any sudden business meetings. As he walked in his office, he stopped in his tracks when he noticed a manila folder sitting in the middle of his desk. His administrator had specific orders to never touch his desk, and this folder was seriously out of place. As he opened the folder, he became even more enraged. He slowly removed the pictures, and rubbed his hands across his face. He was dealing with an even lower class of individuals than himself, and their billions of dollars couldn't gloss over the fact that they were the scum of the earth.

He stared at the pictures of his administrator and sometimes lover. She was strapped to a bed in a complete spread eagle position. She had duct tape covering her mouth, small cuts and blood on her face, and the beginning of bruises and welts on her body. Roy concentrated on one picture of her face up close, and he saw the look of desperation in her eyes. Roy thought about the pictures for a few moments, and then simply threw them in the trash. Roy had his own problems, and wouldn't go down the road of negotiating for her life. *Too bad for her,* thought Roy. *I got my own problems.*

A slow grin grew across Roy's face. He knew the Impending Order tried to intimidate him by these photos, and hoped to increase his sense of urgency. Roy actually felt better than he had in quite some time. The intimidation, the threats, the money, Jim Jackson and now his administrator. All these things were happening around him, but one person was left standing. Gary needed him, and he was going to make him pay. Roy knew money and influence as well as anyone, and the steps Gary took to intimidate him only added to his resolve.

Roy confidently moved around his desk and walked to the closet to retrieve his suit. He opened the door and suddenly saw a handgun pointed straight at this forehead. He took a step backwards as the bodyguard stepped out of the closet. Roy stood there, looking directly past the gun into the eyes of the man. Roy watched as the bodyguard retrieved a cell phone from his jacket pocket with his free hand, and pressed a button.

Roy didn't move a muscle, and never took his eyes off the cocky bodyguard. *He didn't shoot me, they need me,* Roy thought to himself as they gave each other a stare down. Then Roy saw it, a brief look of fear in the bodyguard's eyes. Roy knew the bodyguard was in a trapped situation, where he couldn't hurt Roy. Roy had no such orders.

Roy lunged at the gun, both men now having a firm grip on the weapon. Roy pushed the bodyguard as hard as he could, and they rammed into the closet against the closet wall. The well-trained bodyguard quickly dropped to his knees and dove into Roy's legs, causing him to do a complete somersault. But neither man let go of the gun, causing the bodyguard to fall backwards and land directly on top of Roy, with his ear planted directly on top of Roy's face. Roy opened his mouth and bit as hard as he could into the man's ear.

The bodyguard let out an incredible scream, and shuddered violently while trying to get away from Roy. The man instantly let go of the gun, and then barrel rolled across the floor. Roy suddenly found himself holding the gun while the bodyguard grabbed for his ear. Without hesitation, Roy jumped to his feet and pulled the hammer on the gun. He moved directly to the man, pointed the gun straight at his forehead and pulled the trigger.

Roy closed his eyes, anticipating the man's head to pour open like a watermelon hit with a bat. But nothing happened. Roy stared at the gun and then pulled the hammer again and pulled the trigger. Nothing happened. The gun wasn't loaded!

Roy threw the gun at the man's head, and kicked him as hard as he could. Roy felt the man's ribs giving away under his kicks as he screamed in pain.

"Enough!" said the unmistakable voice of Gary Blackmon.

Roy turned to Gary. He was full of adrenaline and mad beyond his control. Roy lunged with full force into Gary, causing them both to crash into the wall by the office door.

Gary yelled, "We need each other! Don't do this!"

"We need each other." Roy heard the words, and slowly relieved the pressure and backed away.

Gary pulled at his blazer and stretched it back to normal. "We need each other."

Roy gave a knowing look to Gary, "Yes. We need each other."

Both men stood in silence for a moment. Gary gave a disgusted look at the man on the floor, as this was supposed to be the best bodyguard. The man rolled on the floor and screamed like a child with blood all over him.

Roy said, "I only want the money, Gary. No more threats. No more intimidation. I'm ready to die. Nothing you can do will intimidate me. I'll get you what you need, but I only want the money. I've got nothing else."

Gary nodded his head. "I need the refinery dead."

Roy said, "Gary, this thing's gone further than you and I imagined. We're going to need a deeper plan."

Gary slowly said, "Yes. Let's put together a plan."

Roy asked, "The money?"

"It's yours. Just keep moving forward," said Gary.

Roy felt better about the reply, but still had no trust for this man. "Why did you take out Jim Jackson? What possible reasons do you have to kill him? He's my insider."

Gary said, "Was your insider. He gave you the information you needed, and he's no longer necessary. He calls no shots. Brian Larson's the insider now."

Gary paused for a moment and said, "Guys like him can't keep quiet. One way or another, people would've figured he was talking to us."

Roy gave an understanding nod to Gary, and then slowly moved to his desk. He pulled the desk drawer open and grabbed his pistol. Roy cocked the hammer and walked to the bodyguard who was still in the corner, squealing in pain. Without hesitation he shot the man directly in the temple.

Roy watched as the man went lifeless and said, "That's for my admin."

Gary watched the event unfold in front of him. He turned and looked at Roy with a small grin. "Now you're thinking like a member of the Impending Order."

Chapter 36—Remorse

Georgetown Hospital—Washington, D.C.

Agent Womack and Director Beine stepped out of the elevator in the basement of the hospital. They moved into the hallway and immediately walked in the direction of the morgue. The basement was dimly lit, with antiquated beige tile on the wall. Everyone they passed didn't even bother to acknowledge them, as nobody was in any mood for small talk with death being all around them. As they moved down the hallway, the more they walked the longer the hallway seemed.

When they finally reached the morgue, they entered the morgue director's office. They were met by the chief hospital administrator, the morgue director and the White House Chief of Staff. The situation was highly unusual, and the Secret Service required the help of the White House to pull this off.

With the full witness of all in attendance, the morgue director submitted the proper paperwork for Mr. Jackson's death, including time of death and the cause. All watched as the director filled out a web page and pressed the submit button. As far as the world was concerned, Jim Jackson was now officially deceased.

The morgue director completed the official file. Only this time, he printed all the pages in duplicate. After another few minutes he handed Director Beine a standard file folder.

The morgue director pointed across the hallway, "He's in the other room."

The White House Chief of Staff said, "Okay, quiet's the word. We were never here."

Everyone looked at each other with an uneasy feeling, and went their separate ways. Everyone wanted out of this situation as quickly as possible.

Agent Womack and Director Beine gave an acknowledgment of thanks to the others in the room, and then quickly moved to the medical room on the other side of the hallway. There they saw Jim Jackson staring at the ceiling. He had IVs in his arm, and an exceptionally large bandage covering his pectoral muscle where the bullet had penetrated his body.

Jim slowly looked to see the Secret Service agents standing at the end of his bed. His look was to be expected, as these were the last people on the planet that Jim wanted to see.

"I want a phone, Agent Womack," was all Jim said.

"It's not that easy, Jim. Many people want you dead, and it's best we let them think that's the case," said Agent Womack.

"You said you'd protect me. Good job," said Jim in a sarcastic tone but not laughing at all.

Agent Womack walked over next to his bed. "Jim, your safety was my responsibility, and I sincerely apologize for what happened."

"What did happen, Agent?" asked Jim.

Agent Womack looked at Director Beine and then back to Jim. "We don't know yet. All we know is Roy isn't the one that shot you. As I said, many people want you dead."

Jim felt tears start in his eyes. "Roy mentioned my wife. Do you know where my family is?"

Agent Womack raised his hand with a smile, "They're fine and they have no idea of anything happening. Your wife tried to call your cell phone one time. We took the liberty of texting her back saying you're in a late meeting tonight, and you'd call her in the morning. It'll give us some time to sort this thing out."

A huge sense of relief came over Jim. At least his family was okay, and the ghost of Roy haunting his dreams seemed to be fading a bit. Jim leaned back into his pillow while taking a deep sigh.

Jim then suddenly looked up at Agent Womack. "What do you mean let them think I'm dead?"

Agent Womack said, "The morgue director just signed your death certificate."

The look of shock came over Jim's face, "What . . . what . . ."

Agent Womack interrupted him, "Look, Jim. We know you don't realize it, but some very powerful people want you dead. Roy's involved with one of the most influential crime organizations in the world, especially in terms of financial crimes. The information you gave him went directly to this group. Once the refinery moved forward, they couldn't afford a loose connection to their information. With you dead, there's no lead that could connect them. As I said, it's better to let them think that's the case."

Jim shook his head, "No . . . No way. I can't just go off the grid and go into hiding. My family deserves better than this."

Agent Womack interrupted him again. "Jim, listen to me carefully. There're only a handful of assassins in this world, and they're very hard to find. A target left alive is bad for their business, and they'll complete their assignment one way or another. Your assassin's probably on the county website right now looking for your death certificate."

Agent Womack pointed his finger straight at Jim, "I promise you this. If you walk out of this hospital as Jim Jackson, then you're dead."

"What do we do now?" asked a very anxious and confused Jim.

"You're going to get well, and then you're going to give some powerful people a call from the grave."

Chapter 37—Understanding

Plaza Hotel—San Antonio, Texas

The refinery project was nine months into full swing, and the structure began to take definite form. The project was being called one of the engineering marvels of the world, and had become the very symbol of what America could do once she got her act together.

Although things looked good to most observers, Udaya had a very different feeling. He was buried in the computer screen at 1:30 A.M., unable to sleep. He repeatedly studied the process drawings that were in front of him, and evaluated the cause and effect matrix the safety system program had developed. He pulled out every ounce of brainpower he had to understand what Manish was trying to accomplish.

The past months had been the most stressful of his entire life. All the designs, programming, meetings, testing, plans were enough to cause the best employees to crumple under the pressure. But the added knowledge that something wasn't right with the process added exponentially to the situation. They were very close to running the initial tests on the refinery, and Udaya was overcome with fear. Although thousands of people were contributing to the project, only Udaya and Manish had a complete technical understanding of the entire process. Most large refineries had sophisticated computer simulations developed prior to commissioning, but Manish ordered this step to be omitted for the sake of speed. Missing this step didn't provide the empirical data Udaya needed to articulate his concerns.

Others worked on their specific aspects of the project, and had no reason to worry about other components of the massive refinery. Manish had done a masterful job of keeping any additional advanced process control engineers off the project, leaving only himself and Udaya to understand how the system really worked. People were simply connecting equipment and running wires. Details on when and how they operated were up to others, so no real oversight was provided except by Manish, who had Brian Larson's total faith. The Department of Energy and OSHA had their teams to evaluate different elements of the system, but none had the advanced chemistry knowledge to truly understand what was going on.

Udaya struggled to understand exactly what Manish was trying to accomplish, without asking him to explain the designs. To date, all the systems had been installed exactly as planned and on schedule, and now they were only a few days away from beginning initial testing on the refining process itself. The final pieces of the cracking unit were being installed this week, so Udaya figured plant-wide process tests would begin within two weeks.

The more Udaya reviewed the drawings, the more convinced he became that the plant would explode. Over the duration of the project, Manish had inserted several process variables into the control system and safety system, also known as a bypass, which allowed pressures and temperatures to rise to unacceptable levels in the reaction process without the safety system engaging. These variables were data fields on the computer screen that allowed key set points to be overridden. Only Manish and Udaya had password access to this screen, but the fact it was even there made Udaya's heart skip a beat every time he thought about it.

Although the extreme pressure of the catalytic cracking unit was concerning enough, Udaya was absolutely frightened of the process control system on the sulphur recovery unit. Udaya knew an advanced extraction unit was required for this plant, because a wide variety of crude oil would be used to supply the massive refinery. Most all crude oil that entered the refinery would have up to five percent sulphur, so they had to break it down into a usable form.

Among the first separation phases of raw petroleum was to add a catalyst to form hydrogen sulphide. The sulphide created a toxic gas that needed further treatment. The usual process involved heating the liquid again and then condensing the product. The heated stream enters another set of reactors that break down the product into a collection filter.

For every refinery Udaya had been involved with, the sulphur recovery plant went through an extensive shutdown process for any safety issue, but not in the case of this refinery. To make matters worse, the only shutdown process that Udaya could see was the closing of a major downstream valve system. Since the upstream pumps would continue operating instead of shutting down, the sulphur vapors would be routed to a release valve, and would essentially blow pure liquid hydrogen sulfide directly onto extraordinarily hot equipment. The result would be the world's largest sulphur dioxide cloud spreading all over San Antonio. As typical in an emergency, all the employees would evacuate and the system would simply keep running. The cloud would continue to billow as long as there was raw petroleum in the storage tanks, and could last for days.

Udaya came to an unfathomable conclusion. Manish had developed a system that would blow the entire facility, and then would generate a continuous sulphur gas cloud, possibly making thousands of people extremely ill, if not cause death. He would kill the project, and take another step to destroying America's reputation in the world. Not only was Udaya scared for his life, but his career would be over if he lived. All he had worked for was about to be destroyed. Udaya had visions of the Union Carbide accident at the plant in Bhopal, India, where a toxic gas cloud killed thousands of local residents. This disaster would be equally as devastating, and would change the United States' position in the world economy for decades to come.

Udaya felt the small beads of sweat forming on his forehead. He had nowhere to turn. He couldn't look up sulphur gas cloud on the Internet, because he would be questioned. He couldn't call his boss, because he would tell Udaya to shut up and continue his work.

He couldn't call Brian Larson, because he was a close associate and friend of Manish. As far as Udaya could tell, there wasn't another soul on this project who had the appropriate background to discuss his concerns. He was literally trapped. All the bad feelings he had about the project were hitting squarely in his gut now. He had to do something.

"What're you working on so late?" asked Manish.

Udaya almost jumped out of his chair, as he didn't hear a soul enter the room. Udaya scrambled a thousand thoughts in his mind. He was scared to death of this situation, and now he was looking the devil straight in the eye. He sensed Manish knew something was up.

"Just verifying the code to the drawings. We had good field installation tests over the past few weeks, so I have some time to make sure it all matches up. Triple checking," said a nervous Udaya.

"Interesting," said Manish in a curious but skeptical tone. "It looks like the sulphur extraction drawings you're reviewing. That's been completed for a couple of months. Why are you going back to it again?"

Manish leaned on the computer table, and folded his arms across his chest. He positioned himself to look Udaya straight in the eye. Udaya assumed Manish's question wasn't one of genuine technical interest; he wanted a detailed answer to understand Udaya's curiosity.

"I'm going over every system. Here are my notes for the past several nights," said Udaya as he slid over his extensive notebook with all documentation on the different processes.

Udaya continued while trying to avoid eye contact, "I'm making sure all the electrical, controls, and processes reconcile. Making code changes during startup causes huge delays. Just making certain that electrical isn't the cause for holding up things."

Manish pulled the notebook towards himself, obviously looking for something on the pages, "Hmmm. Have you found any problems?"

Udaya slowly responded and looked Manish in the eye, "A few errors. But I'm confident the process will perform the way it's supposed to."

Manish paused for a moment as he felt the tension between them. "Well, that's why they say we're the best. We're going to find out."

Manish gave Udaya a knowing look, then removed himself from the table and exited the room.

Udaya sat by himself in the room for another hour. His concern had turned into genuine fear. He had to do something.

Chapter 38—Priorities

Washington, D.C.

It was close to the end of the day, and Jenny couldn't wait for this evening. She and Brian had a date planned for tonight, and she was excited about an evening alone with him. With him spending most of his time in San Antonio nowadays, their long distance relationship could be stressful sometimes. They spoke every day, but now that he was back in her life, she longed to be with him more. She decided to call Brian about the plans for the night.

Brian answered, "Hey Jenny."

Jenny said, "Hey, what's going on?"

Brian sighed, "You know, the usual. Meetings every 30 minutes, asshole project managers, technical delays, all the typical stuff."

Jenny was puzzled. "What? Wait a minute. Are you in San Antonio?"

Brian said, "Uh, yes. Where else would I be?"

Jenny couldn't believe her ears. "I don't believe this. You made a promise that we'd go out tonight. I've been looking forward to this all week, and now this. We haven't seen each other in two weeks, and you just forget! I guess I should expect this from you."

Brian said, "Oh Jenny, I can't believe it. I'm so sorry. I . . . I can catch a government plane somehow. I can be there in four hours. I'll ask Agent Womack to pull a few strings . . ."

"That's not the point, Brian! You made a promise that our relationship would be a priority, not something you think about every now and then," said Jenny.

The phone was silent, neither of them saying a word.

Brian finally said, "Come on, Jenny. You know how I feel about you. Don't be unreasonable, this is a huge challenge."

Jenny fired back, "Here you go again. You . . . You . . . You. What do you think I've been doing? I've had to deal with no less than five Congressmen today alone. I get official requests for information every day from Congress, the White House, the press, you name it. Just so you're aware, the price of oil is being watched pretty closely. And whose job is that, oh yeah, it's mine. Don't lecture me about challenges, Brian."

Brian said, "Calm down. We've been through too much. Don't make this bigger than it is. I'll be there later tonight, and we can have the weekend. Everything's fine."

"Don't bother," said Jenny as she hung up the phone.

Jenny couldn't believe it. She had fallen again for Brian, and now she was already a second thought to him; his career was once again his priority. Jenny stared at the stack of paperwork on her desk, but just decided to leave it for the day. Her cell phone continuously rang with calls from Brian, but she refused to answer.

Jenny gave a frustrated scream, "Ahhh!"

She quickly grabbed her things and left the office. The Secret Service agent outside her door gave chase. "Dr. Liepert, where are we going?"

Jenny didn't even turn to answer him directly. "We're going to pick up some Chinese food and then you're driving me home."

The agent quickly spoke into his microphone, making no further attempt at conversation. Jenny walked out the front of the office building, and a car magically pulled up for her. She and the agent jumped in the back, and it pulled away. Jenny didn't know what to think. She understood the pressure Brian was under, and felt selfish she expected any attention. But then again, she had been more than patient with their relationship. She had the right to be upset, as her job was just as stressful and she needed him around, if only occasionally. They made a commitment to get through this together, but it was getting more and more difficult.

When they finally got to her town home, Jenny grabbed her purse and food and headed directly toward her door. The agent dutifully followed her, never letting her out of his sight. As they reached the door, he told her to wait until he checked it out.

"No way," said Jenny. "This is my place, my food, and my time. I just need to be left alone."

The agent gave a smile and said, "Okay. Have a good evening."

Jenny hesitated for a moment, as the agent gave up way too easily. She expected a huge fight, as they never let her enter any room without thoroughly checking it out first. Jenny shrugged off the thought, and searched for her keys.

The agent said, "Here, allow me."

He unlocked the door, and Jenny rushed through. As she entered her foyer, the aroma of Italian food was in the air. She slowly walked through the small hallway into the main living area, and saw Brian leaning up against the kitchen counter with a freshly opened bottle of Cabernet and a candlelight dinner ready for her.

Jenny gave him a huge smile. "Oh, you're such a jerk."

Brian said, "You still hang up the phone on me? Are you ever going to quit doing that?"

Jenny dropped her things and sprinted to Brian. As they gave each other a huge hug Brian said, "You're all I think about, Jenny. I won't let you down again, ever."

Jenny got a huge feeling of satisfaction and relief. They were going to make it work.

Agent Womack walked out the door of the apartment, doing his best to stay quiet and not interfere with Brian and Jenny. He gave a smile to the other agent standing outside the door.

Jenny's agent said, "How did it go in there? Man, she was pissed."

Agent Womack said, "Let's just say, I think it's going to be a good night for Mr. Larson."

They both laughed a bit, and then Agent Womack said, "Let them have their fun. The next few weeks are going to be intense."

Chapter 39—Entrapment

Home of Gary Blackmon—Napa Valley, California

As predicted by the President, oil and gas prices steadily declined and the stock market slowly recovered. The President was being considered one of the best leaders since Roosevelt, and Brian was seen as the symbol of American pride.

Everything might be better from a United States economy standpoint, but things definitely weren't good for the oil and gas traders, especially those who invested their entire future on the rise in prices. Several members of the Impending Order were close to bankruptcy, and they were getting desperate. Their financial influence was threatened, and these men had full intentions of putting a stop to it. Dissension within their group was a major possibility, made all the more difficult because of their secrecy. Most members felt that Gary Blackmon wasn't up to the task, and were especially skeptical of Gary's confidence in Roy. The men were frightened for their future, and needed a disaster to happen in the oil and gas market.

Gary Blackmon called another meeting at his estate with the same players attending, including Roy. This meeting didn't have all the formalities of the previous meetings, and none of the men bothered to shake hands.

Gary started the meeting: "Gentlemen, the last nine months have seen the inverse of what we predicted for oil futures, and now we sit on a precipice. We either take immediate and dramatic action, or our investments become worthless."

All the men in the room gave somewhat of a nod, but nobody uttered a word.

Gary continued, "Roy and I have been closely analyzing this project. It's our opinion that dramatic steps need to be taken, and now's the time. The security on the project is extremely high, and all companies and employees involved with the project are under extreme pressure to perform to their assigned goals. Their objectives are clear, and it's very difficult to find a single individual or entity that's not committed to fulfilling their obligations. So much so, we've been unsuccessful finding anyone on the inside that will support our cause."

Roy said, "Killing a project is a much more difficult task than influencing the outcome of a project. Over my career, my job was more to influence who got what project, who sold land, what company received certain orders, things like that. Now we find ourselves in a position of having to cut the head off the beast, and derailing all hope of this project being successful."

Roy looked around the room, and noticed all the men and the different signs they gave. A few of them were obviously nervous, and a few were mad as hell.

Roy said, "Our approach to killing this project is two-pronged. First we're . . ."

Roy paused as one of the wait staff approached Gary. The waiter had a look of concern on his face, as he was seriously breaking protocol by approaching during one of these back porch meetings without being asked. Gary turned to the waiter with a look of rage on his face, as there was no more important a topic in his life than the one at hand.

The waiter moved near Gary and said in a very low tone, "Mr. Blackmon, you have a phone call that's rather important."

Gary responded back in a low voice, "What the hell are you doing? Nobody interrupts these meetings!"

The nervous waiter said, "Yes sir. Your instructions are clear. But I . . . I believe you should take this call."

Gary asked with an angered impatience, "Who is it?"

The waiter turned to look at the men at the table, doing their best to hear what he was saying. The waiter moved in closer to Gary and spoke very low, "He asked for Gary Blackmon, the leader of the Impending Order."

Gary's shoulders slumped and the breath left his chest. He turned and stared at the men. *Somebody at the table is talking* was all Gary thought. He was being set up. Gary quickly came up with a lie.

Gary looked at the waiter, and then back to the men again. "Gentlemen, this seems to be an urgent call from my trading house in Asia. I have to take this call. Please give me a moment."

Gary removed himself from the table without looking the men in the eye. The table let out a collective moan, obviously pissed and concerned as Gary left the table. The men continued to sit there, gave each other uneasy looks and didn't say a word.

Gary rushed into his office. A million thoughts ran through his mind. *Did the men at the table give him up? None of them would be here if this was a setup. Why would they do that? Too much is at stake.*

Gary paused for a moment before picking up the phone, trying to get focused on the call. After a few moments, he picked up the receiver and pressed the line with the flashing light. "Gary."

"Good evening, Mr. Blackmon. How's your meeting going tonight?" said the man on the phone in a flat tone.

Gary spun to look out his office window and saw the men gathered on his patio. They all seemed to still be sitting in their chairs waiting for his return.

"Who the hell is this? What meeting are you talking about?" said Gary.

The man said, "Mr. Blackmon, don't play stupid with me. I know the Impending Order is planning on stopping the refinery. Trust me; nobody knows this better than me."

Gary quit breathing for a moment and contemplated the words. Stopping the refinery? Nobody better than me? Gary didn't know what to make of the comment, but knew enough not to incriminate himself without more information.

"Who is this? You have five seconds to answer before I hang up the phone," said Gary.

Without hesitation, the man said, "This is Jim Jackson."

Gary's mind scrambled. Jim Jackson? The name rang a bell, but he knew so many people. Gary recollected Roy's office, and then the unmistakable memory of the file came to his mind. The assassination. This man was dead. The sniper confirmed the death certificate. Jim Jackson, surely not . . . Gary felt like a punch hit his stomach. The line was silent for several moments.

Gary found it difficult to speak. "Uh . . . the name doesn't . . . I don't recognize the name . . ."

"Just stop. You know exactly who I am. You tried to end my life, and now you'll pay me back for your failure," said Jim Jackson.

Gary had answered the phone while standing at his desk, hoping for a short conversation. He suddenly felt the urge to sit down. Gary slowly moved around his desk to have a seat and collect his thoughts properly. A dead man from the past. Knowledge of Gary's involvement. Knowledge of the Impending Order. How could he have this information? Gary saw his entire life flash in front of his eyes.

"Who . . . How . . . . how do you know all this? What do you want?" was all Gary managed to say.

Jim said, "After spending three months in rehabilitation and a full seven months in hiding, you tend to grow resentful towards the man that ruined your life. I want mine back."

Gary now understood. He had here a mentally unstable man who wanted revenge. Gary had a loose end that could cause a devastating blow to his way of life. This problem needed to be dealt with.

Gary said, "Okay, Mr. Jackson, what do you want?"

"I want what you want. I want money. And a lot more than what Roy paid me," said Jim.

Gary heard the words, but wasn't really listening. Gary pieced things together. Jim said he was in hiding. If Jim was in hiding, then only the government could accomplish such an act as forging a death certificate. This was a setup of some sort. If Jim was in hiding, then he had to be working for the government.

"Why would I give you money? You have nothing on me," said Gary.

"I have nothing? That's interesting. It seems to me I have payment records from Roy Ritchey giving you insight to the refinery. I was having a meeting with Roy when he brought up your name, and then I was shot. I have full access to the refinery now. My efforts to destroy you might be futile, but then again, I might be able to deliver a serious blow to your interests. We can then discover publicly if I have anything on you or not. That's an option if you choose it," said Jim Jackson in a confident voice.

"How are you working for the refinery?" asked Gary.

Jim said, "After your attempt on my life, the government became concerned it was a coordinated attack on the refinery leaders. They hoped that faking my death would cause other actions, and lead them to the real killers."

Gary sat silent on the phone, not knowing how to respond to this.

Jim continued, "Since nothing else has happened, they felt it wiser to move me outside of Washington. It's kind of strange actually, because nobody was around when I got shot except for Roy. Only the Secret Service knows my gunshot was an attempted assassination. To everybody else, I was simply mugged and shot coming out of a convenience store. Other than the three months missed in rehab, I'm still the same Jim Jackson. Not many people pause to look at the coroner's website for death certificates."

Gary tried to comprehend it all. No doubt the man had information that would dramatically affect his interests. One half of Gary wanted to put a bullet in Roy for mentioning his name; the other half had a glimmer of hope as a man on the inside gave him a call.

A still very skeptical Gary said, "You mentioned full access to the refinery. What do you mean by this?"

Jim said, "By full, I mean my office is right next to Brian Larson's office. We're in daily meetings together. I have the highest access as

I'm the refinery's chief legal counsel. I know you want him dead, so maybe we can work out an agreement."

Gary about jumped out of his chair. Jim said the words he had been searching for nine months. Gary heard the words "Brian Larson." He did his best to maintain his composure, still not fully understanding the purpose of the phone call.

"What are you proposing, Mr. Jackson?" asked Gary in a very slow tone.

Jim said, "I've done my homework over the past several months. Your trading houses are overly extended on oil and gas futures, and I know about the SEC investigation into you cornering the energy market. If I was to bet, you didn't short your positions because you would be indicted for price fixing. What's wrong, Mr. Blackmon; did you have visions of Nelson Hunt and his downfall?"

Gary remained silent. Nobody knew of the investigation, not even his senior advisors, and definitely not the other members of the Impending Order.

Jim said, "Wait, now that I think about it, do the other members of your club know about this? Wow, you really should consider my offer or you'll be the one taking a bullet."

Gary said, "What do you want, Mr. Jackson?"

Jim said, "Knowing what I know about your organization, and knowing what I know about Roy Ritchey, I can expect a pretty major event to occur shortly. All magically causing the price of oil & gas futures to rise."

Gary said, "Go on."

Jim said, "I almost lost my life. I've suffered more than most people can imagine. I have been dead, come back to life, and am now constantly looking over my shoulder. I won't stand aside and let others benefit while I suffer. I can help you take down the refinery, but it'll cost you dearly."

Gary listened intently, "Go on."

Jim never hesitated. "Ten million dollars. One million for each month of my suffering. All the money up front. You give me the ten million, and I'll give you the details you need. I'll call back in fifteen minutes."

The phone went silent. Gary slowly put the phone receiver in its cradle, and then looked back at his patio. All the men were still there. They all had equal interest in stopping the refinery, mostly because of their blind faith in Gary. Jim Jackson could possibly give him the break they needed. Coming up with the ten million dollars was more difficult today than it was a year ago, but they could do it. But all of this was based upon a man's word who Gary had tried to murder. Gary was desperate, and he made his decision.

Gary returned to the table and offered no explanation to the group. "We have a man on the inside of the leadership team of the refinery. He's intimately involved with the directions, decisions, schedules and tasks for the project. He'll give us all the insight we need, and most importantly, give us the movements of the key members of the leadership team. We're going to take out Brian Larson."

Some of the men got a grin on their face. Others seemed upset about this comment, obviously the first time they personally had blood on their hands.

Roy was in total shock. Roy worked with Gary closely over the past several months, and Gary never mentioned having anybody on the inside. He cut his eyes to Gary's office, wondering who in hell he talked to. Could Gary be lying? Roy decided against saying anything, and remained silent.

"Our second angle is the major oil transfer station near Victoria, Texas. This station is the primary crude pumping system for the new Corpus Christi Pipeline that feeds the refinery. Roy managed to get access to the station with his connections. He's going to enter the station disguised as a service technician, but will in fact plant an explosive device. The explosion will only delay the pipeline for a few months, but the damage will be severe enough to make a difference."

Gary looked around. "We're going to destroy the pumping station and assassinate Mr. Larson on the same day. Our media insiders will print the proper stories of this being a coordinated terrorist attack."

Gary gave the table a serious look: "Be prepared, gentlemen, as oil and gas prices will rise dramatically. I can't tell you the exact date as of yet, so have your triggers ready for the financial transactions."

The table was quiet for several moments. The men imagined the markets and their response to Brian Larson's death, and then the destruction of the station. These actions would definitely send fear into society, and artificially inflate the price of oil and gas.

One of the men turned directly to Roy. "I remember distinctly you sitting at this very table, promising the derailment of the refinery ten months ago. Why in the hell should we trust you again?"

Roy wanted to get up and punch this guy in the mouth. Instead he said, "I did predict this. I told you what was going to happen, before anyone else. We all have considerable assets at risk in this situation. This thing snowballed faster than anyone imagined it could. I thought it best to take a step back to have the most impact. Listen closer next time."

To Roy's surprise, the man said, "You think you intimidate me?"

Gary had enough to worry about on this night, and wanted no part in a petty alpha-male moment.

Gary said, "Alright, that's enough. I need a million from each of you in the account. Meeting's over. Mr. Ritchey, you stay here as there are some things to discuss."

Jim Jackson hung up the phone after his second call with Gary, only this time, Roy was on the phone as well. Jim informed Gary of the bank account information, and gave a few details on how to find Brian, promising more details once the money was transferred. Hearing the actual sound of Roy's voice still shook Jim to the core. The familiar sick feeling showed up again.

Agent Womack said, "Jim, our initial readings are that they took the bait. Thanks for doing this. This will give us the hard evidence we need to bring them down."

Chapter 40—Apprehension

Department of Energy /Fossil Fuel Division
Washington D.C.

Jenny was working in her office when Glen Abbott walked in the room. She gave him a pleasant smile.

"You know, Jenny, you can't get that smile off your face since you and Brian got back together," said Glen.

Jenny smiled even wider, and waved him off, "We're working on it, but it's always a struggle. Our lives are crazy. I had forgotten how committed Brian is to his work once he gets going. But even I have to admit, I'm thrilled to see him working this time!"

They laughed for a few moments and then Glen said, "Hey, Jim Jackson's here and wants a few minutes of your time. He's been working pretty hard in helping us out on all the pipeline land deals, so I told him I would see if I could twist your arm to spend a few minutes with him."

"Oh my gosh! Jim's here? I haven't seen him since the mugging. Is everything okay?" asked Jenny.

"You know, after the accident, he really became introverted. He just keeps to himself," said Glen.

Jenny shook her head. With all the things on her plate plus her weekend planned with Brian, she didn't have the time for a long meeting, but really wanted to at least say hello to Jim.

"Okay. I've got a few minutes," said Jenny.

Glen said "alright" and left her office. A few moments later she heard a knock, and Jim walked in. Jenny was shocked at his appearance. He had lost a lot of weight, had much more gray hair, more wrinkles, and shocking dark spots under his eyes. It seemed he hadn't slept in months. The usual salesman attitude seemed much lower key.

"Hi Jenny," said Jim in a low tone. "Thanks for taking a few minutes to talk."

Jenny said, "That's alright, Jim. I haven't seen you since the accident. Is everything okay? I'm so sorry."

Jim gave a knowing and appreciative gesture. "Yes, it's been quite a while. Brian and his team keep me pretty busy fighting all the lawsuits. Things are a little stressful right now, but I'll make it."

Jenny and Jim sat there for a few moments, neither knowing what to say next. Jim wanted to tell Jenny to run to the nearest safe house and stay there for the next five years. He was almost in tears, and Jenny sat there not knowing what to say.

"You know, Jim," said Jenny, "everybody needs a little time away. Like tonight, I'm traveling to San Antonio. Brian and I are spending a few days together. Going back to our college days, we used to take frequent float trips down the Guadalupe River, and we're doing it tomorrow and Friday. It's a great time, and a good getaway from everything. Maybe you should do the same with your family. Just get away for a while."

Jim said, "Yes. Maybe I should. Brian mentioned your plans."

When Jim entered the room, he hoped to find a way to let her know how much he cared for her and the project, and her comments only cemented his thoughts more. He didn't want her in any danger, and didn't like the steps he had taken over the past few days to put her right in the middle of the storm.

Jim said, "Your trip sounds great. It's a cool story how you and Brian have gotten back together after all these years. You know hearts are breaking all over Washington."

Jenny smiled, "Jim, that story was for you to take a hint."

Jim said, "I got it, I got it. Take some time with my family before I die of a heart attack or exhaustion. Well Jenny, I just wanted to say hello."

Jenny said, "Okay. Take care of yourself."

Jim stood up from his chair, and turned to Jenny with a sincere look, "You too, Jenny."

After Jim left the office, Jenny sat just staring at the door. She had no idea what to make of the conversation. Jim's appearance, his demeanor and his tone didn't add up. Jenny got her thoughts back together. She had a few more things to finish up before heading to the airport and her weekend with Brian.

On the way out of the building, Jim called Agent Womack.

"Womack," was the answer on the line.

"Hey, I think it's time for the call," said Jim in a depressed tone.

"Okay Jim," said Agent Womack. "Where are you right now?"

"I just left Dr. Liepert's office. I wanted to drop by and say hello. I hadn't talked to her face to face in months," said Jim, knowing what came next.

"Wait. You were in Jenny's office? You're supposed to go directly home and get in hiding with your family! Did you tell her anything you shouldn't have?" asked a highly concerned Agent Womack.

Jim quickly responded, "No, no. I just stopped by to say hello, and catch up. She let me know of her plans with Brian this weekend, and recommended I do the same. She said I looked like shit in so many words, and told me to take a vacation. She didn't tell me more than what you already told me. She's not aware of anything. I simply said hello. I'm just worried about her."

Agent Womack paused on the phone a few minutes, half pissed that Jim would do this; half understanding he cared for Jenny, and was scared to death of what might happen.

"Jim, no more unannounced visits. We're already taking a risk on this thing. No more surprises. Alright?" said Agent Womack in a direct but polite tone.

"Understood," said Jim.

"Okay, conference-call in Roy so we can listen to the conversation. Let him know everything you know about their schedule. After we get off the phone, I want you to take my and Jenny's advice, and take your family on a long getaway somewhere. Lay low until I contact you. Don't let anyone know where you're staying," said Agent Womack.

Jim asked, "What about Brian and Jenny? What's to become of them . . . ?"

Agent Womack said, "We have it covered. Just do your job."

Jim took a deep breath and asked the question he'd been dreading, "What about me, Agent Womack? Should I prepare for a prison sentence once all this is finished?"

Agent Womack didn't have an answer. "Jim. I'm not sure. As a policy, we always follow through on our crimes. No doubt your efforts will be acknowledged, but I have no way of knowing what that really means. Let's just do our jobs right now, and let's get through this mess."

Jim gave an exasperated sigh. He shook again, always getting this feeling when talking with Roy. Jim had had a few conversations with him over the past week, and each time was a dreaded moment. Jim knew this weekend was the end point he had been thinking about constantly, and he was now completely weary of the situation.

Jim dialed Roy's cell phone with Agent Womack conferenced in the call. Roy quickly answered, "The money's in your account. Did you get what we need?"

"Dr. Liepert and Brian Larson are sharing the next two days together. They're meeting in San Antonio. Their plan is to float down the Guadalupe River during the day on Thursday and then to go to a bar called Gruene Hall in the evening. Her flight to San Antonio leaves tonight."

Roy hung up the phone without saying a word. Jim did the same, and hit the power button on his cell phone. Jim almost sprinted to his car, and then hit the road to Maine. He was scared sick about Brian and Jenny, and only wanted the whole situation out of his mind. He hoped to never see Washington D.C. again.

Chapter 41—Anticipation

Guadalupe River—Near New Braunfels, Texas

Brian and Jenny were giddy. Their relationship continued to grow, and now they were spending a weekend together near their college roots. The refinery was a week from initial testing, so Brian wanted to take the time off for a few days. Once the testing started, he figured they would be working non-stop for at least the next month.

Brian had been planning this trip for some time, and had called Jenny last week to surprise her. One of their favorite things to do in college was to float down the Guadalupe River past the Canyon Lake dam. Brian and Jenny, usually with a few friends, would stay at a cheap hotel in New Braunfels, hit some local barbeque joint for food to go, and spend the night in the parking lot of the hotel eating the food and drinking way too much beer and cheap wine. Once they eventually got up on Saturday, they would spend an entire afternoon floating down the river, and then dance the night away to country music at Gruene Hall until early in the morning.

As Brian and Jenny walked out of the door of their room at the Plaza Hotel, Brian was surprised to see three Secret Service agents. He had become used to the security, but this seemed over the top. Brian gave a quick nod of hello to the gentlemen, long accustomed to not arguing about the situation. When they made it out the door of the hotel lobby, Jenny started laughing out loud when she saw the old Jeep CJ-5 waiting for them; it was almost identical to the Jeep Brian had in college. Then Jenny screamed with excitement when she saw Chase Stockton and his wife standing next to the Jeep. Everybody exchanged hugs and hellos and then quickly hopped in the Jeep. Brian apologized for all the security as three other cars pulled out with them from the hotel. Brian had strict orders on the route to take from San Antonio to New Braunfels, but didn't even bother telling everyone these details.

They finally made their way to the river, where Brian and Jenny had several people ask for their autographs. This was the first time either of them had been to a real public place together. All the attention caught them off guard, but made them feel good at the same time.

As they got to the water, the two girls quickly hopped on their tubes and were on their way. They did a masterful job avoiding getting too wet in the cold water. Brian and Chase were not quite as capable in avoiding the cold water, as they had a little more work to do. They laughed out loud while they figured out a way to get the beer cooler situated in a tube. It was always a trick to set it just right so as to not fall through the inner-tube hole. This effort pretty much made up all the work required for the entire day. Once they were floating down the river, they talked non-stop with each other. Chase and Brian talked about all the college days, refinery situations and work stories. Jenny and Chase's wife talked about all the crazy stories on television, and how people were coming out of the woodwork for details of Brian and Jenny in their college days. Brian laughed at the thought of the other agents floating behind them. The more he drank, the less he thought about them even being around at all.

Today was a great day. Brian took some time to notice the environment around central Texas. They were slowly going around a slow bend in the river called Horseshoe Loop. He noticed the trees, the river rocks, and the whole feel of the historic river in the Texas Hill Country. He reflected on how much he missed during his time with GeoGlobal. Now here he was, with Jenny and best friends, and thought he could have had any of this at any time. He and Jenny caught each other's eyes, and she splashed cold water all over him. What a great day. He was just a fool.

The sniper was a little out of his element. Most of his work kept him in an urban environment, and he wasn't accustomed to all the camouflage and outdoor gear required in the woods. But the sniper had a good employer, and he would perform his duty whenever or wherever requested. He was in the Caribbean enjoying his fortunes from the previous kill when Gary called, and was stunned to learn his effort had been a miss. The fact that he was deceived by the government with a death certificate only added to the humiliation. Now, he was more committed than ever about this task, needing to get Mr. Blackmon back on his good side.

Because of the short notice, the sniper didn't have time to gather the required gear. He flew directly from the Caribbean to San Antonio, and arranged his weapons through a local pawn shop. He took a big risk purchasing his weapons locally, as these were among the first places investigated after a murder. But he could go into hiding for a long time. He had plenty of money and just needed to finish this one item. The elimination of Brian would make him a star in the eyes of the Impending Order, and make his life quite comfortable for a long time.

He left the airport in his rented SUV and immediately went to a supercenter. He invaded the sporting/hunting section of the store, and purchased hiking boots, camouflage clothes, energy bars, high-powered binoculars, camouflage cantina and black makeup to cover his face. He was going to be completely hidden in the woods for this activity.

Before leaving the Caribbean, he arranged a late night visit to a local pawn shop. People of his profession had many underground connections to the required equipment. The sniper arrived at the pawn shop late in the evening, and went to the side door. Just as promised, the door was open, and he selected any weapon he wanted. The arrangement was quite simple. Enter the shop, get what you need, and leave five thousand dollars in an envelope. No need for discussions with anyone. The sniper selected a long range rifle and a pistol for his assignment.

After a restless night in his SUV, the sniper drove to his chosen location right before dawn. He dressed for the hike and the task of finding the perfect spot. He put on the camouflage gear and spread the black makeup all over his face. He retrieved his guns and rechecked everything, making sure there was no reason to come back except for a sprint after the deed was done.

As he walked through the woods, he was surprised to see the ground wasn't nearly as covered as it looked in the satellite images. What seemed to be a deep thicket was actually a pretty open space between the trees, and he realized finding a place to hide in the cover was going to be harder than he thought. Suddenly a bush in the distance shook violently, and he stopped in his tracks. He let out a huge sigh of relief when a doe and her fawn started running up the riverbank to get away. His heart nearly quit beating for a moment, and then it felt like it was going to jump from his chest. He cussed out loud that he was that nervous, but also came to a quick realization that he wasn't as mentally prepared as he should be.

He assumed that if the deer felt this was a good spot to hide, then it was a good one for him. The sniper slowly took a seat on the ground, and situated the thick honeysuckle bush all around him. He separated the vines for a nice viewing portal of the river bend, and adjusted his binoculars well enough to see anybody floating down the river. He placed the rifle and the pistol immediately to his right, and felt this situation was as good as it would get.

After several hours, he started to get weary and very tired. The sniper was amazed at how many people were floating down the river. He assumed a few people would come by, but not hundreds. All the guys had on hats and sunglasses, and the women had on bikinis with their hair pulled back. Over time, he could barely distinguish anyone. He had been sitting under the tree in the Texas heat for over seven hours, and his patience ran thin. The sniper had encounters with raccoons, bugs, armadillos and a grass snake, and wanted badly to get out of this place. He thought he'd missed them somehow.

The sniper stayed focused, directing his binoculars at each face on the river, having Brian and Jenny's faces etched into his mind. Then slowly, a group of seven people came into his focus. He adjusted his binoculars and saw the unmistakable face of Brian Larson. Dr. Liepert was floating pretty close to him, with another couple nearby. Surrounding the group were three other gentlemen, who seemed to be concentrating on everything except the river, and weren't drinking. The men had the look of security agents. He'd found his target.

The sniper's adrenaline rose. He put down the binoculars and moved to one knee, setting his body in a stable position. He slowly reached down to grab his rifle, and locked the chamber. His rifle was lifted to put Brian in his scope.

Brian thought about the evening to come. It was going to be a great time. He hadn't two-stepped in years, and wondered if he could still do it. He didn't bother to look at who was playing at Gruene Hall tonight. There was no telling, as a ton of different bands play the bar as they tour through Texas. Cold beer and dancing at the oldest dance hall in Texas. Did it get any better than that? He hoped it was somebody like . . . .

Brian heard the splashes, and turned to look at the commotion. He saw two of the Secret Service agents swimming as fast as they could toward him, as the other agent swam towards Jenny. He just sat in his tube, half drunk, holding his beer as the agents got closer.

What the hell are they doing? Damn, that river's cold, why are they going for a swim? thought Brian.

Suddenly one of the agents dove under the water beneath his tube and lifted one side of his tube, pitching Brian towards the water. The other agent jumped out of the river and pushed down on the other side of this tube, then reached up to put Brian in a total head lock.

Brian was pulled straight out of the tube just like a professional wrestler had a hold of him.

Brian screamed, "What the hell!!!" as he went diving headfirst straight into the water with the beer still in his hand.

"Freeze, drop the weapon!" shouted the Secret Service agent dressed in camouflage almost identical to the sniper's, coming seemingly out of thin air. The sniper turned and saw the agent with his gun focused squarely on him, and he noticed other agents sprinting through the woods toward his position. The sniper grabbed his pistol which he had positioned on the ground for quick access, and took quick aim at the agent.

Brian wrestled as hard as he could underwater, but couldn't get out of the neck hold. Somehow the agent maintained the headlock, but positioned his body directly behind Brian's back. Brian felt them surfacing up, and inhaled as much as he could when they came out of the water. The other agent moved directly in front of Brian, and put another headlock around him and the other agent. They created a three-layer pancake floating in the water, completely surrounding Brian. Brian saw Jenny in a similar situation, essentially cocooned completely by the third agent, just bobbing in the water. Brian was in a total state of drunken confusion.

Then he heard the gunshots.

Without hesitation, the agent pulled the trigger and shot the sniper between his left arm and torso. The sniper spun to his left and landed on the ground, with a perfect view of the river. He heard the agent screaming in the background, telling him to drop it. He then realized the pistol was still in his right hand, and he had a perfect shot. He saw the commotion in the water, and knew Brian was in the middle of it. The sniper took aim. He then heard more gunshots, and felt his internal organs being ripped inside of his body.

As everything faded to black, a vision of a life in the Caribbean was his last thought . . .

They had to finish their float down the river, as there weren't any roads to get off anywhere. The exciting day had turned into a terrible one, and Brian was pissed, disappointed and scared to death about the whole thing. As they pulled to the landing spot, Agent Womack stood there with a pompous grin on his face.

"I suppose you're going to say you knew this would happen all along?" said Brian.

"Ah . . . don't worry about it," said Agent Womack.

Brian gave him a stunned look. He remembered back to the conversation he had with the President, and how he warned Brian that dangerous people wanted this refinery to be derailed, and how he required the best security.

An exasperated Brian shouted, "So you let me and the people I care about the most walk right into this, and use us as bait?"

Agent Womack gave no answer, and just stared at Brian with a small grin on his face.

"Who . . . Who . . . the hell are you to do this? You don't have any right to take advantage of me in this situation! How am I to trust you at all if this is how I'm going to be treated!" screamed Brian.

Brian gave Agent Womack a steel glare. All along, he trusted him to keep him out of trouble. Now this situation had undermined his trust. Brian was pissed beyond words.

Agent Womack turned to Chase: "Mr. Stockton, can you give us a few moments?"

Chase turned to leave but added one comment, "Always a story you're your around. Happy I'm not your fucking lawyer."

Brian and Jenny managed a smile, as the mood was lightened up a bit.

Agent Womack took off his sunglasses. "Look, both of you, I'd appreciate you not mentioning this conversation going forward. It's a long story, so I'm only going to give you the highlights. We had a traitor on the inside, and he was paid a considerable sum of money to influence the project. Usually, having this information would be enough. And we would simply arrest the guy."

Jenny interrupted immediately, "It was Jim, wasn't it. I know it was Jim. He looked really bad when I saw him yesterday. He's the one who gave all the information on our location. I can't believe it; Glen knew a consultant would stab us in the back . . . ."

Agent Womack cut her off, "Yes Dr. Liepert, it was Jim. But you might want to cut him some slack. He's been quite helpful in tracking these guys, and was working with us the whole time. Overall, he made some mistakes, but has paid dearly for them. Plus, I'm certain he cares for you a great deal. Anyway, I doubt you'll ever see him again."

"Why, what happened to him?" said a suddenly concerned Jenny.

"Nothing happened to him. He's fine. He just needs to be out of the picture," said Agent Womack.

Brian and Jenny were completely engaged in the conversation with their minds spinning, and wondered about his gunshot from the convenience store hold-up.

Brian said, "His gunshot. That was no random incident, was it?"

Agent Womack held up his hand and continued, "Don't worry about that. Look, we follow the money, and the money led us to places we never imagined it would. These people never get their hands dirty, so it's easy to say you both have scared the shit out of some big shots. When we get a chance to nail them on something as concrete as attempted murder, then we need to take that chance. There's not nearly as much legal maneuvering."

Brian and Jenny were starting to loosen up a bit.

Agent Womack said, "The agents in the river were in constant communication with us the whole time, and we had their hit man under our watch during the whole thing. Remember, our agents would risk their lives for yours, including me."

Brian nodded his head and said, "Okay. Sorry I lost my cool."

"No worries. We got your back. Now look on the bright side, we don't know of any other direct threats on you. We're going to keep three agents with you, but if I were you, I'd party my ass off tonight without worry."

Jenny got a big smile on her face. "Sounds great. Now I have to go and calm down Chase's wife."

Brian asked, "Three other agents? You aren't going with us?"

"No. I have other things to take care of this evening. I'll see you at the refinery sometime next week."

Chapter 42—Destruction

Six Flags Pumping Station—Near Victoria, Texas

Roy flew into Houston's George Bush Intercontinental airport, and immediately took the shuttle to the car rental facility. He rented a standard half-ton Chevrolet pickup truck in a plain white color. As Roy left the airport area, he entered the Beltway Loop that circled around Houston. As he drove, many memories flooded his mind about the city. Roy saw the different offices and buildings dedicated to the oil and gas industry, all filled with the idiot managers, sales people and engineering types doing their assigned projects, all to make money for some unknown person for some unknown reason.

Fools, just a bunch of white collar fools was all Roy thought to himself.

Roy continued on the Beltway until he reached the I-10 freeway on the west side of the city. He caught a brief glimpse of the downtown area proper, and grinned at the thought of the bankers and world headquarters for the many oil and gas companies. Tomorrow was going to be a nightmare day for them. He exited the freeway at Grand Parkway and found the hotel where his meeting was arranged. Roy entered the hotel driveway and spotted his contact parked exactly where he should be.

Roy pulled his truck up next to his associate. He quickly exited his truck and got in the other truck. His contact had been one of Roy's associates for a long time, and specialized in ground detonations with multiple types of explosives. Many oil and gas companies and aggregate companies used his associate's services when they needed underground explosions to remove a tough land formation of any sort. But this associate also specialized in providing explosives to other customers for the right price, and no questions were asked.

Roy's associate never bothered with formalities, and immediately picked up the rather small box.

The associate said, "Okay, this is a standard 12"x12"x8" electrical enclosure. Inside you can see there's a cellular modem and IP address for the device. Here's the line of terminal blocks tied to the output ports of the modem. To power it, simply connect the 120 volts in the control panel to these three wires, which are tied to these terminal blocks."

The man held up a long bundle of wires. "When you do this, the power supply will light up, and you should see the modem light up as well."

Roy's associate placed the enclosure on his lap, and pointed directly to all the devices he discussed.

The associate continued, "Once it's powered up, give the cell modem about one minute to negotiate to the network. Once it's linked up, a green 3G light will display right here. I registered this device with a public IP address, so you'll be able to access this modem from anywhere on the Internet."

Roy's associate then looked him in the eye. "Now, make sure you have plenty of room between you and this thing when it blows. Most everything within 50 yards will be totally destroyed and you'll be able to feel it from over a mile away."

Roy nodded, not losing focus on this conversation at all.

"What you can't see on this enclosure is the explosives. They're all packed right behind the back plate. If anyone becomes suspicious, just hand it to them. It looks like any standard enclosure," said the associate, sensing that Roy was a little nervous around the device.

"Once you're a good distance away, get to a computer connected to the Internet. Simply type this IP address into your browser. A web page will display asking for a login and password. The login is 'boom' and the password is 'bitch' in all lower case."

Roy glanced up at his associate, and saw the arrogant grin on the face of this redneck type. Roy just shook his head to acknowledge him.

"Once you're in the web page, click on the serial port tab. There will be eight bits you can set to a zero or one. Go to bit 0, and change the bit to a 1, and press submit. For your sake, I hope you're nowhere near when you do this."

Roy stared at the enclosure, trying to comprehend how much financial impact on the world this little box would have. This box would make Roy a millionaire many times over, and would put the oil industry on their ass.

Roy said, "It's simple enough. Do you have the other items?"

"I do," said the associate as he reached in the back of his extended cab pickup. "Here are your steel toes, Nomex suit, hard hat and safety glasses. And here's the ID you wanted."

Roy took a look at everything, and it all seemed to be in place. Roy reached into his back pocket, and handed the envelope of cash over to his associate.

Roy said, "Look. There's a little extra in there. Stay low and don't come up for a while."

The associate saluted Roy with his hand above his forehead, and didn't say a word. Roy exited the pickup and then hopped in his truck. He left in a hurry and headed onto I-10 East, then took the beltway south until he hit Highway 59 West to Victoria, Texas. As Roy looked in his rearview mirror, he saw the faint outline of Houston behind him.

It was about three o'clock in the afternoon as Roy approached Victoria. He spotted a cheap hotel on the side of the highway with Internet access. Roy found his spot to push the button, so he could be relatively close to see the destruction. He continued through Victoria until he found Highway 77 and turned his truck south. About five miles outside of the town, Roy recognized the unmistakable profile of the pumping station.

It was in a very strategic location, as it was designed to pump in raw petroleum for the Corpus Christi ship channel, but also had several other infeed pipelines from the Houston ship channel. The facility was all outdoors, and had the look of several huge air conditioning units placed all over a field, except for the massive pipelines everywhere. The station had impressive manifolds that transfer the multiple pipeline infeeds to a single major pipeline built for the new refinery in San Antonio. Roy slowed his truck and turned to the main entrance. There was a sign at the entrance that read "Six Flags Transfer Station—Victoria Texas." The name of the station came from the history of Victoria County, which was the only county in Texas to fly six different national flags during its rich history.

As Roy pulled up to the security station, an obese younger man leaned out the window of the basic security guard shelter and didn't say a word.

Roy rolled down the window and said, "Mike Wimmer with Infusion Turbines. Here to do the upgrade on the controller."

The guard rolled his eyes. Since Roy was a technician working on equipment, this actually meant he would have to inspect Roy's vehicle, which was way more work than this man wanted to attempt. After a few minutes, the overweight guard managed to waddle out of the building. He walked up to Roy's truck and asked him to exit the vehicle and pop his hood for inspection.

Roy did as instructed. The guard simply looked at the engine and then asked Roy to close the hood. The guard did a very lax job in walking around the truck, but he did at least briefly look in the bed of the truck.

The security guard then walked back to Roy, holding his clipboard, which listed any visitors that had been to the station that day. Roy noticed that only one person had even been to the site during the entire day.

The guard said with his annoyed attitude, "Name."

"Mike Wimmer."

"Company."

"Infusion Turbines."

"Purpose," asked the guard, having to take a moment to catch his breath from the difficult work.

"Upgrade controller."

"Driver's License number."

Roy had the number memorized, "19325643."

"You have all the safety gear?"

"Yes."

The guard looked up with his first really concerned question: "Say, it's coming up on 3:30. How long you going to be in there?"

Roy gave an understanding smile, "What time do you want to leave by?"

The guard smiled back, relieved he had a cool technician who understood his concern. "I like to have her locked up by 4:30 with my truck on the road at 4:31."

"I'll haul ass. It shouldn't be a problem," said Roy.

The guard gave a smile, "You have a good one, boy. Don't blow nothing up!"

The guard reached into his security shelter and pressed a simple button, and the automatic gate opened.

Roy grinned while he thought of the last comment. He took a moment to put on his Nomex fire protection suit, steel toed shoes and safety hat. He then jumped in the truck and headed through the gate, giving a wave to the security guard. Roy was now on the inside.

The transfer and pumping facility had all the features of a major oil and gas gathering station. It was built on a foundation of stabilized soil, with fine gray gravel spread over the entire complex. On one side of the facility, Roy saw the pipelines taking a 90-degree u-shaped turn upwards to the main infeeds of the huge pumps, with several thousand horsepower turbines connected to the main drive of the pump drive shafts. Roy was disgusted when he saw the totalizers in line with all the manifold piping. The totalizers were tracking the exact volume measurements of the petroleum passing through the system, and more importantly, interfaced with the invoicing system for the upstream producers to charge the refinery.

Roy drove around the station until he found the ideal target. One of the turbines had its electrical control panel located about 10 feet from the main engine. Just as critical, Roy saw the 460/120VAC sticker located on the panel.

Roy pulled his truck next to the turbine, and then realized he'd made his first mistake. The sound of the turbine was louder than a rock concert, and was a constant scream. He got out of his truck and the high decibels hit him full force. Roy cussed out loud as he had forgotten how loud these things could get.

Roy retrieved the explosive device from his truck, and grabbed his small tool kit from his notebook computer bag. He put his small screwdriver in the large control panel handle and turned the lock while turning the handle at the same time. The panel door swung open, showing Roy what he had expected. Roy searched the panel until he found the long array of 120 VAC terminal blocks he would use to power the explosive device.

Roy quickly knelt down and uncoiled the wires on the device. He ran the wires through the wire way of the panel, then placed the device on the base of the panel floor. Roy found an open terminal block, and then wired his device to the hot, neutral and ground blocks. He watched the modem begin to light up.

Come on, come on, Roy said to himself, looking for the 3G signal to light up on the modem.

After about one minute, the modem indicated it had negotiated with the cellular network, and now was a live IP address he could communicate with through the Internet.

Roy gave out a huge sigh. He felt so close to accomplishing his goal. His inner alpha-male attitude came up again from his soul. He was going to finally rise to the top of the social elite class in the United States while all the other peasants suffered.

Roy started to close the door of the electrical enclosure. He wanted to get out of there ASAP to finish his task, and to get out of the non-stop screaming of the turbine. He struggled to situate his enclosure inside the larger panel so he could completely shut the door, when a shadow came directly over the top of where he stood.

Roy looked to the sky, but nothing was there. There wasn't even a cloud in the sky. He again returned to his panel when the shadow passed over him again. This time he stepped away from the panel to get a better look. Roy didn't initially see anything, so he rotated around to get a thorough look at the sky.

Suddenly, Roy's heart felt like it would fall from his chest. He stared directly at a black helicopter about 50 feet above his head. The chopper hovered above him with the back door open, and a man in a dark uniform held a rifle giving a waving motion at Roy. He turned and saw several law enforcement cars bursting through the gate while the security guard ran for his life.

Roy had no intentions of giving up this close to completing his task, and they weren't taking him alive. He knew there was no escape, but he could cause a devastating impact. Roy scrambled to his pickup, and saw the bullet impacts kicking up the gravel. Roy started his pickup, and slammed it into reverse. He heard the bullets hitting his truck as he backed up to a good distance. Roy rammed the truck in drive and punched the accelerator. He gripped his steering wheel, knowing his life would end as a part of a massive explosion. Roy crashed into the electrical control panel with all the impact the pickup could deliver.

His world was in a daze, and he couldn't breathe. He slowly looked around, and saw the remnants of a deployed airbag in his lap. Suddenly Roy's door was thrown open, and someone grabbed him and pushed him to the ground. His arms were pulled to his back, and he felt the handcuffs being locked behind his back. Roy was dragged up to his knees as he watched a woman exit the helicopter and walk in his direction.

Director Beine walked up to Roy. "Explosive devices actually work better when explosives are in them. Your associate was quite helpful in stuffing your box with plastic."

Roy knelt even closer to the ground. His life and dreams were over.

Chapter 43—Justice

Home of Gary Blackmon, Napa Valley, California

Gary Blackmon decided to stay around his house that week and kind of lay low. The tasks he put in motion were near, and he needed to respond if anything unplanned should occur. Gary was extraordinarily nervous. If things didn't go well for Roy and his sniper, then his financials would take a further hit, minimizing his influence and his family's standing in the order of things. Gary considered additional steps he should have taken to stop the refinery. It just seemed for the first time in his career, dead ends were everywhere. He had sorely mistaken the impact the economy had on so many businesses, and the extraordinary steps they took to get back on track. All his typical methods like kickbacks, media influence, political support and banking interests just didn't pan out. Any report about the energy market being destabilized was old news to Americans, and the media didn't influence any financial trends at all anymore. Politicians he could typically rely on wouldn't even discuss the refinery with him, distancing themselves from anything but total support for the program. Nothing worked, and Gary needed a homerun, just a brief reprieve, so he could take what money he had left in oil and gas and invest it elsewhere.

Gary heard the familiar voice of his son and others as they walked through the main residence. He looked up and saw his son with two beautiful high school girls, all giggling the whole time. Gary hadn't talked to his son in quite a while, so he decided to take a break for a moment to catch up.

As they entered the kitchen to take the back stairs to the second floor, Gary shouted out, "Hey Bret, come in here a minute."

His son came into Gary's office. "Hey Dad, what's up?"

"How'd the grades turn out?" asked Gary.

Bret said, "All A's. Second in the class again. Fucking Asians."

Gary leaned back in his chair. "Well, did you do what I recommended?"

Bret said, "Yep. He screwed me. I offered him five grand to miss a few questions on the calc final. So get this, he takes my twenty-five hundred up front, but aces the damn test. I told him I wanted my money back, but he just laughed at me for being so stupid. He said he'd never survive his dad, but he's willing to take my money."

Gary asked, "What are you going to do about it?"

Bret smiled, "I told him I'm a Blackmon. He either gives me five thousand back, or we'll get his dad kicked off the board at the hospital. We'll give the hospital a choice, the Blackmon annual donation, or a new medical director."

Gary said, "Good job. What do you think will happen?"

Bret reached into his pocket and pulled out his wallet. "I've already got it, but I spent most of it on the chicks upstairs."

Gary reached over his desk and gave his son a high-five, "That's how we do it. Now, don't get into too much trouble with the girls. I've had my fill of pissed off parents."

His son left the office, and Gary returned to his primary thoughts. He had instructed his staff that no calls were allowed today unless it was an extremely urgent matter. Any unnecessary distraction would only cause him to lose focus on his largest financial risk. He stared at his financial portfolio on the Bloomberg monitor, and the financial news channel on his flat screen mounted on his wall. As soon as the activities of today raised the futures pricing, he would discreetly move his money to other funds. During the day, Gary called dozens of his brokers all over the world, gave them strict orders on the method of money movements, and placed triggers on several different levels in numerous funds.

Gary also called his media insiders, and had commitments for primary story coverage on the dire future of America's oil position if anything newsworthy occurred. The financial collapse of the traditional media outlets made for easy picking in influencing the stories. The murder of Brian Larson, the bomb at the transfer station and a fabricated story of a terrorist plot should raise the prices nicely. He was ready.

It was about 4:00 P.M. California time, so he knew the breaking news on Brian Larson would hit at any moment. He had all his foreign brokers ready to go and all the triggers for tomorrow's trading setting the stage. His attorneys and financial teams evaluated what-if scenarios on his money, and were deep into their forecasting spreadsheets. If Gary were lucky, he would essentially walk away from oil and gas with his original investments intact, plus all the profit he'd made over the past few years. All in all, a 20 percent return for that much money wasn't bad, just bad for those who preferred to influence their outcomes.

Gary thought of his other fraternity brothers, and was certain they were doing the same. Although their backgrounds were considerably different, they all had a knack for being in the right place at the right time, one way or another. Oil and Gas turned out to be a disappointment, and they had to get closer to the dirty work than usual, but no matter, things would work out once again. While all the other idiots in the market were deciding what to do, the Impending Order set the stage as to what people had to do.

Gary heard the familiar thumping of his son running down the stairs.

"Hey Dad, what's going on outside?"

"I don't know. What do you mean?"

"Man, it looks like there are a hundred cop cars coming up the driveway," said his son with a typical teenager grin on his face. "Did one of the staff get caught running drugs again?"

Gary gave him an "I don't know, but don't like it" look. He started making his way to the front door at a high pace. As Gary stepped out he heard the sounds of a helicopter above his house, and saw the undercover federal cars screeching to a halt in his front yard, right in the middle of his lawn.

Gary backed away from the door and slammed it shut. He quickly locked the sizable bolt. Gary turned to Bret, "Whatever happens, don't answer that door."

Gary's son stared at his dad with the look of a lost puppy. "What's up Dad? Nobody can touch a Blackmon. Why are you worried?"

"Just don't open the goddamned door!" screamed Gary.

Gary was frantic. "They found out! They found out! The feds must have caught Roy, and he directed them back here. This can't be happening. They have everything. How did I not know about this?" said Gary out loud.

Bret was stunned, and stared at his father, on the borderline of a nervous breakdown. Then Gary's wife and staff members came running into the large foyer.

"Honey, what's wrong? Why are you yelling?" asked his wife.

They heard the knock on the door. "Federal agents! Open the door immediately!"

Gary backtracked from the door. He heard the sound of his wife's voice yelling at him, and the shouts of the agents outside the door. He turned and ran into his office. Gary had to call his lawyer. It was the only thought on his mind. He couldn't go to jail. He couldn't make it in that kind of life. He picked up his cell phone to find the number in his contacts list.

"Gary Blackmon, put down the phone and freeze immediately!" said a muffled voice.

Gary spun around and saw a federal agent standing outside the windows of his office, and others ran across his patio where he had had so many important meetings.

Gary ignored the demands and scrambled for the number of his lawyer. *I can't go, I can't go* was all Gary thought. Suddenly, he heard the sound of breaking glass come through his office, and heard the screams of his wife as the front door was being rammed. Gary looked back out the window and saw the federal agent with his gun focused squarely on his chest.

"That's it, Mr. Blackmon. Put down the phone," said the agent in a calmer tone, knowing that Gary was a trapped man.

Gary dropped his head and slumped his shoulders. There was nothing he could do. Gary saw his wife and son in total shock. He knew he couldn't fight through this with his typical lawyer smoke screen. All that he had built, all that he had been entitled to as a mogul's son, was vanishing in front of his eyes. Gary couldn't take his eyes off his son, knowing that he would have to live a life without his dad or his family money. It was all lost.

Gary couldn't go on. He couldn't deal with the embarrassment. Pictures of arrested executives being paraded flashed through his mind. His father entrusted it all to him, and he ruined it. Gary saw the looks of his wife and son, shocked with the moment, looking upon the man they had trusted with everything. His family, his possessions, the money and his family name. It was all gone.

Gary slowly said, "I'm so sorry. I did it all for you. I love you both. You'll make it through this."

"Gary, what are you talking about?" said his wife. "What's happening?"

"Both of you leave the house. Go somewhere else. Leave now. Please. I don't want you to see me being arrested."

His family didn't know what to do. The agents yelled through the glass, and other agents banged on the front door.

"Please. Leave now," said an exasperated Gary as he lowered his head. "Leave now."

His family backed out of the room. He heard the agents constantly yelling through the window, telling him to get his hands up. He never acknowledged them, and walked to his office door. He shut the door slowly, almost like he didn't want anyone to hear, and walked back towards his desk. He saw several agents outside the window now, all with their weapons drawn, telling him to put up his hands.

Gary sat back down at his desk, and opened a drawer. The agents screamed at the top of their lungs, telling him not to do it. Gary pulled out the pistol, cocked the hammer, put the gun in his mouth and pulled the trigger.

It was all lost.

When the news of the suicide of Gary Blackmon and the takedown of five influential financial players in the United States hit the wire that evening, the media outlets went into full overdrive. Conspiracy theorists were having a field day, being vindicated for their years of paranoia. The Sunday news shows had many financial experts on their panels to predict energy prices for the following weeks and months. Senators were doing their best to take credit for the Secret Service funding, and how their party promoted security better than the other guys. The investigative journalists researched deep into the history of Gary Blackmon and his global financial ties. The History Channel promoted a program for the following week that discussed the history of secret societies and the rumored history of the Impending Order. It was a media zoo.

Agent Womack and Brian were doing their best to hide from the reporters. They were in Brian's new office at the refinery, glued to the Presidential press conference on his 55" flat screen. President Rhea was on the steps of the Department of Justice, giving his speech to hundreds of reporters.

President Rhea started, "Earlier this year, we initiated bold steps to protect our economic future. We expressed several grave concerns with our plans, including the risks of criminal activities to try and destroy our dreams and hopes. As extraordinary as it might seem to the average American, we have many on our own soil who see reward in financial instability, and will go to great lengths to collapse enterprises, ruin lives, shatter hopes and quash dreams. This destruction has a singular purpose, and that's to protect a lifestyle. A lifestyle of privilege, a lifestyle of arrogance and isolation from the realities of building something special. These individuals absolutely don't care for the greater good."

President Rhea paused for a moment, and then leaned forward with one elbow on the podium, his other hand pointing towards the media to give more purpose to his next words, "Well, my fellow Americans, I'm proud to say we got the bastards now."

The media let out a collective gasp. Not only had they caught a great sound bite, very seldom did a President use such direct language. The bottom of Brian's TV screen almost immediately displayed a text banner, "President Rhea: "We got the bastards now!" The media actually gave out applause, and was a scrum of activity.

President Rhea let the crowd calm down a bit, and then stood back in a standard position, "I'll let my Attorney General give the details here in a moment, however, I want to take time to thank the Secret Service for their tireless efforts in breaking this case. They've been building an extensive file on this criminal activity for over nine months."

As the President continued his press conference, Brian turned and looked at Agent Womack. "You're a hero!"

Agent Womack grinned, "Yeah, and the rewards are following your sorry butt all day long."

Brian smiled while looking back at the screen, and then turned back to Agent Womack. "So, you aren't aware of any more threats?"

Agent Womack thought about the question, and then looked at Brian. "No. That's what concerns me most."

Brian gave a nod to Agent Womack, not really knowing what to say about the comment.

The room was silent for a few moments, and then Agent Womack asked, "So, the refinery's going as planned? Everything's good here?"

Brian said, "It's better than good. Every single skid and sub-system passed the initial tests with flying colors. The preliminary tests on the system integration are going very well. If I was a betting man, I'd say we make kerosene on our very first day of commissioning."

Agent Womack said in a casual tone, "Great. Hey Brian, how's Manish doing? It seems to me that he works like crazy, never taking any time for himself."

Brian's face lit up. "Ah, man, he's an animal. It's unbelievable what he's pulled off here. He essentially designed the entire plant process system by himself, other than a few AutoCAD designers. And he's ridden herd over the control system. It's amazing."

Agent Womack said, "Yeah. I hear you. I mean, over the past year, you know he hasn't made a single personal phone call? To my knowledge, he watches no TV, no movies, no dinners with the team, no e-mails, no Internet surfing. I mean he has no personal life or personal entertainment."

Brian was curious about where this conversation was going. "What are you saying? You concerned about Manish for some reason?"

Agent Womack thought about his response for a moment. "Well, not really I guess. Well, I should say I'm concerned about everyone. Hell, I even follow up on your activities. It's my business to be concerned. But, in my entire career, I've never seen anyone like this. All he does is work."

Brian knew Agent Womack had uneasy feelings about Manish, reflecting back to when they first started the project.

Brian said, "Like I said the first day I met you, he's the best process engineer on the planet. He looks at this plant like a conductor looks at his orchestra. The plant is a direct reflection on a lifetime of work. I'd say he's focused, no different than a medical researcher that is locked in his lab for several years."

Brian paused for a moment and said, "You're thinking about this too much. He's just a focused individual."

Agent Womack just nodded. Something didn't feel right.

Chapter 44—Commissioning

Refinery Control Room—San Antonio, Texas

Brian and Manish walked down the hall to the new control room together. As they finished entering their security data to open the door, Brian turned to Manish: "You ready for this one?"

Manish stared at Brian and paused a minute before answering, "Brian, I've been planning on this day since the moment you called."

Brian put his hand on Manish's shoulder, "Okay. Let's go."

There were six people in the control room for the big day. The past few weeks had been intense getting ready for today. All the work, engineering, testing and installation culminated to the full system test now upon them. The refinery team had painstakingly gone through extensive functional testing for each major piece of equipment, and now the team felt they were ready for a plant-wide run through. For today's comprehensive testing, each different component would move to an operational state, and the first runs of kerosene would begin. The Six Flags station pumped crude to the refinery, and the raw petroleum tank farms were filled. Although there were a few technical glitches the refinery components seemed to be performing well, and for the most part each company that contributed to the refinery was breathing a big sigh of relief. Nobody wanted to hit the media as the reason the refinery was delayed.

As per Brian's direct orders, the control room was a state of the art facility with the latest in industrial technology. It had three rows of computer stations that cascaded downward, with each side of the center aisle housing two large monitors. The room was dimly lit, and was a deep industrial gray color. The front of the room had a large wall covered with eight different huge flat screen displays, providing a great overview of the entire refinery process. Each computer station had an integrated IP phone and IP camera screens built right into the software, so communications or visuals anywhere in the facility were easy to accomplish. Overall, the control room had complete diagnostics, status overview and direct system access to run an exceptionally efficient refinery with minimal staff. Access to the control room was strictly guarded; there was an electronic door with retina scanner and keypad, and a security code that changed on a daily basis. Additionally, a large slide bolt was used to lock the stainless steel door once you were inside the room.

Everyone was unusually quiet today, with little need for chitchat. All knew what was at stake. One associate was needed for refinery status overview, and was the first line of defense for any system alerts or faults. The second associate was the production operator, who was essentially the pilot for the plant, and commanded and controlled the primary system processes including refinery set points. The third associate was strictly for safety and security, and spent his entire time viewing the many different cameras located throughout the facility. These associates had complete authority over the refinery process, and any one of them could choose to stop it at any time.

For the testing today, Manish developed a detailed process step diagram for commissioning of the refinery, and directed the production operator to initiate the different process steps through the control screen on his computer. If for any reason the system wouldn't respond as expected, Udaya had immediate access to the control system code, and could diagnose and modify any part of the control system almost immediately. As for Brian, he was here as an observer, and he didn't want to miss this moment.

At precisely 9:30 A.M., Manish instructed the production operator to begin the separation process. Brian felt the hair on the back of his neck stand up as the large screens on the wall came to life. He saw the major pumps begin to increase their load, and the raw petroleum stream approaching the sulphur extraction unit and the risers. As the petroleum exited the sulphur extraction, he saw the furnace begin to light up on the large screen. Brian smiled at the thought of pure liquid turning to an immediate gas.

Manish looked completely under control. He studied his notes and the large screens to verify what he knew had happened.

Manish then said to the operator, "Activate condenser manifold E14."

The production operator clicked the button on his screen. Brian looked up at the E14 valve on the large screen, and saw its sensors begin to activate to the open position. The gas then floated to the condenser. Brian felt it now. Suddenly, the spectrum analyzers displayed a dizzying array of numbers. Just as planned, kerosene was the chemical being produced.

Brian let out a quick "Yes!" and jumped out of his chair. The other men in the room gave out quick smiles, but Udaya and Manish stayed in their seats. They had passed the first phase of testing, and the plant performed just as planned.

"Hold here for five minutes," said Manish.

The refinery now produced raw kerosene prior to the catalytic cracking process. For the moment, the raw kerosene was being diverted to the holding tanks. The process was running about 25 percent of its production capability, and the other men in the room gave out a collective sigh of relief, knowing they'd passed a major milestone in the process testing. The plant seemed to be running well, with all process variables running within nominal and predicted ranges.

The production supervisor used this time to call various parts of the plant, and verify things were running as they should. The security manager combed over all the camera screens, looking for signs of anything out of the ordinary such as vibrations or mechanical issues. For both, everything looked good.

Brian paced back and forth, unable to contain his excitement. Things were going as planned, and he knew they were just a few minutes away from producing pure kerosene. Brian gave a quick look at Udaya and Manish. Neither said a word, and both were deep into their notes and computer screens.

At exactly five minutes, Manish once again gave out process orders: "Initiate catalyst process."

The room vibrated as the huge catalytic cracker ramped up.

"Divert valve C-12," Manish said in a cool tone.

Brian watched the valve open on the large screen as the raw kerosene diverted to the cracking process. Once again, Brian focused on the spectrum analyzers, giving him detailed component breakdowns of each element being created. Although Brian knew what happened, he was a little disappointed that the kerosene still needed considerable modifications to be a sellable product, but it looked better.

Manish gave a quick look at the screens, and then said, "Increase volume to 50 percent, increase temperature of FCC to 1300 degrees."

The room tensed up. This was the first time the fluid catalytic cracking unit had been raised to this temperature with high volumes of petroleum. Brian watched his analyzers, and then he saw kerosene morph to a sellable product.

"Yes, yes, yes!" shouted an exuberant Brian.

The petroleum was now in Jet-A form. Brian immediately picked up the phone and dialed the number Agent Womack gave him.

"President Rhea."

"Mr. President, we're making Jet-A here," said Brian, almost giddy.

"Outstanding, Brian! I'll be damned. We actually might make it!"

Brian laughed, "We just might. We want to keep this quiet for now, but I would think a press release this evening would be ideal."

"Okay, we'll get your buddy Bill Pence on it," said the President as he chuckled out loud.

"Oh God, Mr. President, you just ruined the moment!" said Brian laughing out loud. "I need to run, but I'll let you know of any other developments today."

As Brian hung up the phone he gave a quick shout to Manish, "Manish, you're the man! Great, great job!"

Manish turned to look at Brian, but instead of giving an enthusiastic response, Manish gave him a look of disgust, and then turned back towards his notes.

That's odd, thought Brian. Manish had been killing himself on this project non-stop, and now he reacted like that? Brian sat down in his chair, not knowing what to say next. The more Brian thought about it, the more he thought Manish was pissed about his premature call to the President. Manish must not want any feedback until the plant was up and running. Brian turned to look at Udaya, who also watched Manish's response. Udaya gave a quick look at Brian, and then turned back to his computer screen.

No big deal, thought Brian. He would get with Manish later and apologize for being so euphoric at the moment. Brian turned his attention back to the large screen, and once again got excited. Even at only a 50 percent level, his refinery was now one of the largest kerosene producers on the planet.

Brian was consumed with his refinery, and gawked at all the plant diagnostics on the screens. Most people would be thrilled at becoming one of the wealthiest men on earth. But not Brian, he was much more excited about getting the refinery running and, just as importantly to him, he'd helped Jenny get her life back with a stable energy supply. He had done his part, and contributed to a major effort to put America back where she belonged.

Brian then heard a mumbling, and looked down to see Manish sitting in his chair, with his elbows on his knees and his head bowed. Manish seemed to be in prayer, and spoke in a dialect Brian didn't understand. He gave a quick glance around the room, and noticed everyone just stared into their monitors and tried to ignore this strange event. Brian never knew Manish was even very religious. Brian kept to himself, and thought this was Manish's way of giving thanks for a successful project. Brian had no personal feelings one way or the other on the subject, but certainly thought this was an awkward situation.

Brian watched Manish closely as he removed himself from his seat and walked to another computer monitor in the row directly below Brian. Brian's personal radar was now on high alert, as something didn't feel right. Manish's response to him earlier, now the awkward prayer gave him a strange feeling. He watched Manish's computer screen as he logged into the plant control system, and entered his security credentials. The system administrator screen immediately came up, and Manish navigated to a screen Brian had never seen before. Brian slowly stood out of his chair and pressed his palms up on the table, giving himself a very good look at the monitor and every single move Manish made.

Once again, Manish started a prayer, in a much louder voice. Brian watched him select a data field with no description, type in 2200, and then press the Enter button on the keyboard. Manish then stepped away from the computer.

What the hell? Brian thought to himself.

Brian then heard the boiler on the cracking unit begin to ramp up, and felt the vibrations of the equipment all the way in the control room. He slowly looked at the screens on the wall, and saw the temperature of the cracker unit begin to rise.

Brian was confused and very nervous. *2200? What in the hell is 2200?* thought Brian. *Surely that's not the temperature setting on the cracker unit. At those pressures, it'd blow sky high.*

Brian quickly turned to Manish, and now saw him holding his hands outward and upward to the sky, praying loudly and more pronounced.

"Manish, what the hell's going on?" said Brian very aggressively.

Manish ignored him, and prayed with his hands raised to the sky. Brian saw the rest of the men looking at this scene in stunned silence, not knowing exactly what to do.

Brian quickly turned to the production operator and shouted, "The boiler control screen. Get to it immediately. Override the set point!"

The production operator scrambled as quickly as he could to get to the screen. Once it came up, he selected the data entry field. But this time the field was grayed out, and he couldn't change the set point. He was frantically clicking his mouse, but nothing was changing.

"I can't change it! It won't let me change anything!" shouted the operator.

Brian looked at the screen, and could see the cracker unit approaching 1500 degrees. "Emergency shut down! Emergency shut down!" shouted Brian. "Shut it down, now!"

The production supervisor clicked on the large emergency stop icon button that was displayed on every screen. The screen just locked up. The supervisor turned to Brian with a stunned look on his face, "It's locked out too!"

The other two gentlemen in the room were now out of their chairs. Nobody knew what to do. They could tackle Manish and take him down, but what good would that do?

Brian looked to Udaya, who just stared at his computer screen. "Udaya! Do something! Override the data field in the control system!"

Udaya continued to stare at his computer screen, not acknowledging Brian. Then the large screen lit up with alerts and alarms.

The plant operator screamed out, "High pressure and temperature alarms! The system's ramping up past the limits! Why in the hell isn't the safety system engaging!"

Brian was in a total panic. He didn't know what else to do. There wasn't enough time to do a manual shutdown. He had to order an evacuation, as hundreds of his employees were about to be incinerated. Brian picked up the phone to dial emergency services, and then he noticed the praying had stopped. He quickly looked up and saw Manish staring at the large screen on the wall. Brian looked at the screen to see that the temperatures were ramping down.

Manish continued staring at the screen as his shoulders slumped. He didn't say a word; he just stood there, looking as if the energy had totally left his body. Brian and the refinery team watched Manish intently, while Udaya continued to look at his computer screen.

Suddenly Manish ran to his computer bag, pulled out a pistol, and pointed it directly at Udaya.

Brian screamed, "Manish, what the hell are you doing with a gun!"

Manish ignored him and walked at a brisk pace back to Udaya. "Reverse it. Reverse it now!"

The security associate in the room sprinted towards Manish, trying to take him down. Without hesitation, Manish pointed the gun at him and put a 9mm caliber bullet directly through his skull. The blood went everywhere, pasting brain parts all over the new computer systems. Brian let out a gasp as blood splattered all over him.

Agent Womack sat in the break room down the hall from the control room, and enjoyed a cup of coffee while reading the local San Antonio newspaper. He was confident Brian was safe with the door security and bolt locked. Suddenly, "bang!" Agent Womack leaped from his chair as he recognized the unmistakable sound of a gunshot.

Agent Womack ran as fast as he could down the hall towards the control room. His subject was out of his sight, and he couldn't get there fast enough. Agent Womack drew his gun as he ran, and saw the agent from the other end of the hall coming as well. He made it to the control room and looked through the large window into the room.

Agent Womack couldn't believe his eyes. Manish held a gun to Udaya's head, with Brian and the other two gentlemen standing in a line in the row above Manish, all with their hands up. Agent Womack saw the body lying on the floor, with blood splattered everywhere.

Agent Womack saw an open computer bag in a chair. *The computer bag* was the first thought through his mind. *Oh God, Manish's computer had been behind their security screening ever since the project started. The gun's been here the whole time.*

He'd been digging into Manish's background for the entire duration of the refinery project, obsessed with finding something about him. Now it made sense; there was no information because Manish wanted it that way. No outside help, and totally integrated on the inside. Manish was a martyr for his cause. Agent Womack had let a terrorist get to the very heart of their project.

Agent Womack typed in the pass-code to the door and put his eye in the scanner. The door unlocked but he couldn't open it. The bolt lock was engaged from the inside.

"Shit!" shouted Agent Womack.

He quickly scanned the window, but knew shooting the glass wouldn't do any good, as it was built to take a severe refinery blast and still be operational. He looked into the room again, desperate to get inside. He saw Manish look up to the window to see who tried to get in. Brian looked to the glass with a look of desperation.

Brian turned back to the scene in front of him. Manish screamed at Udaya, "Reverse it, or everyone here dies, one at a time!"

Udaya sat at his desk and felt the hot barrel of the freshly shot gun next to his temple while tears ran down his face. "I can't do it. I can't let you kill thousands with a sulphur cloud. I'm not going to let you do it."

Manish screamed, "How did you know! How did you know?"

Manish was in a raging fury, and swung the gun back, then came down on Udaya's scalp as hard as he could. Udaya rolled to the ground and screamed in pain.

Manish reached down, grabbed Udaya by the shirt, and forced him back to his chair while the blood gushed down his forehead. Manish turned to the production operator and pulled the trigger. The bullet was a direct hit in the middle of his chest. He immediately hit the floor in a quick death.

"Do it. Do it now!" screamed Manish.

Brian yelled out, "God damn it Manish! What the hell are you doing! We've been friends for years. Talk to me. What's happened?"

Manish immediately turned to Brian in a rage, "I'm not your friend! I'm not your friend! I'm another pawn you and your government used to gain an advantage! Do you think I'm going to sit back, and watch you and your country continue your imperialism! You represent everything I hate! I'm not your friend! I'm going to ravage your plant, and destroy this city. Maybe then, you'll understand your greed."

Brian was in total shock. All along, he was worried about the outside, when the enemy was with him the whole time. Manish had been planning this whole thing. Total control, total process design, total safety design. Brian was stunned.

Manish turned back to Udaya. "Reverse it, or they die."

Brian's panic turned into complete rage. Brian had let this bastard use him to achieve his goal. Everyone was going to die and the refinery would be a failure because of his choices. Jenny, President Rhea, the American people all would suffer because of Brian's poor choices. He looked down and saw Udaya was now bleeding badly and his hands shook uncontrollably. Brian watched as Manish slowly turned to the production supervisor, who started screaming and tried to run away. Manish put a bullet directly through his back.

"You fucking coward!" screamed Brian.

Manish ignored him and turned back to Udaya. "Brian's next. Once I kill Brian, then I'm going to slowly torture you until I get what I need. It's your choice."

Udaya slowly nodded his head, still shaking badly while blood streamed over his face. Brian looked from Udaya to Manish, who grinned maniacally as Udaya reached for the keyboard to change the status of the code. He typed on his computer and brought up a function called "Udaya Bypass." The field was set to "1" for true. Manish smiled as he was very near to completing his mission.

Something inside Brian clicked, and he launched himself across the room. Brian's shoulder slammed into Manish's chest, and the two of them went flying over the table and did a somersault down to the next row. Manish scrambled like a madman, only focused on getting to the computer keyboard. Brian got Manish in a body lock with one arm as his other hand reached for the gun. Manish started doing body roll after body roll, managing to break free of Brian's hold. Manish scrambled to his feet, and jumped back over the top of the computer row, trying desperately to get back to the computer. Brian got to his feet and jumped back over the computer rows, trying to tackle Manish before he reached the computer.

The explosion blew Brian and Manish off their feet again, and threw Udaya straight to the floor. Brian's head rang, and all he could see was sparks and smoke in the air. Brian leaped up, dazed and confused at the moment. He saw Agent Womack and another agent screaming at Manish while running through the disintegrated control room door. Manish quickly got back to his feet.

"Freeze! Now!" screamed Agent Womack.

Manish stared at Agent Womack, having to make a choice. Manish saw the computer screen, still displaying the computer code with a "1" selected. He made his decision, and dove towards the computer. Manish felt the bullets drilling holes in his body and the compression from the hits blew him sideways to the table. Manish landed on the tabletop and rolled to his side with his hand extended towards the keyboard. With all the strength he could muster, Manish pressed the 0 key and the Enter key.

Manish smiled, as he knew nothing could stop it now. His arrival to Allah would be glorious. He'd outsmarted the infidels, dedicated his life to his mission, was dying a glorious death for his cause. Manish felt his body starting to shut down. He was prepared.

Udaya slowly walked up to the computer screen, covered with blood and soot from the explosion. He looked at the monitor, and then at the large screens: "Shutdown sequence started."

Manish felt his very soul leave his body. Udaya had tricked him again. Instead of raising the temperatures, the entire plant was going into a standard shutdown. Manish was fooled, dying, a failure.

Brian walked up to Manish and put his lips right next to his ear, "You failed, and we won. Your conversation with your god should be an interesting one here in a few moments."

Manish repeated over and over "You failed" as everything faded to black. He was no different than his brothers.

Chapter 45—Conclusion

Jim Jackson was just about finished with the hike. He was impressed that his son was doing the more difficult trails. It was everything Jim could do just to keep up with him. As they rounded the bend for the last half-mile, his son talked about taking a different trail head tomorrow. Jim laughed out loud, and turned to enjoy the beautiful views of the mountains.

When they finally exited the trail, they paused for a moment to catch their breath. Jim saw a handmade log bench and walked towards it to take a rest. His son said he was going to the creek to see if any trout were in the water.

Jim said, "Okay, but only a few minutes. We need to head back to the cabin or Mom will ground both of us."

His boy ran towards the creek. Jim couldn't believe all the energy his son had.

"Good looking boy you got there."

Jim quickly spun around, and immediately recognized Agent Womack. Jim was frozen, not knowing what to say.

Agent Womack walked slowly towards Jim. "You know, I've been thinking; there're several kinds of people in this world. But for me, it boils down to three types. The ones who take care of the problem, the ones that cause the problem, and the ones that wish the problem would just go away. Which one are you?"

Jim stared at Agent Womack, not knowing where this conversation would go. He looked around, and there didn't seem to be any other federal agents.

Jim finally said, "I want the problem to go away."

Agent Womack quickly said, "Right. I think you're that kind of guy as well. I mean, for example, as a lawyer, you never really solved problems. You give tools to make the problems go away. And this situation with your refinery kickbacks, you just want the problem to go away, correct?"

Jim just stared at Agent Womack, scared to say anything.

Agent Womack said, "Now, running away from a problem isn't that big of a deal in itself. It's how you're wired. Maybe a little cowardly sometimes, but, that's who you are. The issue is when people like you cause the problem and then run away from it. It leaves a big pile of shit for people like me to fix. This leaves you in two of the three categories. You get what I'm saying."

Jim nodded his head. "Yes, I think I know what you are saying."

"So," said Agent Womack, "that leaves someone like me in a dilemma. It seems like you're a pretty good guy, nice family, great dad and appreciate the simpler things in life. But, you created a big shit pile of problems, left me to fix it while you live this life on the very money you got from your pile of shit that I had to fix. Do you think that's fair?"

Jim dropped his head towards the ground. He had nowhere to run, and Agent Womack called him out.

Agent Womack sat directly next to Jim. "Look, what are you going to do with your life now?"

Jim continued to look at the ground. "I was thinking of opening a small office in town. I'm going to advise people on property issues, land development, mineral rights and things like that. Maybe sign up to be a coach on my boy's baseball team. I'm going to help others solve their problems, and help kids understand how to solve problems. I hope to learn how to be in your category."

Agent Womack shook his head. "Okay, Jim. You can call this unofficially official, but bringing you in now will only cause more problems, and you know how I feel about that."

Agent Womack said in a low voice, "You stay out of Washington. You stay out of oil and gas. If I find you're causing any problems, I'll fix the source of the problem immediately. Understood?"

Agent Womack stood up from the bench and started walking away. Jim said, "Agent Womack. I never heard your name on the news, but I know what you did. Congratulations on the refinery and keeping everyone safe. Thank you."

Agent Womack acknowledged Jim with a nod, "You better get going. Don't want mamma grounding you tonight."

Brian needed to get gas for his Jeep. As he pulled into the convenience store, a big smile came across his face when he saw gas prices. The sign read $2.99 for regular, $3.09 for mid-grade and $3.19 for premium.

Jenny hopped out with Brian when they stopped at the pump. She asked him if he wanted anything. He said he'd take a fountain Dr. Pepper and Lance crackers. Jenny rolled her eyes, as his healthy eating habits were sometimes lacking.

Brian stared at her backside as she walked into the store. Her figure was as good as ever. Her faded blue jeans only added to her looks.

As they pulled out of the store, Jenny asked, "What's the plan?"

Brian had a puzzled look on his face. "What plan?"

Jenny had an exasperated expression. "Brian, you always do this. You never think anything through. What am I supposed to wear? Where are we going to eat? Where are we going to stay? I mean, you plan everything to a tee for work, and then just let things go with everything else."

Brian got defensive. "Why are you so uptight all of a sudden? I don't know, I just wanted us to come to the mountains and have a good time. We always said we wanted to take a trip to the mountains. Hell, I got us the airline tickets, got the Jeep, got us to Denver. Let's just ride it out."

She turned to Brian: "Do you even know where we're staying? Do you even know the town?"

"No," said Brian with a big grin on his face. "Chase said Estes Park is really nice. I just kind of figured we would find something. I guess I should get a map."

Jenny shook her head. Brian quickly pulled the Jeep over on the side of the road.

Brian leaned in to her, "You know, I do have a plan. I plan on not letting you get away from me ever again. Everything else seems pretty trivial beyond that."

Jenny said, "Now that's a good plan."